1010 Freeman Street

Dona Rae Octavia Chatman

Pen & Pulse Consulting LLC

Disclaimer: This book is based on true events experienced by the Chatman Family,

Certain names, details, and scenes have been dramatized for storytelling purposes.

Contents

Dedication Page

The Chatman Family

I dedicate this book to my beloved parents, Ophelia Mae Guillory Chatman and Raymond Chatman Sr. They taught me the importance of education, self-respect, and independence. I admire their courage, strength, and wisdom.

Born and raised in Opelousas, Louisiana, they lived through segregation and Jim Crow laws. Yet they overcame every obstacle placed in their way. They never gave up and believed anything was possible, instilling those same values in me.

Today, my mother is 86 years old, living with Alzheimer's. My father, at 89, although he has prostate cancer, remains strong, and remembers life's moments as if they were yesterday.

I also honor those who came before them my grandparents, August and Pearl Guidry-Guillory and Louis and Octavia White Chatman, along with all my ancestors. I honor you for the things you were not allowed to do because of the color of your skin. I promise I will do them. Thank you for passing the torch and paving the way. I promise not to let you down.

To my beautiful children, who have always encouraged me, Devonte Ray Driver, Albert Norfleet III, kendal Rae Norfleet Ebrecht, Kelby Rae Norfleet, Tierra Chanel Driver, Radien Dean Driver, and Alliyah Rae Norfleet.

Always remember, if there is a will, there is a way. Get it done. You come from the background of amazing warriors.

Introduction

T he house on 1010 Freeman Street held secrets buried deep into its walls and rooted in the fireplace within. Shadows moved regardless of whatever anyone was looking or not, Whispers slithered through the night like an owl in the forest, wicked fingers brushing against bare skin as the family slept. What once stood as a hospital had become something else entirely, something restless, something evil. The spirits inside didn't welcome the Chatman family; they tormented them. Lurking in corners. Shattering their peace, waiting for the perfect moment to remind everyone *inside: you are never alone.*

The parents, Raymond, and Ophelia Chatman, along with their children, Terricita, Raymond Jr., Betty and Sandra, knew that the horrors of 1010 Freeman Street weren't bedtime ghost stories. They were real. Friends and cousins refused to spend the night, too afraid of what they might see...or what might reach for them from the dark. Only the power of prayer kept evil at bay, shielding them from something unseen, something relentless, something determined to drive them out.

As for the father, Raymond Sr., the house stirred something far worse than fear; it awakened memories. A fragile childhood trauma he had tried to bury: a severed head floating in the canal on Grolee street. a nightmare that had haunted him for years and now, within this curse house, the past was crawling its way back to life.

The house has since been destroyed, reduced to nothing but an empty lot. All that remains is the rusted pipe from the outdoor faucet, still protruding out of the ground like the last breath of evil refusing to die.

But even now, those who dare to step into the land don't ever leave alone.

They carry something back with them, something unseen, un-forgettable. a force both good and evil.

The Chatman family has placed artifacts from the home in a case such as an eighty-year-old seashell and a Pinocchio bank. This seashell should never be tampered with; it holds both good and evil.

These events are based on a true event.

Mona and Dona were the youngest of the Chatman children. They didn't grow up in the house in Louisiana, just their siblings before them, however they heard of the stories and felt the fear, the kind that lingers in your heart and mind and never leaves. Dona Chatman a Christian and psychic medium, with persistent motivation of her twin sister Mona, has chosen to bring this story to life and share it with you.

There are things in this world we can't explain. Things that exist outside the physical realm and once you have encountered them you are never the same.

One

The Sound of the Sirens

Raymond

I t was 1943. The sound was loud blaring in our ears. The whole house shook and trembled like it was fixin' to cave in.

Mama burst into our room, breathing heavily, her voice tight with worry. "Quick! Blow out them lamp lights!" She said, her eyes scurrying from one child to the next.

Daddy was already running around the house, boardin' up windows like a mad man. Sam and Perry took off toward the back porch to help. Their hearts filled with fear. Jules ran right behind them, gathering food items we might need. There was never a way to determine how long we would be in hiding or if we would even survive. Dorothy and Hazel stayed in the bedroom, blowing out the lamps fire light wick like Mama said.

Once we got back in the room, Mama grabbed each one of us by the arm, quick as she could, and rushed us into the bedroom closet.

"Move, now! Hurry!" she whispered loud enough for us to feel the fear behind it.

We ran inside the closet, nine of us all packed in together, breathing hard, hearts beating so loud it felt like drums in the dark. My skin was clammy from the Louisiana heat, and the air was sticky and moist, felt like I had hot sticky Carmel clinging to my body refusing to let go.

Mama wrapped her arms 'round us, tryin' to be strong, but I could feel her tremblin'. Daddy stood close, his breath comin' fast. It was pitch black.

We sat there for what felt like forever, thirty minutes, even more, until finally, the siren stopped. It just cut off suddenly. Silence fell like a heavy blanket.

Daddy gently pulled his arm away and cracked open the closet door, peekin' out slowly. He turned back to us, holding' a finger to his lips.

"Shhh…" he whispered. "Y'all stay put. Let me make sure it's safe."

He looked again, his body tense like he was ready to fight. Then he turned around and nodded. "The coast's clear y'all can come on out."

We all let out one big breath together, then stood up and crawled out that closet like we'd been reborn.

Sam was the first to speak. "Whew! Y'all sure was scared!" he said with a grin.

We all started laughing, a little too loud, at least to loud for a neighborhood that had fallen into silence, but it felt good to release that fear.

Dorothy, the smallest and sassiest of us all, crossed her arms and huffed. "I wasn't scared," she said, nose in the air.

Hazel, who towered over her, laughed. "Sure, you weren't, Sally," she teased, calling her by her nickname.

"I wasn't! Stop laughin' at me!" Dorothy snapped, giving Hazel a quick shove.

"Keep your hands to yourself!" Mama called out. "And stop that foolishness."

Truth be told, we were *all* scared. But right then, we laughed together like we'd just survived the end of the world.

"It'll pass," Daddy said, his voice calm and low. "This ain't gonna last forever. And when it's over, we'll be singin' that song instead of whistlin' it."

Perry couldn't help himself. He broke into a chant, grinning big: *"The German in the grass, with a bullet in his ass, pull it out, Uncle Sam, pull it out!"*

"Nope!" Daddy said, steppin' in sharp. I wasn't talking about that song "You can't be singin' that mess. I don't care how wrong folks act out there we gon' walk in integrity in *this* house. Y'all hear me?"

"Yes, sir," we all answered together.

"We might be fightin' to be free in this war, but don't forget we ain't free in this country. Remember that."

"Yes, Daddy," I said, and everyone else echoed the same.

"A'ight then. Go wash up. Supper's ready."

"That night, like so many others, I thought would be one of the scariest nights of my life. But life... life got a whole lot more frightening especially after that visit to the canal.

Four years later.

Two

MONKEY WRENCH

Raymond

Once upon a damn time, on a scorching muggy day, it felt like the sun had picked a personal fight with me. The air stuck to my skin, heavy as syrup, but all I wanted was to be outside, free to run wild. My brothers and friends had all the freedom in the world. Why couldn't I? My parents always told me I was too small or young.

My best friends were my cousins on Daddy's side, Willie and Francis Louis. Truth be told, they were more like brothers than cousins. But that day, neither one of them was around to play.

We lived on a narrow country road, snugged into an acre of land on Bellevue Street and when I say *we*, I mean me and my six brothers and sisters, Louis Jr., Sam, George, Dorothy, Hazel, Jules, and me. To the left of our yard stood two giants: an old fig tree and a pear tree. The figs were ripe and fell every day, covering the ground in a sweet-smelling, mushy mess that drew bees and flies.

Our house sat back away from the road; the backyard stretched out like it went on forever. Filled with chickens, ducks, and a big garden with corn, tomatoes, greens, and about everything else daddy could grow. I loved slipping into the chicken coop to gather warm eggs, and I reckon my parents loved it too, it saved them more than a little money.

Like most Southern homes back then, ours was painted white. My favorite place of all was the screened in back porch. That porch held so many warm evenings, filled with laughter, stories, and the hum of cicadas. There were three doorway entrance one led into the backyard the other, you could walk right into the kitchen and right beside that door, you could slip straight into Mama and Daddy's bedroom.

Inside, the walls were a soft peach, and the wooden floors gave a low crackle and groan with every step. My parents slept separately, their beds were tall, made of metal frames. Between the beds on the wall hung a string of prayer beads, along with a big wooden cross. Every morning, without fail, they knelt by their beds to pray.

Daddy, Louis Chatman Sr., was a devout Catholic who worshipped at the Holy Ghost Catholic Church. Mama, Octavia White-Chatman, was a faithful Baptist over at Little Zion Missionary Church. Two faiths under one roof, yet steady in prayer.

The rest of the house carried that old 1940s charm, full of character and warmth. Mama's white leather couch sat square and sectioned in the living room, elegant in its own way. Against the wall, a long brown record player gleamed, polished so bright it looked new. The walls were dressed in family photos, each frame holding a story we never wanted to forget.

Once you step out of that room and look right, you'll see the bathroom. Look straight ahead, and there it was: Daddy's recliner. A worn brown leather chair, handles split at the seams, but it was his throne. He ruled the house, parked right in front of the television.

Beside the TV to the left sat the side door, the *real* entrance to our home. The front door was for company, for special occasions. But that side door stayed propped open most days, held by nothing but a metal screen. That was the door everybody used, neighbors, family, and friends. Daddy liked it that way, from his recliner, he could see exactly who was coming and going, never missing a thing.

My mother filled our home with love. She sewed all our quilts by hand, making sure each bed was covered with cozy warm blankets. Even our pillows were specially made. They were stuffed with feathers from our own chickens, making them soft and cozy.

Our house was simple but full of love, every creaky board and handmade quilt telling the story of our life there. We were poor but my parents were educated, humble and loving. They instilled in us morals, values, and self-respect.

I played outside sometimes, but not with all the kids in the neighborhood. Some folks didn't let their kids mix too much, and truth be told, sometimes I didn't feel like I fit in anyway. Still, when I got the chance, I'd run barefoot down them cracked sidewalks like I had wings on my feet. We used to play Steal the Flag 'til the sun dipped low, and the mosquitoes came out singing.

Lord, knows, some days it was just too hot. That deep, swampy kind of heat that makes the air feel like a soggy wet blanket. On days like that, we didn't bother with soda or Kool-Aid, we drank just cold ice water and sweet, juicy watermelon. We'd sit under the shade of the pecan tree, legs dangling off the porch, spitting seeds as far as we could, laughing like we didn't have a care about anything in the world.

Now when I wasn't allowed outside or when that heat had everybody lying low, I'd park myself right at the window. Nose smushed up against the screen, eyes wide as deer in headlights, just watchin'. Cliff, Arthur, and Gerry in the street tossin' that old beat-up baseball like they were in a real baseball game with Jackie Robison at bat. I didn't understand how they could play in this heat. But if we were trying to be like our hero Jackie Robison number 42 for the Dodgers, anything is possible.

Then, sure as day, Gerry did it again. He let one loose throwing the ball hard, crazy as all get out and that ball smacked Arthur *right* in the face. You could almost hear the *thud* from inside. Arthur didn't miss a beat, he lunged at Gerry like a bull in a rodeo, and next thing you know, they were scrappin' in the middle of the road.

My heart was beating like a drum as I watched 'em roll around, kicking up dust and yellin'. I followed every bit of it, head swingin' side to side like I was watchin' a tennis match. And let me tell you, it wasn't just a fight, it was the most exciting thing I'd seen all week. I felt like I was right there at a Floyd Patterson and Ingemar Johannson fight, right outside my window.

I was caught up in that moment; I turned around as I sensed someone behind me. I nearly jumped outta my skin when I realized Mama was standing right behind me. She laid her hand gently like on my shoulder and said, "See there, Raymond? That's exactly why I don't like you runnin' with them boys. Always fightin', carryin' on. The Lord knows what other foolishness they're up to. I sure hope they don't go wanderin' down to Old Man Jesse's property and messin' around in that canal. I better not *ever* catch you down there, you hear me, boy?"

"Yes, ma'am," I said quick, knowin' better than to argue.

She gave me a look that said she meant every word, then turned back and walked to the stove, where she was stirring a pot and working on her roux for gumbo. The smell filled the whole house, makin' my stomach growl somethin' brutal.

Mama looked nice, wearin' her light pink dress with nude stockings and white shiny clunky shoes. Over it, she had on her white apron, just as neat as could be. She was a tiny woman, four eleven on her best day and about one hundred thirty pounds, but don't let her size fool ya, Mama was little, but she was feisty.

I turned back to look at my boys out in the street, and sure enough, they caught me peeping out the window at 'em. Gerry hollered, "What you lookin' at, punk? You want me to give you a knuckle sandwich like I just did Cliff?"

"I ain't lookin' at you!" I shot back, snapping my head around quickly to see if Mama was listening. She must've gone on to the back room 'cause I didn't see her.

When I turned back, Gerry, Cliff, and Authur came, stompin' right up to the window. I just stood there, lookin' down at 'em.

Gerry smirked and hollered up, "Yeah, you were lookin' at us, you little pussy."

"I ain't no pussy!" I yelled back, my face heating up.

Cliff laughed and said, "Well, prove it then jive turkey." "Meet us at the canal!"

I was mad now, cheeks steaming' under my milk-chocolate skin, my nose scrunched up, puffin' air like a bull ready to charge. "Aight then! I'll see y'all at the canal over by Grolee Street," I snapped.

"Uh, I ain't goin' over there..." Authur said anxiously.

"Oh, yes, you is," Gerry shot back, givin' him a shove. "And y'all better be there. We 'bout to show this chump what's what." I gave them one last mean dog look. They quickly turned and walked simultaneously, their movements stiff with frustration, fist balled up tightly.

I took a deep breath and exhaled as they walked away.

What had I just done? Not only was I scared, but my mom is going to kill me, that is if the thing in the canal doesn't kill me first. If my dad, Louis, finds out, it's over, I thought to myself. The weight of the day's challenge just might be the end of me tomorrow.

Three

Don't challenge me

Raymond

I sat in class, starin' at the clock, tappin' my number two pencil against the desk. Everything Ms. Hammond was sayin' turned into a blur. She always ended class with our homework assignment, but my mind was somewhere else.

I glanced around the room. Some kids were paying attention, while others were already stuffin' their backpacks with old, torn-up textbooks, ready to bolt. My eyes landed on my classmate's arm, he had a big scar, from one of these busted-up desks.

Back in those days, we were still living under segregation. There wasn't no mixin' of races, not in schools, not in churches, not even at the water facet, bathrooms, and swimming pools. In Opelousas, the line was clear as day and ran right through town, and they served as the unspoken border between two different worlds.

Black folks lived mostly on the north side, and that's where we had our schools. White folks were down on the south side, with their big brick buildings and polished schoolyards. Nobody ever had to remind us; we all just *knew* where we belonged and where we didn't.

I went to St. Landry school through the seventh grade. The district later called it Pecan Grove before naming it J.S. Clark High School, one of the few places we felt was truly *ours*. That school held a lot of memories for me. In fact, if I'm remembering right, that's where I met my very first girlfriend, Ophelia Mae Guillory. If you let her tell it, she will say, we met on the railroad tracks. Lord, she had the sweetest smile you ever saw... but that's a story for another time.

Now, let me tell you black schools didn't get any proper funding. Not even close. We got all the handy downs from the white schools once they were done with 'em. Our desks were that old metal frames with wooden tops scratched up, stained, full of cravings and cuss words from racist kids long gone. Some of their desks wobbled so bad, you'd spend the whole class tryin' to keep from fallin' over. Others had missing parts like no back, no seat, or the little book tray hanging halfway off.

Still, we made do. I kinda liked the little cubby underneath the desk, though. It was just enough space to stash your textbooks and a bag of lemonheads or a cold bottle of Nehi if you were lucky.

We'd sneak snacks into class when we could, passin' 'em around under the desk when the teacher turned her back.

Was it rough? Yes. But we were tough and fearless. We had pride in what little we had, and we leaned on each other. That school, during that time, shaped us and made us courageous.

Ms. Hammond was still on the chalkboard, writing down our assignment. The board was so worn; you could barely make out what she wrote most days. It was always cold in that classroom, but today, it felt hotter than the devil's ass. It could have been that the wood-burning stove was actually workin' for the first time in months or it was just my nerves. One or the other.

Sunlight spilled through the dirty window, hitting my face exactly right. I could feel little beads of sweat popping up on my forehead. Then finally, the bell rang.

I jumped up, slingin' my backpack over one shoulder, ready to meet Gerry, Author, and Cliff's challenge. I was almost at the door when suddenly I heard her voice.

"Raymond! Not so fast, young man. Come back here." Ms. Hammond called.

I stopped dead in my tracks and turned around slowly. "Yes, ma'am?"

She stood there, tall, and thin, dressed in that same khaki-colored dress she always wore, thick stockings, and the big, clunky black shoes. Her hair was pulled up, with some kinda fancy clip holdin' it together.

"I noticed you was preoccupied at the end of class," she said, eyeing me. "Everything alright?"

"Yes, ma'am," I answered quickly.

"Did you write down tonight's homework assignment?"

"Yes, ma'am, I did," I said again, tryin' to sound sure of myself.

She narrowed her eyes a little. "Alright now, you best have it by mornin', ya hear?"

"Yes, ma'am," I said, nodding' fast.

She let me go, and I turned back toward the door, my backpack barely hangin' on my shoulder. I wasn't waitin' around for no more questions. I had places to go and places to be.

I bolted down the poorly lit hallway, my footsteps echoing against the worn wooden stairs as I ran out. The humidity stuck to my skin as I stepped outside, searching the front of the school for Gerry, Arthur, and Cliff. My stomach turned when I spotted them hanging out near the broken stop sign, right where they always were. They looked rough- filthy hands, ashy knees, and not a backpack in sight. Had they even stepped foot in school today?

I straightened my shoulders and strutted toward them, chin high, my nose curled in disgust. I was ready: bad, bold, and fearless. My heart pounded, but I didn't blink. I locked eyes with each of them, our faces mirroring the same hardened frown. The air between us thickened, resilient and reluctant, as we stood locked in the unspoken challenge of who would break first.

Then Gerry smirked. "Let's go," he garbled.

No hesitation. We moved as one, slipping into the shadows of the unknown, heading straight for Grolee Street right to the canal.

The one place I swore to my parents I'd never ever go.

The place where, once you approached the canal, the rules changed.

And people disappeared like they never existed.

Four

EYES IN THE WATER

Raymond 1949

*T*he atmosphere felt heavy and thick as I found myself running through the cornfield, my legs pumping as fast as they could carry me. Every green leaf and husk seemed to lash at my face, but I didn't dare slow down. The streetlights would come on any minute, and I knew I had to be home before they did. Somewhere in the distance, I could hear my mother's voice calling loudly through the humid Louisiana air, trembling with fear. "Raymond! Raymond, where are you, boy?" Her cries only made me run faster, the crunch of dry soil and husks beneath my feet pulsating in my ears. But it wasn't just her voice or the thought of her wrath that I feared when I *got home. It's not what made my heart pound. It was the unknown lurking from the canal, the memory of what I'd seen, and the thought that it might be following me.*

We walked in silence down the long stretch of Grolee street, the only sound was the crashing of gravel beneath our feet. The energy was thick, and all we could smell was hot asphalt and distant honeysuckles. The giant white oak trees arched over the road, their twisted branches gave us shade, but they did little to break the heat. Sweat trickled down my neck and back.

My pulse kicked up the moment we stepped over the train tracks. We had crossed the line and there was no turning back now.

Gerry led the way, strutting fast, full of confidence, his shoulders swinging in rhythm with each step. His cut-off overalls flapped at his knees; dirt smeared on his legs like he stepped in a hog pen. I glanced down at myself, my best shirt, green and pressed to perfection the one momma made me wear this morning. If I got it dirty, she'd know I didn't come straight home from school.

Gerry picked up the pace. I stayed right behind him, taking a deep breath and swallowing my spit, southern stickiness clanged to my skin. Something made me glance back. Arthur and Cliff had slowed down, dragging their steps. Their faces were unreadable, but something about the way they lingered made my stomach twist. *Were they scared? Were they having second thoughts?*

I almost wished they were.

Afterall, we are getting closer to the canal on Grolee street.

The closer we got to the canal, the worse everything felt. The dirt beneath our feet turned into a slammy mud sucking at our shoes with each step. The trees leaned in heavy, their moss draped limbs reminded me of bony fingers reaching for us. Mosquitoes swarmed thick in the air, their buzzing-like whispers in our ears. Love bugs clung to our skin, drawn to the sweat dripping down our faces.

And the smell, good God all mighty, the smell.

The water was murky, thick with filth. Tadpoles wriggled near the bank of the canal, but there were other things too, things that didn't belong like old shoes and ropes that dangled from the tree. Bloated fungal bubbles drifted just below the surface, shifting like they were alive. The stench of rotting and stagnant water hit me in my face, forcing it into my throat, I held my breath, but not long enough before I swallowed it down.

We stepped closer. The mud sloshed beneath our feet.

Arthur's foot slid out from under him, and he fell forward, nearly tumbling in. Cliff grabbed his arm at the last second, yanking him back just in time. Neither of them spoke, but I could see it plain as day, they were scared. Hell, we all were. My heart slammed against my ribs so hard I thought it might bust through my chest.

I cleared my throat, trying to sound braver than I felt. "So… we here. What's the big deal? It's just a dirty ol' creek." My voice shook, betraying me.

Gerry turned, his eyes glinting with something I didn't like. "Throw some rocks in," he said, his voice aggressive. "Watch Old Man Jessie appear."

A cold shiver shot down my back. I forced out a laugh. "Man, there ain't no such thing."

"Do it," Cliff yelled.

I hesitated. Then I held out my hand. "Fine. Gimme the biggest rock you got."

Perry dug through the mud and handed me one. I pulled it back and threw it into the water. We all stared. Nothing. I let out a breath I didn't realize I was holding.

"See? Ain't nothin' "

"Do it again," Gerry interrupted, his grin gone with look of evil on his face.

Cliff shoved another rock in my hand. I threw it harder this time. The splash echoed, water rippling out in circles. Still nothing. We all exhaled, the tension breaking just a little.

Then Gerry bent down and picked up the biggest rock he could find. He pressed it into my hand, his grip firm. "One more," he said with a mean condescending tone in his voice.

I swallowed my salvia even harder this time.

We stepped even closer to the edge. The mud covering the tip of my shoes. I took a deep breath and threw the rock with all my strength.

For a second, everything was still.

Then the water started bubbling.

Big, angry bubbles, rising up slow, popping thick and wet. The trees behind us shuddered, their branches rattling like window shutters in a storm except there was no wind. I couldn't get a deep breath. I couldn't move. None of us could. Something was holding us there, locking our feet in place, forcing our eyes to stare into the water.

Then it came.

A head burst up from the canal, breaking through the surface with a sickening slurp. The eyes, Lord help us, the eyes. were bulging, blue and red like fire, burning with something evil. Its skin was gray, slick with slime, its mouth stretched big and wide, filled with jagged, rotting teeth. Its curly, matted gray hair clung to its head and face, dripping black sludge back into the water.

Old man Jessie was looking right at us.

I tried to scream, but no sound came. My lungs wouldn't work. My feet wouldn't move.

Something yanked at us, pulling us forward, dragging us toward the water's edge. My shoes slipped closer, sinking deeper into the mud. I could feel it, whatever it was, wrapped its arm around my body, tight like invisible hands.

Then, through the fear of silence and a near premature death, a voice came through, piercing my ears, commanding but loving and real.

"Raymond! Where are you, boy?!"

Mama.

The moment I heard her voice; the invisible grip released me immediately. My body lurched back like I'd been released from a noose.

"RUN!" I screamed.

Arthur grabbed Cliff, who had slipped in the mud. Gerry stumbled; his foot caught on an old fishing line. His breath gone, unable to scream for help. We quickly looked back, he couldn't escape, He reached his hand out begging for help. I doubled back to untangle him. Gerry was crying, his hands shaking so badly he could barely move. I yanked him free, and we tore off running, legs burning, lungs on fire.

Behind us, the growling started.

Deep, Low, and angry.

We didn't dare look back.

The growl was closer now, a deep, jarring snarl that rattled my entire body. No matter how fast I ran, it was gaining. My lungs burned, each breath a high pitch wheeze, my legs heavy like bricks. If I could just get over the tracks, maybe I'd be safe. But my body was failing me. My feet felt like they were sinking into the earth, dragged down by exhaustion and terror. If I stopped, if I so much as stumbled, that thing, old man Jessie, or whatever the hell it was would tear me apart and drag me back into the canal.

I didn't care where Gerry, Authur, or Cliff had gone. They got me into this nightmare. Let them fend for themselves.

Just as I reached the tracks, my foot caught, and I went down hard, slamming onto my stomach. The world spun. The hot metal rails burned against my skin. I tried to lift my head, but everything was a blur, my vision flickering as I stared at the heat rising from the ground, Had I passed out? I didn't know. All I knew was that I was weak, wheezing and drenched in sweat.

I forced myself up, my limbs trembling. I looked at my hands, they were covered in abrasions, stinging with small bits of gravel embedded deep in my palms. The metallic taste of warm blood dripped from my lips. I wiped my mouth and felt a sharp sting from my busted skin.

I got to get home, I thought to myself.

Stumbling forward, I veered off the road, cutting through the cornfield. The stalks towered over me, swaying in the wind, their dry leaves scratching at my arms like clawed fingers. The streetlights ahead flickered, their glow barely piercing the darkness.

Then I heard it again.

"Raymond!"

Momma's voice this time sharp and desperate.

She knew something was wrong. There was panic in her tone. She called my name again, this time screaming.

I forced myself forward, each step slower, heavier, like something unseen was dragging at my ankles.

And then, just beyond the rows of corn, something moved.

Waiting!

Watching!

 I knew I wasn't alone.

It was my daddy.

"Boy, git yo' ass in that house!"

He had a belt in one hand and a cigar in the other, smoke curlin' up into the night air. Daddy was tall and skinny, always wearin' the same pair of jean overalls, no matter what the weather. He pulled that belt back, ready to let me have it, but his arm froze mid-swing when he got a good look at me ,blood dripping from my mouth, eyes wide like a deer caught in headlights. It would be the first time daddy had ever spank me. He wasn't the disciplinary parent.

"Boy, what in the hell you done got yo'self into now?" His voice was sharp, but there was something' else in it,somethin' close to worry.

He jerked his head toward the house.

"Git in there to yo' momma, 'fore I change my mind 'bout whuppin' you."

I nodded at my daddy and headed straight for the house. My momma was already standing outside, hands on her hips, her face twisted with worry.

"Oh, Lord have mercy, Raymond! Boy, I'm so glad you alive!" She grabbed me in a tight hug, her body shakin' as she cried against my shoulder. Then, just as quick, she pushed me back, holdin' me by the arms, her eyes searchin' my face.

"I know you went down to that canal," she said, her voice tight with fear. "Didn't I tell you not to go down there? Didn't I tell you, huh?"

I opened my mouth to speak, but all that came out was a wheeze.

She frowned, leanin' in closer. "Raymond, you wheezin'?"

I nodded, barely able to get a word out.

"Come on, baby," she said, takin' my hand. She led me out back to that old tree, Grandma Mary's tree, Old Ma, the one she swore she had the power to take sickness right outta you. Every year, Old Ma, mark my height against the trunk, sayin' it was watchin' me grow. Her legal name was Mary M. Fontenot, she was my daddy momma,

"Stand right here," she said, guiding me under the line, Old Ma had drawn last time.

I leaned against the rough bark, chest retracting, my breath labored and tight. Then, just like always, the wheezing started to ease up, my breath became smoother, stronger.

I didn't know what kinda hoodoo or herbal remedy lived in that tree, but it worked.

"Some folks say it's voodoo," Momma murmured, watchin' me close. "But it ain't nothin' but natural medicine, passed down from our ancestors."

I closed my eyes, lettin' the night air cool my skin, lettin' that old tree do whatever magic it did. Momma just stood there beside me, hummin' soft under her breath, like she was prayin' or maybe just thanking the spirits that I'd made it home.

Mary Fontent Chatman born December 8th, 1872- died April 16th, 1962, her son Louis Chatman Sr, Born August 10th, 1898- died Feb. 2nd, 2002, have been buried together at St. Landry catholic cemetery next to the Holy Ghost catholic church in Opelousas Louisiana

Five

THOUGHTS BE GONE

The next day: Raymond Sr.

There are some things in life you just can't change like what happened yesterday and what's comin' tomorrow. My grandma Old Ma, Mary always said, *"Don't do nothin' today you'd be afraid to read about in the paper tomorrow."*

I can't lie; I'm still shaking up from seeing that head in the canal yesterday. I didn't sleep a wink last night. I kept my eyes open, listening, watching my heart thumping every time the wind rattled the window.

In a way, I felt safer after Momma prayed over me. But I also saw her out on the porch, sprinklin' salt near the front door. A Louisiana ritual, folks say keeps bad spirits out and since Momma believed damn near everybody had some kinda evil in 'em, we kept plenty of salt.

I got up outta bed and pushed off the quilts my mama made, the kind stitched with love but worn from years of use. The feathers were coming out of the pillows she made for us just yesterday. My skin was clammy, and when I stood up, my legs felt wobbly, like they didn't want to move and I did. I slid my slippers on and took a deep breath.

The smell of grits, eggs, and bacon drifted through the house, makin' my stomach dance. Mama was already up, fixin' breakfast like she always did. Goodness, I was starving' couldn't wait to eat.

But my gut was twistin' for another reason. It was gonna be a long weekend, especially knowin' I had a whoopin' coming for not listening'.

"Raymond!" Mama's voice echoed through the house.

"I'm comin', Ma!" I called back, but my feet didn't move just yet.

Instead, I stepped to the window and peered outside, hopin' to see Gerry, Arthur, and Cliff playin' in the street like they always did. But there wasn't a soul in sight.

My heart skipped a few beats as it tightened.

Oh, shit, I thought. *I hope the man in the canal didn't catch them.*

I walked into the kitchen, my parents already sittin' at the table. My plate was set, with a glass of orange juice right next to it. In the center of the table sat a plate of buttered toast and the homemade jam Mama canned every year. Oh my God, my mama was the best cook Opelousas had to offer.

The kitchen was small, real small. You could reach the stove from the table without even gettin' up. The round, dark brown wooden table had scratches from years of use, and the chairs creaked every time you sat down.

Mama reached out, grabbin' my hand and Daddy's for prayer. We all bowed our heads as she started talkin' to the Lord, givin' thanks for the food, for wakin' us up this mornin', for keepin' us safe. I scrunched up my forehead and peeked one eye open only to find Daddy starin' straight at me.

I shut my eyes quickly and bowed my head lower.

"Amen," Mama said, lettin' go of our hands.

I wasted no time stuffin' my face. The eggs were fluffy, the bacon crisp, the grits creamy just how I liked 'em. But Daddy wasn't touchin' his food. He was lookin' dead at me from across the table, sittin' tall and serious.

"So," he said, his deep voice fillin' the room, "what happened? What did you see yesterday, Rimen?"

He never called me Raymond, always Rimen.

"Not now, Louis," Mama cut in, her voice sweet and calm.

"No, Octavia," Daddy said, sittin' back in his chair. "Now is the perfect time. We gon' talk about this."

I swallowed hard, my appetite disappearing. "Well," I started, shiftin' in my seat, "Arthur, Gerry, and Cliff dared me to go. They kept callin' me names, sayin' I was too scared. I wanted to show 'em I wasn't."

"I told you not to play with those boys, Remin!" Mama's voice shot up, her face twistin' with worry.

Daddy held up a hand, his long fingers touchin' her arm lightly. "Let the boy talk, baby. Let him finish."

I nodded and took a breath. "After school, we walked down the railroad tracks and crossed over to Grolee Street. We walked all the way down until we reached the end of the canal. We were just throwin' rocks in the water when."

"My tongue was tied". My hands started shakin', my chest had a knot in it. I couldn't get the words out.

Mama stood up, her hands coverin' her mouth, tears wellin' in her eyes. Then she turned and rushed outta the kitchen.

Daddy took a slow sip of his coffee, then wiped his mouth with his handkerchief. His face was calm, but his eyes weren't.

"Daddy…" My voice cracked, tears spillin' over. I pushed back my chair and walked around the table. He pulled me into his arms without a word, his long, skinny arms wrappin' around me like a shield.

"It's okay, son," he mumbled. "It's okay."

I sobbed onto his chest. "I'm sorry."

He pulled back, holdin' me by my shoulders, his face lined with worry. "Don't you ever do that again, you hear?"

"Yes, sir," I said crying my eyes out.

"Good, son." He nodded, then sat back down. "Now, go on outside and do your chores. We'll talk later."

His voice was steady, but that look on his face told me everything.

This wasn't just about me sneakin' off.

This was somethin' bigger. Somethin' they weren't tellin' me.

I left my remaining breakfast untouched and stepped outside, the hot Louisiana sun hittin' my face as I went to do my yard work, my mind still stuck on that canal.

I stepped outside into the backyard. The chicken coops lined the left side of the yard, hens and roosters walked around clucking, while the garden stretched quietly to the right, blooming under the blue sky. I made my way into one of the coops, the wooden door creaking open like a warning. The hens clucked softly, cute golden things always laying eggs. Sometimes, I'd hide a few, hoping to hatch a baby chick.

As I scattered the feed across the ground a sound cut through the stillness. A low, raspy grunting like a wild pig, but not. This wasn't a sound that belonged to any living thing I knew. It was weird unholy, vibrating through my bones.

A sudden shadow crawled over the coop as a dark cloud descended from nowhere, swallowing the light. My legs trembled beneath me. The sound grew louder, crawling closer, it was scraping its claw against the wired chicken coop, with each movement I felt an electric shake run through my body, I tried to scream, my mouth gaped open, but no sound came out.

Then, from the far corner, a rooster emerged. But this... this wasn't any rooster I'd ever known. It lunged forward, talons scraping the ground like metal on bone. The other chickens scattered in terror, feathers and corn exploding into the air.

Its eyes were enormous, jet black like marbles, soulless, bottomless. Its beak was jagged and dripping with thick, green stuff. The body... twisted, malformed, like it got caught in an axle.

It reared up, screeching, and attacked me. Its beak tore into my skin bite after bite, peck after peck. I felt warm blood soaking through my clothes. My vision blurred. The last thing I saw was the creature towering over me, wings outstretched like a demon's shroud, before I knew I fainted. However, I could still feel fear impulses going through my body.

My mama, she could always tell when something was wrong. She ran outside screamin', just like that, and that's when my daddy,

Louis, got all startled. He was sittin' in that old brown leather recliner, sippin' his coffee when he heard her screamin'. Spilled it all over himself. He jumped up like he'd seen a ghost and rushed right out behind her.

They found me there, layin' unconscious inside the chicken coop, my body limp. My daddy, he didn't think twice. He scooped me up and started runnin' back inside, his feet barely touchin' the ground.

Mama, she was frantic. She grabbed the phone and dialed my grandma, Mae Temple Glaze White, we called her Tippy, she was a midwife and delivered babies in Opelousas. Momma knew with her skills she could stitch me up, Tippy was married to Martin White, together they had fifteen children, but it wasn't just Tippy who came to the rescue. My mama had another call to make.

She dialed my other grandma, Mary Fontenot, Old Ma, who knew all the right herbs and homemade remedies. The folks in town knew to see Old Ma for all their healing needs, herbs prayers and rituals. Her Husband's name was Jules Chatman. My brother, the one we call Rat, was named after him.

Anyhow, my mama, , told me later that when daddy picked me up, the chicken head had been cut off and was layin' right there on the ground. She knew, right then, that I'd been cursed by something evil from the canal.

Old Ma and Tippy got right to work on me, fussin' and prayin', doin' all the things they knew how to do. After a while, I started to come around. Old Ma, bless her heart, put somethin' strong under my nose, and that's when I woke up, starin' around the room, hoping I wouldn't see nothin' else.

"Lay down, baby. Keep still," Old Ma said, her voice soft but firm.

Grandma Tippy, though, was sterner. "Keep yo' ass still like she said, boy," she snapped. "Now didn't you mama and daddy tell you, Raymond? Didn't they tell you to keep yo' bad ass away from that canal? I oughta spank you right now, boy!"

"Don't spank him, Tippy Mae," Mama jumped in, her voice strong but full of concern. "I'm gonna have a long talk with him tonight."

The next day we went to church, I remember it like it was yesterday. Daddy, he was Catholic, and he always went to Holy Ghost Catholic Church down on Union Street. Mama, though, she was Baptist, and she'd head over to Little Zion Baptist, the one that's been standin' since 1892.

After church, when we sat down for Sunday dinner, it was like the air changed. Mama and Daddy finally decided it was time to tell me about the canal on Grolee Street, the one folks don't talk about. They told me why it was banned, why no one ever went near it. I ain't sure if I'm more scared now that I know the truth, or if it was better when I didn't.

Mama made me swear, swear on my soul, that I'd never speak of it to anyone, that it'd be a secret buried deep, never to see the light of day. She said there are things in this world, things you just gotta take to your grave.

And 89 years later, I still can't bring myself to speak of it. I get chills just thinkin' about it. I can't even tell the story of that cursed canal on Grolee Street, not without fear, not without shivers runnin' down my spine. There are some things, some stories, that should never be told.

To this day, I can't speak of it, not even to you. Telling it might bring a curse on the ones who hear it and for your protection, I won't. Some secrets don't belong in this world. Not now, not ever.

Mae Temple Glaze born 1870 died 1948. Mother born enslaved as Celeste Glaze.

Mary L Fontenot, Old Ma born 1865, Her parents were Froncois Fontenot and Margrete Fontenot

Six

WHISPERS IN THE HALLWAY

Raymond

I t started like any school day… but something was off.

Monday morning rolled around again, and that meant it was time to haul myself back to school. I hadn't seen Gerry, Arthur, or Cliff all weekend. I figured I'd catch up with 'em by the water fountain or hangin' around outside the cafeteria.

I got dressed in my best outfit, blue jeans, and a light blue striped shirt. Mama had ironed 'em out exactly right, creases sharp enough to slice bread. She didn't play about lookin' decent for school, rain, or shine.

I peeked out my bedroom window, and I be dog-on, the sky looked heavy like it wanted to slap me. You could just *feel* one of those Louisiana thunderstorms brewing' and let me tell you, when it rains down here, it doesn't play. The sky turns black; the wind starts howling and the rain hits you sideways like it's mad at you.

Now, back then, Black kids weren't allowed on the school bus. We had to walk, rain or not, and don't think for a second they slowed down for us either. One time, that school bus came barreling through street, hit a puddle the size of the Grand Canyon, and splashed muddy water all over us kids walking to school. We looked like soggy biscuits as we watched the bus continue down the road.

I remember looking up at that bus, ready to cuss somebody out, and all the white kids inside were laughing like it was the funniest thing they'd ever seen. But then I spotted two girls sitting in the very back, quiet as church mice. That's when I did a double take.

"Wait a minute," I thought. "Ain't that Miss Pearl's sisters?"

Sure enough, it was. But something didn't sit right with me. I mean they weren't white. However, with skin pale as biscuit dough and hair straight as a hot comb could get it, they were sitting there riding that bus like they belonged. Back in those days, you did what you had to do to survive.

They were passing and slipping through the cracks of a racist system, trying to make their way just like the rest of us. Shit, I'm here to tell you, things were different back then. Strange, messy, and sometimes plain unfair but we found a way to laugh through it.

I stepped out of the house wearing my yellow rain jacket and black rubber boots. Mama always said, *"if you didn't have shoes on you would catch a cold"* and Lord knows, with the storm brewin', my boots were going to come in handy. I slung my backpack over my shoulder and started walking to school.

Momma and Daddy had already left for work they didn't baby me none. They believed in raising us to stand on our own two feet. I was the baby of the bunch, but my brothers and sister were long grown and gone. That left just me, the rain, and the long walk ahead.

By the time I reached the school yard, the wind had picked up, blowing sideways and whipping tree limbs like switch canes. I shook the water off my coat and stepped inside the building. The hallway was short and dim, the kind of dim that made the flickerin' overhead lights feel more like candlelight than electricity.

I spotted Gerry down the hall. He didn't say a word, didn't even look me in the eye. That boy always had somethin' smart to say, but now? He looked like he'd seen the Devil himself.

He passed me slowly, and I turned to glance back at him. His face was pale and drawn, and there was a fresh abrasion across the side of his cheek like something had clawed him. My stomach turned. He'd been actin' up bad Friday after school, but this? This was different. He looked scared and ashamed. I couldn't tell which.

I made my way to class and paused when I saw Arthur sittin' in the back row. That didn't make a lick of sense he wasn't even in my homeroom. I stared at him, trying to figure out what he was doing there, but when our eyes met, I almost shit my pants.

He was smiling but not like Arthur usually smiled. This was a wide, twisted grin stretched across his face and his eyes... they were black. Not just dark. I mean *black*, like pitch black, like the bottom of a well black.

I blinked and turned away, my heart pounding. A chill slid down my spine like ice water. When I worked up the nerve to glance back, he was gone. The seat was empty and the rain outside started falling harder. I jumped at the sound of the thunder; I turned my head quickly to the left and right scanning the room for him.

Ms. Hammond must've sensed the storm was more than just severe weather. She dismissed us early that day, saying the rain was coming down too hard, and it wasn't safe for us to be walking home. I was glad to leave, felt like the walls of that schoolhouse were collapsing on me anyway.

As I walked, my boots splashed in puddles of water. I glanced toward the street that led to the old canal. I picked up my pace, my heart starting to beat a little faster, like it always did near that place. From a distance, I could see the train tracks cutting across the road, fog rising from the ground,

Then I heard it, soft at first, like the wind was calling my name, "Raymond…"

I froze.

I wasn't imagining it. That voice… it came from the direction of the canal.

Fear wrapped around me like the thick Louisiana humidity. I heard the train's low rumble in the distance. My bronchioles tightened, my asthma was kicking up. Still, I ran. My breath came hard with a wheeze like I was breathing through a straw. I felt dizzy, the world tilting sideways.

I stumbled and fell, my hands sinking into the wet pavement. I pushed myself up, and when I looked up, I was five feet from the tracks.

That's when I saw him.

A man stood on the other side.

If you could call him that.

His skin was gray... dusky, like old ash. His hair looked like it was made of scattered wool, wild and tangled and his eyes were dark blue and empty. He stared at me with a look that felt evil, like he knew every wrong I'd ever done. My knees buckled, and my eyes widened in pure, soul deep terror.

Then he stepped forward.

Just as he was about to cross the tracks, the train came rolling down like a demon from Hell.

The impact was horrific.

His head, oh my God, his head flew clean off. It rolled across the wet ground... straight toward me.

I turned and ran, the rain slamming into my face like cold needles. I didn't stop. I couldn't. My chest burned, but I kept running till my house was in sight.

When I got there, I didn't go inside right away. I collapsed onto the porch and cried quietly, snot everywhere trying not to make a sound. I couldn't tell Mama and Daddy. They'd never let me leave the house again if they knew.

I didn't call Grandma either.

Instead, I walked over to the asthma tree where Grandma had drawn a line around it just for me, she always said stand there when my lungs get tight. I stood under the line, trying to breathe, trying to believe what I saw wasn't real.

Once I caught my breath, I went inside, changed outta my wet clothes, and pretended like nothing happened.

But I ain't never walked by Railroad Street again and I never will.

Life went on, you know, just like it always does. I graduated high school, Gerry and Cliff went off to join the military. As for Aurthur, well, he got himself into a mess and was arrested for being an accessory to a robbery at a local store. Last I heard he was on trial and if convicted he would be sentences to Angola State penitentiary.

Now, me? I ended up marrying that cute Creole girl, Ophelia Mae Guillory on June 29th, 1955. Before I could blink, she was pregnant with our first little one, Terricita. It didn't take long, and I got myself a job at the Greyhound bus station, loading and carrying all the bags and whatnot. I made one hundred and fifty dollars a month, but that was enough to get us a place to call home over on Ross Street.

Seven

Echoes of the Unborn

Ophelia

I stood out on the porch, rubbin' my belly. I was pregnant with our first baby. It was hot in Opelousas, Louisiana. Like always a thick kinda heat that sticks to your skin and makes the kids smell like rabbits and syrup.

Raymond had just gotten us a place to live on Ross Street. It wasn't much. Just a small two-bedroom house sitting on a big, lonely lot, with one tree standin' out back looking as if it was going to fall any minute. The Bathroom was outside, which I hated, but it was what we could afford. The house had that quiet hum of something'...or maybe something else.

Ma'mu, my mother, Pearl she wasn't happy 'bout me being pregnant. She said she already had too many mouths to feed. Potoon, which is my father, August, was always workin', and when he wasn't, he was out in the shed cookin' up moonshine or mixin' that so-called" man herb" he sold to folks who couldn't keep up in the bedroom.

I had a whole mess of siblings, Theresa, Velma, Clifton, Walter, Authur, David and Bobby. Bobby was named after our father August Guillory. They were kinda supportive, I guess, except Velma. Good lord, Velma couldn't stand Raymond.She said he had something' evil hangin' on him. something from the canal.

I walked back inside the house, wiped the sweat from my neck. And I swear to God, I saw somebody pass by the back window just a quick shadow, low to the ground, like it was crawlin' more than walkin'.

Scared me near to death. But we ain't got nowhere else to go. So for now, this is home.

I went on into the kitchen to bake Raymond's mama, Maw'ma, a birthday cake. It was April 14th I'll never forget that date as long as I live. I planned to write "Happy Birthday to Octavia White Chatman" right across the top of that big white sheet cake.

She was up there in age, born back in 1890. Folks said she had roots deeper than the cypress trees. She and my grandmother, Amelia LeBlanc Guidry, were close friends goin' way back. That kind of friendship don't come 'round too often.

The kitchen was small and worn-down, with faded yellow cabinets that didn't close all the way. The floor creaked no matter where you stepped, and the air always smelled faintly of grease and dust. A single bulb hung from the ceiling, swayin' just a little, like it had caught a breeze but the windows were all shut. The sink dripped steady, tickin' like a clock. It was quiet otherwise. Too quiet.

I opened the lower cabinet and pulled out the old cake pan. a heavy cast iron, blackened from years of use. It had been passed down from my grandma Ophelia Durousseau, Daddy's mama. That pan had a long history. I set it down on the counter with a thud and turned to get the flour and eggs.

Then came the crash.

Loud. banging. Sudden.

I spun around, my heart pounding. The pan was on the floor, spinning like somebody had thrown it. Like it didn't want me near the stove. I blinked a few times, confused, and bent down to pick it up, my hands shaking. And just as I set it back on the counter, I felt it right there on my shoulder.

A hand.

Hot and scaly. Not like any human hand I'd ever known.

I froze. My breath caught in my throat, and my skin went cold despite the heat in that little kitchen. I turned slowly too scared to move fast and before I could even face it, the pan flew off the counter again. Like somethin' didn't want me there or maybe something didn't want that cake baked.

I screamed loud and wild then ran for the phone to call Raymond. My hands wouldn't stop shakin'. I kept hearin' Velma's voice in my head: He got somethin' evil on him, from the canal.

God help me... she might've been right.

I grabbed the phone and started dialin'. That old rotary dial spun round and round, slow as molasses. It felt like it took forever just to connect.

"Raymond! Raymond!" I hollered into the receiver, breathless. "There's somethin' in this house .I'm scared out my mind! Please, baby, come home!"

He answered like he always did when he thought I was overreactin'. "Aww, woman, ain't nothin' in that damn house."

"No, Raymond! I'm tellin' you ,Velma was right! There's somethin' here... somethin' evil. It's attached to you! We need to see Miss Aladyse . She can break it she knows how to get rid of curses from the canal!"

"I ain't cursed, Ophelia," he snapped, his voice low and stubborn. "Ain't nothin' followin' me out no damn canal."

"Raymond!" I cried, tears runnin' hot down my cheeks. "I ain't playin'. That pan flew across the room twice! I felt somethin' touch me, and it wasn't human."

There was silence on the other end. Then he softened just a little.

"Alright, baby... just calm down. I'm on my way."

The line clicked.

I stood there, hand shakin' on the phone, starin' at that dark hallway like it was breathin'. Whatever it was... it was still here. Waitin'.

I sat out on the porch, rockin' slow in Mama Pearl's old chair, waitin' for Raymond to get home. The baby was turnin' flips in my belly like she felt the tension too. The night air was thick, still holdin' on to the heat of the day. The only sound was the buzz of cicadas and the creak of the porch boards beneath my feet.

Then I saw the headlights bright and low comin' down the gravel road. Dust kicked up behind his car like smoke. My heart eased up just a little.

As he pulled into the driveway and turned off the engine, I didn't wait. I ran to him barefoot, gravel cuttin' at my feet, and he caught me in his arms, pullin' me close like he knew how bad I needed it.

"I don't wanna go back in there," I cried, still shakin'.

Raymond leaned back, brushin' the hair from my face. "Baby, come on now. I'll protect you from the monster," he said with a grin, then chuckled low.

I couldn't help but smile too, thinkin' how ridiculous I must've sounded talkin' 'bout ghosts and curses and flyin' pans. Maybe I was just wound up.

We walked back inside, the screen door slammin' behind us. The house was calm. The air felt cooler somehow. I looked toward the kitchen and sure enough, the pan was sittin' right where I'd left it. Like nothin' ever happened.

"Raymond," I said, turnin' to him, "please tell me you ain't cursed."

He took my hand, his thumb brushin' slow over mine. His voice was steady and calm.

"Listen, Ophelia. When I was young, my grandma Mary, old Ma made sure I was protected. She knew about the canal, and what was down there. She told me things can attach to you, but not if you know how to stop it. She said we're covered. You don't have nothin' to worry about Ophelia."

I looked in his eyes and believed him. Folks always said Old Ma knew how to keep evil away. She was a strong believer in Christ, but she still did her rituals said her gifts came straight from God, and she used 'em the right way.

Still, just to ease my mind, Raymond went with me to see Miss Aladyse the next day. She read over us, waved that bundle of herbs through the air, and lit a white candle that smelled like sage and lemon balm. Her eyes got soft, like she saw peace already settlin' in.

"You got nothin' to fear, child," she said. "Ain't nothin' here but a little leftover energy. It don't want y'all. It's just passin' through."

And just like that... I felt lighter. Safer. Like maybe we'd be alright after all.

The rest of that day passed quietly and peacefully like the house was holdin' its breath. Miss Aladyse words had soothed me some, but a part of me still felt... watched.

Raymond stayed close, workin' in the yard most of the evening, tryin' to fix the old clothesline that sagged like a tired back. I stayed on the porch, shellin' peas and hummin' gospel tunes under my breath, watchin' the tree in the yard sway just a little even though there wasn't no wind.

That night, we went to bed early. I laid there beside Raymond, one hand on my stomach, feelin' the baby twist and nudge. Her movements had settled some, but every now and then, she'd give one strong kick sharp and sudden, like a warning.

I was just driftin' off when I heard it.

Scratch... scratch... scratch.

It was faint, like nails draggin' slow across the wood floor. My eyes flew open.

"Raymond," I whispered, nudgin' him. "You hear that?"

He mumbled somethin', turned over, and kept right on sleepin'.

I sat up, strugglin' to listen. The sound had stopped but the air felt different now. Heavy again. Like the house remembered.

I slid out of bed, careful not to wake him, and padded barefoot down the hallway. The boards moaned beneath me. I crept past the bathroom and toward the kitchen, the moonlight spillin' in through the back window just enough to see shadows.

The pan was still sittin' there.

Right where it should be.

But the cabinet door underneath it? It was wide open.

I hadn't opened that cabinet. And I never left it like that.

I stood there, frozen, heart thuddin' loud in my ears. Then

Clink.

The faucet. One single drop of water hit the sink basin.

Then another.

Then a third.

And then, the lights flickered.

Not all at once. Just the kitchen bulb. Like it was struggling' to stay lit, like something' didn't want me to see. I backed away, eyes never leavin' that dark, open cabinet. I didn't breathe 'til I was back in bed, pullin' the covers up to my chin like a child.

Raymond never stirred.

And the baby? She was still as stone.

The next mornin', the pain hit me hard.

My stomach was tight as a drum, hard as a rock, and then whoosh my water broke right there on the kitchen floor. I let out a cry, grippin' the counter, and Raymond jumped like he'd been struck by lightnin'.

"Go get Tippy!" I hollered. "Now!"

He didn't ask any questions, just bolted out the door barefoot, runnin' up the dirt road to fetch his grandmother, Mae Temple. She was Octavia's mama and the only midwife anybody trusted around here. Delivered just about every baby born on Ross Street and beyond.

The sun was barely up when they came back Raymond breathless, and Miss Tippy walkin' steady like she'd done this a thousand times, which she had. She came in carryin' her old black bag and that calm look she always wore, like nothin' in the world could shake her.

"Boil some water, get me clean towels," she told Raymond. "And hold her legs when the time comes."

I was already breathin' heavy, curled up on the couch with a pillow clutched to my chest. Sweat rolled down my face, and the baby pushed low, real low.

Raymond did just like he was told he grabbed the towels and water, then knelt down and held my legs, his hands were shakin' worse than mine.

"You're doin' good, baby," he said, voice crackin'. "You got this."

Miss Tippy knelt between my legs, calm and steady, talkin' me through every contraction.

"Alright now, Ophelia. When the next one hits, I want you to push, ya hear?"

I nodded, teeth clenched. Then it came a wave of pain like fire rollin' through my spine. I screamed, bore down, and pushed with everything I had.

And just like that she was here.

Our baby girl.

She let out one sharp cry as Miss Tippy caught her, wrapped her in a towel, and placed her in my arms. She was bald-headed, light-complected, and the prettiest thing I'd ever seen. So tiny… but already strong, like she came into this world with purpose.

We named her Terricita Chatman.

Raymond cried. I laughed and cried at the same time. Miss Tippy smiled, wiped her hands, and said, "She came through the veil clean. That's a good sign."

But somewhere deep in my gut… I wasn't so sure.

Life moves on Fast forward.

Time goes on, and things settle down. I take a job working at Goodwill. Raymond thinks it's real funny, so he starts callin' me Fefe Goodwill. He doesn't know that's where I have been findin' all the fancy clothes he wears.

While Raymond and I are workin', his mama, Maw'ma, Octavia, watches the babies. LJ and Sibby Raymond's brother and sister drop their little ones off too, so our Terricita always has someone to play with. Brenda Joyce and Ann are always running around with her. They play for hours in the front yard, pickin' pears off the tree, eatin' figs, and whatever else they find growin' out there.

Raymond's folks got themselves a real sweet home right there on Bellevue Street. They been livin' there all their lives just like my folks. My mama and daddy, Pearl and August Guillory, got their house over on Melancon Street. That house got passed down from my grandparents, Ernest Guidry and Amelia LeBlanc.

Of course, now, it didn't take long 'fore I ain't workin' no more. I found myself pregnant again with our second child. This time, we had a baby boy. I named him after his daddy: Raymond Chatman Jr. We call him Bode, 'cause he got a little cherry mark on his behind. My husband is over the moon proud to have a son. Because we were doing better money-wise, I was able give birth at Lafayette General Hospital. Six weeks after giving birth, I found myself pregnant again with our third child. You see, I ain't got access to birth control not as a colored woman in the South.

Seven months later:

The house is feelin' crowded now. Toys are all over the floor and not enough bedrooms. Raymond and I sleep in one room, and all the children pile up in the next one.

Betty was born on June sixteenth, and Lord have mercy, she was so tiny she could've fit right inside a shoebox. We didn't even bother with a crib just tucked her in that box with a soft little blanket and set her right next to our bed. She came early seven months along.

When she arrived, I felt another strong urge to push. Something else came out... something that didn't feel quite right. Maybe not even human. I asked the doctor what it was, but he looked at me with fear in his eyes and said, "You don't want to see this." He turned away quick and rushed whatever it was outta the room. The nurse looked at me, I could feel her hand trembling on my leg. It was obvious she was scared; her skin was pale as a ghost.

I cried.

But when they placed Betty in my arms, and I looked down into them big, almond shaped eyes of hers and wrapped my fingers around her little hands, all that fear just melted away.

The doctor came back in, cleared his throat, and looked at Raymond and me really seriously. Told us Betty probably wasn't gonna make it through the night. I cried even harder then.

Was the spirit in the birth canal comin' back to haunt Raymond?

But Betty... she made it. She lived through that night.

When we brought her home, everybody came over to see her. Auntie Vertie walked in, took one look, and said in her thick French accent, "Oh my... she so small, sha bébé. Your belly was so big, I swore you had two in there!"

I didn't dare say nothin' about that other thing that came out before Betty.

Auntie Yvonne said, "We need to get that baby to Holy Ghost Catholic Church and get her Christened right away." So, two days later, we loaded up the car. The sky was dark, wind pickin' up fierce like the whole world was holdin' its breath. Raymond drove us to the church, and all the family came too. Sally Raymonds's sister and Dot his brother were her godparents, I don't know why we called his sister Sally. Her real name was Dorthy Emily Chatman; she was married to a man with the last name of Greene he was the plumber for Opelousas and Dot his brother well his real name was Austin Chatman.

We had a big dinner after, over at Mama and Daddy's house, Pearl and August's. But we had to cut it short. There was a storm brewin'. Hurricane Audrey was comin'.

"Come on, Fefe Goodwill! Pack the children up ,let's get outta here before that storm hits," Raymond called. Momma had already gotten up, fixing food for us to take home. We had more than enough of her oxtail stew. It was the best oxtails. Rich, slow-cooked, and seasoned like only she could do. I got the babies' coats on and went around giving hugs, one by one. Raymond went outside to bring the car 'round to the front.

That's when the sky cracked open.

The clouds hung low and heavy, bruised purple and gray, like something angry was pushing its way through. Thunder rolled slow and deep ,like a growl from the belly of the earth and the rain came down in sheets, cold and fast. It was pouring cats and dogs. I stayed on the porch, watching Raymond run back and forth through it all, grabbing Terricita, Bode, and Betty Ann.

Daddy handed me an old umbrella, the kind that clicked when you opened it. The wind yanked at it like it was tugging me. Lightning sliced through the sky, bright and jagged, and I couldn't help but look up at the sky. The water was falling on my face, I took a deep breath, my chest tightened, scared of what I might see.

Then I heard Raymond holler, "Come on, woman! Let's go!"

I bolted down the steps, dress clinging to my legs, rain in my eyes and just like that, my foot slipped straight into the mud.

I started to limp, pain shooting up my leg. Raymond jumped out the car to help me, his boots splashing through puddles. The wind was pushing hard against us, like it had something to prove. We were soaked through, clothes sticking to our skin like they'd grown there.

We drove slow down that dark road, the wipers barely keeping up with the rain. It slapped the windshield like angry hands, and I could tell Raymond was on edge. He leaned in close, both hands gripped tight on the wheel, eyes squinting through the downpour.

By the grace of God, we made it home.

Raymond had to carry all four of us inside, me with my sprained ankle, and the babies half-asleep. He set a fire to warm the place up, the wood crackling as if it were speaking.

I managed to get the children tucked in, and laid little Betty in her shoebox bed right next to us. Then Raymond and I crawled into bed, his arms around me, the weight of the storm pressing on the roof above.

We laid there quiet, just whispering to each other about the christening. It was pitch black in the room. The only light came from the fireplace, but even that dimmed after a while.

Then, plink, Raymond felt it first. A drop of water hit his cheek. A second later, it hit mine.

"Did you feel that?" he asked, his voice low.

"Yeah," I said. "I think the roof's startin' to leak."

I get up with Raymond right behind me. We're so tired we can barely move. We shove the bed over, away from the leak, and I hobble over to the kitchen to grab a bucket to catch the water.

It's so dark in the house you'd think night never left. I grab a lantern one Raymond keeps for when he's fishin' and lit it up. That soft glow cuts through just enough of the dark.

I peek in on Terricita and Bode. They're laid out, mouths wide open, sleepin' like they ain't got a care in the world. I smile and tiptoe away.

I slide under the covers, and just like that, we drift off to sleep.

When I wake up, it's near 'bout nine in the mornin'. Still dark. Still rainin'. The eye of the hurricane's done passed, but the mess it left behind is just gettin' started.

The roof's leakin' worse now. I hear that water plinkin' steady into the bucket. I look outside, and my heart drops streets flooded like an ocean, water rollin' over sidewalks and front steps.

This right here, I think to myself, is the worst storm Opelousas done seen. 1955… a year I'll never forget.

As the days roll by, Raymond keeps on workin' at that roof. Patchin', hammerin', prayin' over it but it still leaks. No matter what he does, that water finds its way in.

Word spreads that four, maybe six hundred folks done died because of Hurricane Audrey. Louisiana has always had its share of haunts, but now? Now it feels like the whole state has been overrun with spirits.

Our house is fallin' apart, plain and simple. After years of Raymond tryin' to fix it, one day he walks in, dusty and tired, and says,

"Baby, listen here. I been workin' and savin' up. I found us a big ol' house and I'm going to buy it. Needs a little work, but it's got plenty of room for all the babies."

I turn to him, my heart jumpin'. "Really, Raymond? I love you! Well where's it at?"

He grins wide. "Right on Freeman Street."

I freeze, my smile droppin' just a little. "Freeman Street?" I say, puzzled and wary.

"Yeah," Raymond says, actin' like it's the best news in the world.

"You mean that big house been sittin' empty for years? The one nobody wanna touch?"

Raymond had a nonconcern look on his face like it didn't matter. "Don't you worry 'bout all that, Fefe. We got us a good deal. I'm fixin' to go put the money down. 1010 Freeman Street, here we come!" he says, proud as can be.

I smile, but deep down, I'm uneasy.

Nobody talks about that house. It's like it's been sittin' there, waitin'... and not for something' good.

Eight

Hitting the Road

Ophelia

Today was movin' day, and Lord have mercy, the Louisiana heat was something terrible. It was the kind of heat that sat heavy on my shoulders like one of Maw-ma's wet quilts. The cicadas were singin', which were these big-eyed, big, winged insects with stocky bodies and short antennas. The air was thick with the sweet scent of magnolia trees, their blossoms droopin' like they couldn't take it no more. Even the Spanish moss looked tired, hanging lazy in the breeze that never quite made it to my skin.

I'd been packin' all week, tryin' to clean as best I could in that sticky heat. Still, I was excited, Raymond had worked hard to buy us a house, and I was grateful. I just wished I had somebody to help me pack. Velma didn't care much for Raymond, and Theresa, bless her heart, was pregnant again.

Now Sally, Raymond's sister, is pregnant. Green kept her full of babies. She was a little feisty thing, barely four-foot-eleven, with smooth, red-brown skin and a tongue sharp as a switch.

Raymond had called on Green, Duke Norman, and some of his brothers Louis, LJ, and Perry to come help with the heavy stuff.

I felt nauseated, and Lord, I hoped I wasn't pregnant again. It'd been five years since I last had a baby, but I knew this feelin'. My breasts were tender, and my belly feels off. Still, I kept packin'.

"Terricita! Stop playin' with them baby dolls and get your stuff in the box!" I hollered.

"Okay, Momma!" she yelled back.

"And make sure Betty and Bode finish eatin', and get their faces cleaned up!"

"Yes ma'am!"

Terricita was my little helper around the house. She'd follow me like a shadow, tryin' to be grown before her time. Honestly, I need the help, she does such an excellent job.

"You ready, woman?" Raymond hollered from outside.

"Yes, I'm ready!" I called back.

"Well, jump in the truck! Let's go!"

I turned to Terricita, heart flutterin' with nerves and excitement. "Go get Betty and Bode your daddy's ready!"

"Okay, Momma!" she said, then took off toward the back room, her little feet tappin' quick against the floor.

I stood there for a second, watchin' her run off. That baby girl of mine was growin' up fast way too fast. I could see it in the way she moved, how she carried herself. Lord, I'm gonna have to keep a close eye on her. I won't let what happened to me happen to her. Not my baby. Not by nobody, especially not by somebody close.

We all piled into the truck it was rusted and dented, like a tired ol' mule that done seen too many seasons. Green brought it over, one of his old plumbing work trucks. The thing looked like a rusted-out breadbox on wheels, paint chipped and grill bent, ridin' low with all our life packed in the back.

Raymond slid into the driver's seat, and I sat close beside him with the kids squished in like sardines. His big hands gripped the wheel; fingers stained from years of labor. He turned the key once nothing. Tried again clack-clack-VROOM COUGH! Still nothing'.

The engine made that tired coughing' sound like it was protesting' moving us one more mile. I looked at Raymond's hands shifting' gears on the side of the wheel, his brow furrowed with concentration. Sweat rolled down his temple. I sat quietly, sayin' nothing, but the Lord knows what I was thinkin'.

Why in the hell would Green bring one of his broken-down work trucks to help us move? I thought with my lips pressed tight trying not to say it aloud, this is a sign that the house doesn't want us.

Then ROAR! The engine finally kicked to life with a deep rumbling growl, shaking the whole cab. Raymond gave it a few pumps on the gas, and the whole truck jerked like it was wakin' up from a long nap.

I looked at Terricita, and she looked right back at me, eyes wide and shinin'. She smiled, and I smiled too.

"Okay, kick it into gear!" Green hollered from behind us. "We'll meet y'all over on Freeman Street! Don't stop!"

Raymond looked in the rearview mirror and shouted, "Okay!" loud enough to wake the dead.

As we pulled off, a big ol' cloud of dust came up from the gravel, coverin' Green and LJ like flour on a biscuit. Terrie and I busted out laughin' as we rolled down the road, their arms wavin' like they were tryin' to swat off a swarm of bees.

That was the start of a brand-new chapter. And Lord helps me, I hoped it'd be a good one.

As we were travelin' down the road, Terricita and Bode sat in the back seat, their little faces pressed to the windows. Betty was curled up in my lap, light as a feather. All three of their heads turned in unison as we passed Dairy Queen, Abdalla's, and the old Delta Rexall Pharmacy.

"Daddy, can we go to Dairy Queen?" Bode asked, his eyes wide and hopeful.

I looked back and gave him a soft smile before glancing over at Raymond. He was already lookin' at me, a crease forming between his brows. I knew that look. It was the look of, "we don't have the money for ice cream today." He didn't have to say a word.

Raymond looked up into the rearview mirror and met Bode's eyes.

"Not today, son," he said, his voice calm but firm. "We gotta get this furniture in the house and get ourselves settled."

Bode's face fell just a little.

"But I tell you what," Raymond continued, his tone warming, "give me a little time, and I promise we'll get ice cream every Friday night. Just you wait and see."

A smile crept across my face, and when I looked back over at him, he smiled too. His brown skin glowed under the heat of that old truck's cabin, sweat glistening on his forehead. Even with the windows rolled down, the air was dense and stagnant, clingin' to us like glue or a second layer of skin.

We kept on driving', the truck bumpin' and rockin' along the worn country roads of Opelousas. The wheels dipped into every crack and groove, and with each jolt, our heads bobbed side to side like bobbleheads on a dashboard.

After a while, the only sound left was the muffler, rattlin' and clangin' underneath us, hanging' on for dear life as we rolled on toward our new beginning.

We turned off Burr and made a right onto Freeman Street. I could see the house from a distance tall, old, white, and big as ever. As we rolled down that dusty road, everything felt like it was happenin' in slow motion. The neighbors stood out on the sidewalk, staring' at us like where are they going?

There were two ladies and an older man wearin' a big ol' hat that shaded half his face. One woman had on a black-and-white striped dress, tight around the middle like it'd been ironed into her shape. The other one wore a faded flower print muumuu and a pair of worn-down slippers, her hand pressed against her forehead like the sun was eating her face and the other hand sittin' firm on her hip, like she was ready to ask questions before we even got out the car.

Sure, enough she did, I wasn't out the truck good and before I knew it, she was walking towards me. I stepped out sitting Betty down on the ground, to her feet, Terricita and Bode hopped out the back, Terricita get your brother and siter and watch them, while I speak with these folks, okay momma. Terricita replied.

Nine

Patrick

I got up early that Saturday morning, ready to ride my bike on the first day of summer. The sun was already beating down. So hot you could fry an egg on the sidewalk. I couldn't wait to meet up with my boys Charles and Bryant Chatman. We all went to J.H. Augustus Elementary, back when our backpacks were super heavy, and we had to walk back and forth to school in the rain, shine, or snow. Our scrapped-up knees and ashy skin was a clear representation of that.

They lived over on Hiram Street; I was on Williams. Most days we'd meet at the corner where our streets crossed, the place where we planned out our little adventures bike rides, marbles, whatever kept us busy 'til the porch lights came on.

Only thing was... we weren't allowed down on Freeman Street.

Too many stories and whispers of the unknown.

But like most things' kids ain't supposed to do we did 'em anyway.

That day, we made up our minds. We were going. I hopped on my bike, feeling the gravel crunch under the tires. Bryant was behind me, tossin' rocks from his back pocket like some outlaw. I was laughin', dodgin' 'em, pedaling faster just to get away.

"Hey! What up, Bryant!" I yelled back, grinning.

"Quit throwin' rocks and catch up, fool!" Charles was dying laughing. Now Charles had ten fingers, his father Charles Sr. had twelve, he was Louis Chatman Sr. brother.

I stood up on my pedals and turned hard onto Freeman Street.

That's when I saw the house we were forbidden to go near.

Two stories tall, sitting still and silent. Something about it was just... off. Always empty and quiet. Like the land itself didn't want it there. Even the lot next to it was bare, all that stood was a pecan tree, no grass, nothin' but dirt and the metal plate labeled water sewage.

We stopped, all three of us starin'.

"I'm going inside," I said, like the words weren't mine.

Charles' voice cracked, "Patrick, what the hell are you doin'?"

But I didn't answer. My feet moved on their own, like I was being pulled. I could barely hear Bryant and Charles yelling behind me. My heart was slamming in my chest. My head was screamin', *What the hell are you doin'?*

Nobody ever went near that house.

Nobody.

But my feet hit the porch anyway.

The wood groaned under me.

Then... the front door creaked open.

There wasn't any wind or breeze. Just that long creaking sound slow and long, like the house was takin' a breath.

I remember the stairs. They were worn down in the middle from footsteps that hadn't been there in decades. They looked like they could whisper secrets if you listened close enough.

I stepped forward.

Inside it was dark. Not just lights-off dark. But the kind that questions your reality. The kind that settles in your gut and doesn't let go. It felt like the air itself disappeared or didn't want me breathing it.

Folks said the place was cursed. Said it wasn't meant to be lived in. That terrible things happened to anyone who tried.

Those thoughts were racin' through my head, but my feet kept moving.

I looked back once, I could still see Charles and Bryant on the sidewalk, yellin', eyes wide frozen in fear.

I raised a finger to my lips. Shhhh.

Then I turned back...

And that's when it happened.

A black shadow came fast and slashed across my vision like lightning.

My heart nearly stopped.

I damn near peed myself.

I spun around, bolted off the porch, and leapt on my bike like hell was on my heels.

One thing about us Black folks, we don't wait to ask why someone's runnin'. We just keep runnin'.

And that's exactly what Charles and Bryant did. No questions. No hesitation. Tires hittin' gravel like we were in a race for our lives.

We didn't stop 'til we were three blocks away.

When we finally did, I doubled over, laughin' 'til my ribs hurt. But my hands were shaking, and so were theirs. They looked at me like I'd lost my damn mind.

Maybe I had.

All I know is...

We never played marbles near that house again.

Well until we seen the new family moving in, I couldn't believe what I was seeing the house that was forbidden has been sold.

Later that afternoon, after the sun started going down, I made my way to the corner store. I rode my bike through the sweet smell of honeysuckle and motor oil.

The corner store was Mr. Baptiste's Place. It was one of them old-time shops with creaky floors, one flickerin' light in the back, and a dusty ceiling fan that did more squeakin' than coolin'. The bell over the door jingled like it was warning folks who stepped in instead of warning him. At times it felt like the walls were listening. However, it had every piece of candy, chips, and soda pop I needed.

I pushed through the door, tryin' to act normal, but my legs still felt like rubber bands. I grabbed a grape soda and a bag of hot fries. It was my favorite. But really, I came to talk.

Mr. Baptiste stood behind the counter, tall, thin, and older than the building itself. His suspenders hung loose over a sweat-stained white shirt, and his eyes were two faded blue marbles that had seen too much. This man had a deep voice, dry and rough with a memory long as the Mississippi.

He looked at me, nodded once. "Afternoon, boy."

"Hey, Mr. Baptiste," I said, settin' the stuff on the counter.

He started ringing me up, his fingers slow and deliberate. "You look like you seen somethin' crawled outta the swamp."

I hesitated. Swallowed hard feeling the frog in my throat "You ever hear about that old house on Freeman Street?"

Mr. Baptiste's hand froze as he punched the keys in the cash register.

The silence in the store stretched long and thin, like a string 'bout to snap.

He didn't look up at me when he finally spoke. He kept starin' at the cash register like he was lost for words. "What the hell you doin' down there?"

"I, I didn't go in, "I lied, but my voice cracked bad. "Just rode past it."

He looked up, slowly, and sharply. His eyes weren't just old they were haunted with fear.

"You go near that place, that's bad enough, "he said, voice low and mean. "That house ain't right. Never was. It was built wrongly and was placed there centuries ago. A bad house placed on bad ground. My daddy told me his father said, the earth tried to swallow it once. Damn thing just came back up."

I blinked. "Swallow it?"

Mr. Baptiste nodded, slowly. "Storm of '49. Flood waters rose up, like the river had a grudge. Wiped out two whole blocks. But that house was still standing spooky as ever. Not a shingle touched."

I felt a chill snake down my back. "Why ain't nobody ever lived there?" Oh, they tried, "he said, leaning forward, his voice not much louder than a whisper. "Family moved in back in 'fifty-five. Whole family. Momma, daddy, two kids. Week later, folks found the daddy out in the front yard, sittin' in a rocker, rockin' back and forth... but his neck was broken. Clean through."

My mouth went dry.

"What happened to the rest of 'em?"

Mr. Baptiste looked at me for a long time. "Ain't nobody knows. They were just... gone. Dishes were still on the table. Toys in the yard. Lights on. But not a soul inside."

The soda in my hand felt like hot lead.

"You sayin' it's haunted?" I asked, though I already knew.

"I ain't sayin' nothin'," Mr. Baptiste said, leanin' back, arms crossed. "But I am sayin' I wouldn't go pokin'

around there no more. Spirits don't like bein' stirred up. Especially the kind that don't know they gone."

I didn't say anything else'. Just took my soda, hot fries, and a stomach full of doom.

As I turned to leave, Mr. Baptiste called after me. "Boy."

I stopped.

"If that house looks at you again... don't look back."

Months later, after the family moved in, we felt comfortable enough to go near the house and play.

When the sun dipped down just low enough to cast our shadows, we'd gather by the house to play marbles. Raymond, Davis Edmond, Evan Brown, and myself. We'd lay our marbles on the ground, start counting, and watch the sore losers come out. You either lost to Edmond fair and square... or you lost with a few bruises to prove it.

Now Bode? He didn't like to lose either. Not without throwin' hands. He kept marbles in a tin can, and some in a sock. I swear that sock swung like my daddy's belt quick and fast. But Bode never used them in a fight after losing the marble game.

Cathy was another neighborhood friend of ours. She would come out to play sometimes, tossin' chalk and playin' hopscotch, her laugh contagious and loud. Terricita though, she was different. She's Raymonds older sister, Ain't nobody messed with her. I remember clear as day she looked me dead in the eye and said, "Why you lookin' at Cathy like that?" And I knew right then, sayin' the wrong word could get my teeth knocked in. Although I continued to play with Terricita, Betty and Raymond Jr. I never went inside their house again.

1010 Freeman Street

Terricita

This had to be the happiest day of my life. I was finally gonna have my own bedroom. A real room, with a door I could close. A yard big enough to run around in with my brother, sister, and cousins.

As we rode through the neighborhood, I pressed my face to the window.

"Look at all these pretty houses!" Right here in Brickyard, I squealed. "I hope the one Daddy got us is just as nice."

Before I could blink an eye, "Yes! We're here!" I cheered as the truck rolled to a stop.

I jumped out quick and landed hard on the sidewalk, starin' straight ahead.

There it was.

A big, two-story white house, standin' tall like it wanted to grab me and suck me in. It was bigger than anybody's house I'd ever seen. But the closer I looked... the less excited I felt.

Something about it gave me a chill.

The white paint was chipped in various places. The shutters hung crooked like worn out eyes. The brown wooden stairs that led up to the porch creaked even when nobody was on them. The windows, oh girl, the windows looked like eyes watchin' us, unsure and uninviting.

I placed my arms across my chest and stepped back a little.

Just then, a boy came rollin' down the street on his bike, kickin' up dust and hummin' to himself.

"Hi!" I called out. "What's your name?"

He slowed down, gave me a quick look. "Patrick," he said. "I live over on Williams Street."

"I'm new here," I told him. "Do you know Cathy?"

"Do you know Cathy?" he shot back.

"Yes...well no, I don't think so. What school you go to?"

"J.H. Augustus."

"I go there too," I said.

"I ain't never seen you there."

"Well," I said, squinting. "Just 'cause you ain't seen me don't mean I don't go."

He smirked a little. "You play marbles?"

"Sometimes."

"Can I come play with you and your brother?" he asked.

"I guess so. I gotta ask my momma and daddy first."

Patrick looked past me, up at the house. "Why y'all movin' in there?" he asked. His voice dropped a little, like he was tellin' a secret. "I heard that house got ghosts."

I felt like a had a frog in my throat. "My momma and daddy said there's no such thing as ghosts," I answered, but my voice didn't sound too sure.

"What's your momma and daddy's name?" he asked.

"Raymond and Ophelia Chatman."

"Ohhh," he said slowly. "Y'all must be kin to Charles and Bryant Chatman. They live over on Hirman Street." "Might be," I shrugged.

"Well," Patrick said, pushin' off on his bike again. "I'll see you later."

"Bye," I said, my voice in a hush tone.

As he rode off, I stood there, starin' at the house again. Patrick's words rolled around in my head like a dice game on the pavement.

"I heard that house got ghosts."

I turned toward the brown wooden stairs again. They creaked now, and nobody was even standin' on 'em. My heart pounded hard, loud enough I swore someone else could hear it.

I took one shaky step forward and then another. Then off into the house I went.

Once inside, I got excited all over again. The house was big built differently than most homes I'd ever seen. I stood there, frozen for a moment, just looking around. Slowly, I walked in, eyes wandering over every wall, up and down. I was drawn to the olive-green walls.

I ran my hands along them. They were warm. I could feel something, an eerie energy, maybe a presence beneath the surface. I felt as if I'd stepped into another world, one where I was completely alone.

Faint echoes of my parents' voices drifted in from somewhere laughing, talking. Their sounds felt miles away. To my right stood a grand staircase, deep brown and towering. To my left, the kitchen opened up like a memory I hadn't lived yet.

I stepped into it cautiously. The sink was enormous, porcelain white and old. The olive-green walls continued here, wrapping the room in an earthy, unsettling stillness. I turned on the faucet.

A loud groan cracked from inside the wall.

Startled, I looked up just as brown, rusted water poured out of the tap. I twisted the handle off fast.

Behind me, the refrigerator stood big, outdated, humming low. We're gonna have plenty of food in there, I thought.

I turned to the window. The white shade barely clung to the rod cracked, stained, and broken, like it had been hanging there for decades.

To the right, a short hallway led toward the back of the house. As I passed, I opened a narrow closet door just out of curiosity. I had to know what was in the closet. How big or small it was.

That's when it hit me suddenly, sharp, and cold.

I felt it rush toward me, fast, desperate, though I saw nothin'. My chest tightened like a fist was squeezin' the breath right outta me.

"Nope," I whispered, backing up quick.

I slammed the closet door hard enough to rattle the old frame, then hurried down the narrow hallway, heart poundin' so loud I could barely hear my own footsteps. Whatever was in the closet wanted out badly.

The porch door creaked open like it hadn't been touched in years. I stepped inside.

It was long and kinda dark. Oddly one side was a lot darker than the other end. It Smelled like damp wood and mold.

I reached up and yanked the rusty metal chain hangin' from the ceiling light. The bulb flickered once... then buzzed to life with a weak orange glow.

The walls were made of thick, black-painted wood solid and silent. I shivered.

"If anybody ever got locked in here," I muttered, "they'd never be heard again..."

Something about that thought sat heavy on my chest.

My eyes scanned the porch until they landed on a washing machine tucked in the corner.

"Well, look at you," I said softly to myself, walkin' over. "Ain't you somethin'?"

It was one of them old ones with big rollers on top to wring the clothes out, and a pipe leadin' outside for the water to drain. I ran my hand along the metal edge, still cool to the touch.

"This is real nice," I smiled, just a little. "Ain't gotta wring our clothes out by hand no more. Mama's gonna like that."

I turned to the window.

Outside, a single clothesline stretched across the whole yard, saggin' just a little in the middle. The trees swayed as the wind blew through them..

I sat down on an old wooden bench by the window and stared.

In my mind, I saw her a cow, big and white with black spots, trottin' through the yard like she owned it.

"I'm gonna call you Daisy," I said out loud, still starin'. "You look like a Daisy."

I smiled, but it didn't last long. The quite pressed in again thick, still, and watchful.

Then I heard 'em my mama and daddy callin' out through the house.

"Terricita! Where are you, girl?"

"I'm back here, Mama! You gotta come see this washin' machine!" I hollered back, excitement in my voice.

"A washin' machine?" she called, her tone liftin'. "I'm on my way!"

I could hear her footsteps hittin' the old wooden floors, clacking through the house loud and fast. She came in through the opposite door. I hadn't even noticed there was another entrance. Momma stopped right in the doorway.

"Aww no, sha tee-Bae-Bae!", she gasped, eyes gleaming, we got a damn washin' machine!"

She had the biggest, brightest smile on her face like she'd just won at the bingo hall. I grinned too, proud to show her.

"Look over here, Mama," I said, pointing to the window. "Check out our clothesline."

We stood there, side by side, lookin' out that dusty window. The clothesline stretched clean across the whole yard like it'd been waitin' just for us. We both smiled, imaginin' what was to come fresh linens blowin' in the wind, sun-kissed and clean.

Just then, Daddy came walkin' in, swipin' sweat from his brow.

"What the hell y'all doin' back here?" he asked, smirkin'. "Terrie, you need to come on and watch your brother and sister."

"Okay, Daddy," I said quickly, still half-laughin'.

"And woman," he added, turnin' toward Mama, "I need you to unpack them pots and pans and get that dinner started."

Mama just looked at him and let out a laugh, one of them warm, easy ones that said she'd known him all her life. "Mmm-hmm," she said, rubbin' his cheek as she passed by. "Ain't you just full of orders today."

He stood there grinnin', sweat shimmerin' on his forehead from a day's worth of movin'. But behind that sweat was a look of peace. Finally, all this hard work was finally payin' off.

The grass was high and ticklin' the backs of my knees as I stepped off the porch, the sun warm on my neck. I made my way out to where Bode and Betty Ann were sittin' in the front yard, messin' with dandelions and dirt. "Come on now, Bode," I called out. "Grab Betty's hand. Let's go inside and see your room!" He looked up at me with a deep frown, his lips poked out like he'd been suckin' on a lemon.

"Don't call me Bode," he muttered, squintin' in the sun.

"Well, fine then, Raymond Junior, grab Betty Ann's hand."

"That ain't my name either," he huffed, arms crossed.

I stopped in my tracks and blinked at him. "Well what should I call you then?"

He stood up proud, stuck his little chest out, and said, "Noon. My name is Noon."

I stared at him with a ridiculous look on my face, trying not to laugh. "Noon? Where in the world is that comin' from?"

"Ma-Maw told me," he said matter-of-factly. "She said I should tell everybody to call me Noon, not Bode." Now Ma-Maw was what we called our grandma,Pearl. And Mamou was Octavia, our dad's mom. That French blood ran deep on both sides of the family.

"Alright then," I sighed. "Noon, grab Betty Ann's hand and come on in."

"That's not my name either!" Betty hollered, arms flailin' like she was swattin' a fly.

"Oh Lord, not you too," I said. "Well what's your name today then?"

She stuck her chin out defiantly and said, "Bean Face."

"Bean Face?"

"Yep," she said, noddin' like it was the most natural thing in the world.

I just laughed and threw my hands up. "Alright, Bean Face and Noon ,let's go see the house."

It's funny to me that, my little brother and sister don't know that when I was born Maw'ma and Ma'mu use to say I was a little girl with unique gifts, like a psychic.

They both started marchin' toward the porch like little monsters that had just accomplished, a big scare. Weeds stuck to their clothes and dirt smudged on their cheeks. The house stood before 'em, still, evil, and quiet, waitin' for all the noise and life we were about to bring inside. I could sense it was angry. Once they got inside the house, Bode and Betty were full of excitement which might have made the house even more mad.

"Aw man, I like it!" Bode shouted, his sneakers echoing off the dusty hardwood floors. "Where's my room?" "C'mon, I'll show you," I said, wavin' him on.

Our rooms sat dead in the middle of the house, like the heart of it. They were split by a pair of old doors with foggy glass panes shaped like ladyfinger cookies thin and curved, kinda delicate, but off somehow. Like they didn't belong.

The walls inside the bedrooms were painted this deep, blood-colored burgundy, thick and dark like honey left too long in the sun. All along the wallpaper were birds' long, lean things with jagged wings with sharp, twisted beaks that curved like hooks.

Betty squinted, pointin' at one near the corner. "What kinda bird is that?" she asked, her voice soft, uneasy.

I stepped closer, draggin' my fingers lightly across one of the beaks. It felt raised almost like it had grown into the wall.

"I ain't real sure," I muttered. "Ain't like no bird I've ever seen."

The air in the room had gone still, heavy like a blanket laid across your chest.

"Come on," I said, tryin' to shake the feeling. "Let's go check out the livin' room."

We left the bedrooms behind, but not before I gave that bird one last glance. Its eye looked painted on... but somehow, it felt like it was watchin'.

We tore outta them bedrooms, feet poundin' down the hallway, passin' right by Mama and Daddy's room without even lookin' in. We made a beeline straight for the livin' room and the second we crossed that threshold, we all just froze.

Right there in front of us stood the biggest damn fireplace I'd ever seen.

It stretched from the floor clear up to the ceiling, made of rough gray stone, like it had been carved straight outta a mountain. The thing looked old, older than the house itself, like it'd been waitin' for us.

Why is everything in this house so big? I thought, my heart thumping and palms sweating.

The three of us crept closer, drawn in like flies on poop, only there wasn't a fire to look at.

I leaned in a little, squintin' into the dark long open fireplace. "Is this even a real fireplace?" I whispered.

But what I saw inside made my stomach twist.

It wasn't just a fireplace. This thing had depth. I mean real depth. I looked closer. I saw what looked like a tunnel narrow, low, with stone walls and spider webs. A secret hallway or passage, disappearin' straight back into another part of the house.

Bode and Betty peeked in, one on each side of me.

"What's in there?" Bode asked.

"I don't know," I replied.

"Let's run through," Bode said.

"NO!" Betty yelled. "I ain't goin' in there!"

"Well, I am," Bode said.

He ducked under my arm and took off runnin' full speed, laughin'. His voice echoed.

"Come back here, Bode!" I hollered.

"That ain't my name!" he shouted back.

"You're gonna get me in trouble! I'm s'posed to be watchin' y'all!"

He just laughed and kept runnin'. I could hear his footsteps slappin' against the cement... but there was somethin' else too—a second set of footsteps. And another laugh.

That's not my brother's laugh, I thought.

I looked down at Betty. "Wait here. I gotta go get Bode."

She looked up at me, eyes wide and almost in tears. "Okay," she whimpered.

I started walkin' through, pushin' cobwebs off my face and arms.

"Bode!" I called. No answer.

Just then, it felt like the whole world went silent and dark.

"Bode!" I yelled again, louder this time. "I'm supposed to be takin' care of y'all, come on!"

Then, outta nowhere, I heard a soft voice.

"I'll take care of him. Go back."

I looked around, startled but not scared. The voice was calm and reassuring.

I turned around and ran back out as fast as I could, the sound of my feet echoing through the hollow stone fireplace. When I reached the end, my mother was standing there with one hand resting on her hip. Bode stood next to her, laughing, and Betty was just behind him, her index finger pressed to her lips, chin tilted toward her chest with that look on her face that said, she told on me.

"What are you doing inside of there?" Momma asked, narrowing her eyes.

"I was looking for Bode. He ran inside," I replied, still catching my breath.

"Really? That's odd," Momma said, glancing at Bode. "So how did he get out?"

I stood there, silent.

Then momma's eyes went even lower and her mouth twisted before she yelled out.

If you don't get your little ass out of there before your daddy, see you. Go sit down on the truck until we are done. Momma said assertively.

We all walked over to the truck, our faces hangin' low like a deflated balloon. Sadness clung to us like tics on our backs. We plopped down on the tailgate, fussin' and arguin', while the heat rose up from the gravel beneath our feet like steam off a skillet. There wasn't a lick of shade to be found.

Bode reached down, grabbed a handful of them little gray rocks, and started chunkin' 'em out into the field.

"How'd you get outta there?" I asked, squintin' at him.

He shrugged, eyes on the ground. "I dunno," he mumbled, voice laced with shame.

"Don't give me that," I snapped. "You do know. Quit lyin'. You got me in trouble with Momma and Daddy!" He gave a small sigh. "Sorry."

Betty Ann just sat there, swingin' her skinny legs back and forth off the tailgate, kickin' up dust. I turned to her. "I know you told on me. Didn't you?"

She didn't answer right away just barely lifted her head and cut her eyes at me, then looked back down at her lap. Quiet as a mouse.

Meanwhile, Bode kept throwin' rocks, each one skippin' across the gravel like they had somewhere to be. Then somethin' strange happened.

One of the rocks he'd thrown... it rolled back toward us. We all went still.

At first, we figured it just bounced funny. But then came another one. Slow and deliberate, rollin' right up to our feet.

"Y'all seein' this?" I whispered.

"That ain't normal," Bode said, his voice now a little shaky.

"There's no wind," Betty Ann mumbled, eyes wide open.

We all stared down at the third rock, sittin' there like it chose us. The air went from being hot to suddenly cold. And then we heard it, an odd whistle-like sound comin' from somewhere far off. It wasn't the wind. Nor a bird. It was somethin'... else. And It was getting' closer, fast.

Our hearts beat as one loud, scared, and pounding like drums in a band.

Then we saw it.

Eleven

I Remember

Raymond Jr aka Bode

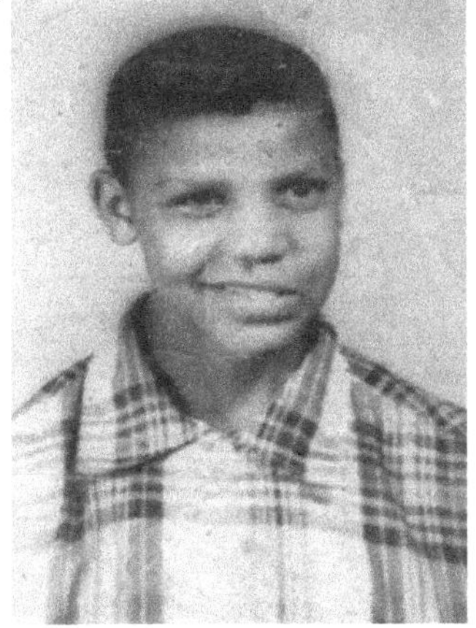

I sat there in silence, sweatin' under the hot sun, scared. Terrie couldn't protect us this time. I didn't know who or what it was. That whistle was annoyin' and sharp on my ears. Ever since the accident, my ears have been really sensitive.

As it walked by us, Betty stopped swingin' her legs. Her eyes got big and wide like saucers. I swallowed hard, tryin' to get rid of the lump in my throat. I looked over at Terrie, sittin' on the other side of Betty. I could tell she was scared too. Her fists were balled up tight, restin' against her thighs. Sweat glistened on her golden skin, and I could see the vein in her neck throbbin'.

That whistle,Lord, it was piercing', sounded like it was comin' faster and closer, but the figure didn't seem to be in no rush. It looked like it was just strollin' slow. But then, suddenly, it sped up and passed right in front of us. It was a woman.

She wore a long, dirty white dress and had nappy black hair hangin' down her back. Her skin was pale as a ghost, and she looked like she hadn't slept in days.

As she walked past, we all heard her whisper:

"Toto Pret."

"Did you hear that?" I asked, my voice barely above a whisper.

"Yes, I did," Terrie replied.

Betty started cryin'. Terrie reached over quick and covered her mouth.

"Shh! Be quiet, stupid, before she comes back," she whispered.

Tears rolled down Betty's cheeks, her eyes still wide with fear, Terrie's hand pressed firm over her mouth.

"Listen," Terrie said, her voice low and serious. "Wipe your tears. Let's go in the house and don't say nothin' to Mom and Dad, ya hear?"

"Yeah, I agree," I said, noddin'.

"Be quiet, Betty. Let's go."

As soon as we got in the house, we could smell the food cookin'.

Momma had made some fried chicken, black-eyed peas with rice, and cornbread with Daddy's favorite dessert: lemon meringue pie.

It smelled so good in here.

Daddy, Uncle Green, and Uncle LJ had done a respectable job gettin' all the furniture in the house. But I wasn't so sure about our bright orange couch sittin' next to them olive-green walls.

"Momma, that food sure smells good," I said.

"Thank you, Bode. Now y'all go take a bath and get cleaned up for dinner, you hear?"

Terrie, Betty, and I took off runnin' toward the bathroom.

"Ladies first, Bo-Scott," daddy yelled out.

Just like that, I had a new nickname.

Terrie took forever in the bathroom, then Betty. Finally, it was my turn.

Wow, I thought, this bathtub is huge. It was shaped almost like a big ol' claw.

Betty and Terricita had left a ring around the tub. My face scrunched up for a minute, but I quickly jumped in and took my bath. I filled the whole thing with so many bubbles usin' Palmolive.

I played for a minute with my toy, but I still couldn't get my mind off the lady we saw an hour ago.

In the back of my head, I was thinkin'... I'd seen her before. I wondered if she was real or a spirit. Was she the one who lured me close to Uncle Green's truck?

All I wanted to do that day was play.

As always, the family was busy either cookin' or workin'. Uncle Green was the plumber for Opelousas. He was married to my Auntie Sally.

I don't remember much, but I remember hearin' a voice.

My ball rolled away, and I ran to grab it.

Here came Uncle Green, rollin' fast in his truck.

He didn't see me.

I could see the bumper and the tires comin' toward me really quick, dust kickin' up all around.

Before I knew it, I woke up in the hospital several months later.

My face was disfigured on one side.

Uncle Green had run my head over.

Ever since then, I have been Mama and Daddy's favorite though I'm sure that's mostly 'cause I'm their only boy.

I climbed outta that bathtub, reached for my towel, and started dryin' off. Water dripped down on the cold tile floor, and I dang nearly slipped. Caught myself just in time

I looked over at the windows in the bathroom door and shook my head. Terrie's right, I thought. Those windows do look like ladyfinger cookies. Kinda strange, though, havin' windows in a bathroom door. Never did make much sense to me.

I put on my clothes real quick and bolted outta there, slidin' into my seat at the dinner table. Dad blessed the food, and we all got to laughin' and carryin' on, talkin' 'bout the day like nothin' happened. Not a soul brought up that woman in white we saw earlier. It was like we all agreed without sayin' a word best leave that part out. Then Daddy cleared his throat and gave us the lowdown.

"Alright now," he said, setting' his fork down. "Tomorrow, we're cleanin' up the yard and takin' care of some things around this house. So soon as y'all finish up dinner, get on to bed and get some sleep, ya hear?"

"Yes, Daddy," we all said together.

We finished our supper and started to get up from the brown wooden table. Daddy pushed back in his chair its legs screeched loud against the hardwood floor.

"Put them scraps together for the dogs and go on out back and feed 'em," he said, full and happy.

I stood up and scraped the leftovers onto one plate. Mama was already putting the rest of the food into the refrigerator, moving slow and careful like always. Terrie and Betty started gathering the rest of the plates to wash.

The water pipes let out that usual stutter and groan sounded like an old man clearing his throat before the stream came rushing into the sink.

Daddy talking about what we all must do tomorrow.

"I sure hope he fixes this sink," Terrie muttered under her breath.

"You better hush before Daddy hears you," I whispered back.

"Shut up," Terrie snapped.

I shot her a look, grabbed the plate of scraps, and headed toward the back door. As I walked out, I glanced over and saw Daddy sitting at the big black piano.

I still don't know where my parents got that giant thing, it looked too grand to belong in our house, but Daddy loved to play it before bed. His fat fingers and big hands danced over the keys, soft and slow, the sound curling through the air like the smell of freshly baked biscuits.

I stepped out onto the porch. The cool breeze hit my skin, and Lord, it felt good.

It's so dark out here, I thought to myself.

I moved slow down the wooden steps, careful not to get my foot caught on the broken cracks, balancing the plate of scraps in both hands. The wood creaked under my weight, loud in the quiet.

Admit it, I told myself, I'm scared.

I rounded the side of the house, each step cautiously. I could barely see my own hand in front of my face. The only light came from the stars and the moon, which was mostly hidden behind thick clouds, casting nothing but a faint shadow across the yard.

I must admit, I whispered again to no one, I'm scared.

Black and Bell were our dogs, Bell, a wiry ol' hound Daddy used for hunting, and Black, a broad-shouldered boxer with a bark that could make your bones rattle.

"Black! Bell!" I called softly, listening.

Nothing.

Usually I could hear them panting, huffin', rustlin' around in the dirt. I swallowed hard, hoping I'd tied them down good like Daddy told me. I'd used that coat hanger and the rusted chain he left near the back steps.

Still, no sound. Not a bark, not a snort.

The night was dead quiet, save for the crickets singin' and frogs croakin' somewhere out by the creek. The air was still and heavy so still it felt wrong. Chills ran up my spine like cold fingers.

"Black! Bell!" I called again, a little louder now, my voice shaking.

The dry grass crunched beneath my feet as I stepped closer to where I'd left them. My heart was thumpin' so loud I could hear it echo in my ears.

Then, there it was. That can't be dogs, I thought to myself.

Two white eyes gleamin' in the dark, floatin' like they didn't belong to no body at all. Hollow lookin', empty. Then came the growl low, deep, and mean.

I froze, my eyes big.

Teeth,shining in the dark like knives, suddenly they snapped out from the shadows.

I screamed and dropped the plate of scraps. Food went flyin' every which way but the right way. I turned on my heel and ran, legs pumpin' like they never had before.

The porch steps groaned as I hit 'em hard, nearly trippin' on the top one. I flung the front door open so fast it slammed against the wall with a bang.

Inside, I bent over, hands on my knees, gasping' for breath.

Daddy looked up from the piano.

"What's wrong with you, boy?" he asked, brows raised. "Did you feed the dogs?"

"Yes, sir," I panted.

"Good. Now bring your scary ass to bed."

I put my head down and hurried off to my room, my feet thudding against the floor.

"Don't be stompin' your feet in this house, boy! You hear me?" Daddy hollered from the other room.

"Yes sir," I mumbled, already halfway down the hall.

Before jumpin' into bed, I glanced over at the window. The broken shade was still up, lettin' just enough moonlight spill through to cast a silver glow across the floor.

I walked over and peeked out, holdin' the edge of the frame like it might bite me. I didn't wanna see nothin' strange out there not after what just happened.

My eyes scanned the yard.

There they were Black and Bell, both of 'em, gnawin' away at the scraps I'd dropped. Bell's long ears flopped down as she chewed, and Black looked up once before goin' back to his food.

I let out a breath I didn't know I'd been holdin' and stepped back.

Thank the Lord.

I walked over to my bed and hopped in, pullin' my old yellow blanket up over my face, just enough to feel safe but still breathe. The mattress was lumpy, but it was mine. We all slept on moss mattresses ain't like Maw Maw's fancy feather bed, but they did all right.

Moss mattresses were made from the dry leaves off them Spanish moss trees. They crinkled a little when you moved, and every now and then, you'd find a twig pokin' at your side, but it was home.

I laid there in bed for a while, starin' at the soft light spillin' through the window. It danced across the floor, gentle and quiet, like it was tryin' not to wake me.

Before I knew it, I was out cold deep asleep.

Next thing I knew, the morning sun was pourin' through that same window, stretchin' across the wooden floor in long golden stripes. Dust floated in the light, twirlin' slow like tiny fairies.

My eyes fluttered open. I rubbed 'em, gave a good stretch, then let out a big ol' yawn.

That's when I smelled it.

Mama was already up. I could smell Daddy's strong black coffee, sweet and bold, and Mama's homemade buttermilk biscuits floatin' through the air like a black butterfly

Lord have mercy it smells like home. I said to myself.

I bounced outta bed, my feet barely touchin' the cold wooden floor as I slipped on my slippers.

I hurried down the hall and into Terrie and Betty's room, they shared a bed. Standin' in the doorway, I looked over and saw the bed was already empty. The only thing left was a tangled mess of covers, bunched up in the middle like somebody'd fighting in their sleep.

I stepped a little further in, my eyes driftin' over to the vanity in the corner. It was a gold-varnished thing, old as methuselah, with little cracks along the edges like spiderwebs

Looked like it had been there a hundred years, if not more. Still, it sure was pretty and fancyl like something' out of one of them old-time movies Mama liked.

Just as I was admirin' it, I heard footsteps behind me.

It was Terrie.

"What you doin' in our room?" she asked, her tone sharp and bossy like always.

"I was lookin' for y'all," I said, turning to face her.

"Well, Daddy wants you outside. Now," she said, hands on her hips.

"But I ain't even had breakfast yet," I mumbled.

"Well, it's too late. Should've got up earlier," she snapped.

I gave her a gentle shove out the way just enough to pass and she nearly tripped over her own feet. I didn't wait for her to come back with more sass. I walked quickly across the hall and into the kitchen.

"Good mornin', Mama."

"Good mornin', baby. Grab you a biscuit and some cocoa and get on out there to help your daddy 'fore it gets too hot," Mama said, her back turned as she worked the stove.

"Yes, ma'am."

I grabbed a biscuit off the plate and dipped it straight into my cocoa. It got soggy just how I liked it. I slurped it up while standin' by the table, then turned fast toward the front door.

I swung the door open and ran down the steps, the boards creakin' under my feet.

Then I noticed it, Mama's good plate shattered on the ground. I froze. It was the one I dropped last night in the dark, runnin' from Black and Bell. I'd forgotten all about it.

My stomach sank.

That wasn't just any ol' plate.

Mama always said it came from her grandmother, the one she was named after Ophelia Durousseau. Now, Miss Ophelia was from her daddy's side, August Guillory. Word is, that plate had been passed down for generations

all the way back to the 1700s. And that's why I'm more than a little scared to admit I broke it. Lord. knows what kind of spirits might've been attached to that thing.

It wasn't just a dish it was heavy, thick, with a deep blue and white print that looked part Native American, part French, even Spanish. It was beautiful, really old and pretty. Not just a plate, it was more like a platter. Big as a serving tray, with a presence that filled the room.

They say it was gifted to my great-great-great-grandparents, Jean Baptiste and Gertrude Ramon. Jean was born in 1820 and passed away in 1886. His father was a Du Rousseau, and Gertrude was a LaCase. Gertrude Ramon's parents were Trinidad Ramon and Maria Vasquez, born all the way back in 1766.

Now, legend has it, we were supposed to use that platter every single night at supper, said it would keep evil spirits at bay and bring abundance into the home. When Jean and Gertrude passed on, they left it to their daughter Clara Durousseau and her husband Augustin Durousseau. When they died in 1893, the platter went to Ophelia Durousseau (1879–1939), who married Auguste Guillory (1871–1951). Together, they had my sweet grandfather, August Guillory we called him Patoon.

Patoon married Pearl Guidry, and they held on to that platter for years. Swore it brought them good luck until the year his mama, Ophelia, passed away in 1939. Funny thing that was the same year my mama was born. So, August and Pearl Maw-Maw and Patoon, we called 'em , named my mama Ophelia after her grandmother. And when Mama learned to cook, they gave her that platter. Said it was hers now her inheritance, her blessing. She's had it since she was a child. That plate has been in our family since the 1700s. And now... I've gone and broken it.

I just stood there, starin' down at the pieces, wonderin' if I'd shattered more than just ceramic. Did I break the veil of protection that'd kept this family safe for generations? Did I invite some kind of evil into our lives? My chest felt heavy, like all the ancestors were watchin'.

Truth is, I never knew much about that woman Miss Ophelia or the folks she came from. People say they might've been Native American, Mexican, maybe French. One thing's for sure: she wasn't Black like the rest of us. But round these parts, we're considered Creole anyway, a little bit of everything mixed in.

I walked toward the platter, eyes still wide. I bent down and peeked behind me to make sure no one was watching.

The coast is clear, I thought to myself.

Quick as I could, I ran over and tossed the plate under the house. Our new home stood on white stones, so there was plenty of space to slide the platter underneath. I dropped to my knees and looked under, just to be sure it was well-hidden. Satisfied, I stood and wiped the dirt from my hands onto my pants.

"Bo-Scott!" I heard Daddy holler.

The sound of his voice startled me, and I jumped.

"Get out here and help me get this yard together!"

I took off running around the back where Daddy was. He stood beside a shed full of old junk, digging through it. Sweat poured from his forehead, the sun was already blazing hot. He wore a faded yellow shirt and a pair of jeans he'd cut off at the knees. His legs were dusty, and his knees looked dry and ashy. He looked over at me and shook his head.

"You still got your pajamas on? How you gon' work in your night clothes, Bo-Scott?"

I squinted up at him, my nose crinkled, and my shoulders hunched from the sun.

"Oh, just forget it," he said with a sigh. "Just get over here. Let's start with all this stuff in the shed."

We got to work pulling everything out. There were some of the oddest things in there old medical supplies, strange tools I ain't never seen before. One of them was a heavy hunk of metal, which looked like giant pliers with sharp, rusted edges. There were Bibles, a chair with wires sticking out of it... Daddy looked mighty concerned. I couldn't blame him. That shed gave off a feeling, and not the good kind.

Once we'd cleared it all out, we loaded the truck. Daddy climbed inside, and I slid into the passenger seat.

"Oh, go close the shed doors and put that lock on it," Daddy said.

"Okay," I replied, hopping back out of the truck. I ran across the dry, crackly grass toward the shed.

Just as I reached for the doors, one of them swung open inward. I had to step inside to grab the handle. The old wooden frame groaned a little as I moved. Sunlight filtered through the cracks in the boards, and thick spider webs clung to the corners.

I grabbed the handle, my back facing into the shed. As I started to pull the door closed, I heard it.

A low gnawing sound.

Like something chewing through the wood behind me.

My breath caught. I didn't want to turn around.

Then came the sound of claws skittering across the floor. Fast. Coming toward me.

My hands trembled. Sweat pooled in my palms. I yanked at the door, heart racing.

Before I could even shut it, something slammed into me.

I screamed.

A high-pitched cry escaped me as pain lit up my back and neck.

"Mama! Daddy! Heeelp!" I hollered.

I twisted and squirmed, trying to see what was on me. Claws scraped my skin, teeth sunk into me rats. Big, ugly, mean rats. They bit and scratched, crawling all over me.

I fell, mouth hitting the hard ground. Blood squirted from my lips. Dirt filled my mouth. I looked up and saw Mama through the kitchen window, changing the curtains. Her eyes met mine and went wide with terror.

"Raymond! Oh my God, RAYMOND!" she screamed.

Daddy was still in the truck, picking his chin with those little tweezers like he always did. He hadn't heard my screams, but he heard hers. He looked up and saw me lying there, bleeding in the dirt.

He flung the truck door open and came running, slamming it behind him. His legs flew across the yard, yellow grass whipping against them, dust kicking up in his wake.

"Daddy!" I cried.

He didn't stop. Couldn't. He hit the brakes near me, feet skidding, knees bent, hands reaching. He grabbed me and yanked me up to my feet, swatting and beating at the rats with his big, strong hands.

Then Mama came flyin' around the corner with the biggest cast iron skillet I ever seen. For half a second, I wondered which grandparent she got that from. She wore her yellow house dress, white apron tied tight, and her hair was curled up high and neat.

"Get away from my baby, goddammit!" she yelled.

By the time she reached us, Daddy had already pulled most of the rats off and thrown them to the ground. Mama smashed the rest with that skillet, not holding back one bit.

Once they were all gone, Mama wrapped her arm around my shoulders and walked me inside. I was dirty, bleeding, shaken.

"What happened to you, Noon?" Terrie asked, her voice soft and shaky.

I looked up and cut my eyes at her, mad. Betty stood behind her, hand over her mouth, trying to hide her laughter.

"It's not funny," I snapped.

"Stop it, y'all. Finish these curtains," Mama said sharply.

She took me into the bathroom and cleaned me up, dabbing at each wound one by one. Her hands were gentle, but her face changed. Something came over her, something strange.

I looked up at her, then glanced at my shoulder. I couldn't see what she saw, but the pain that had been burning in me just... vanished. Like it had never happened.

Twelve

THE TOUCH

Betty

I'm so mad! Why'd he have to go and ruin our whole day?" I huffed under my breath. "I don't like havin' a big brother," I thought to myself, arms crossed tight across my chest.

All I wanted was to play with my baby doll, Frances. Instead, Momma had me scrubbin' floors and helpin' hang curtains all 'cause I laughed at Bode. And I only laughed 'cause Terricita did first. She started it! Then she went and pretended to care when Momma and Daddy brought Bode back inside the house.

Terricita was the first one to run to the window, peekin' out and gigglin'. I wouldn't've even known what was goin' on if she hadn't turned and hollered, "Betty, come look!" Next thing I knew,

Momma was runnin' 'round the yard swingin' a skillet, tryin' to kill them rats. Bode was screamin' bloody murder, but he's alright now so why I'm the one on punishment?

I sighed, picked up Frances, and gently brushed her golden curls with my fingers. Her little eyes looked up at me like she understood. "It's alright, baby," I whispered, "we'll play later."

I walked back into the kitchen, determined to finish the curtains like Momma asked. I climbed up the step-ladder slow and careful, reachin' high over the window frame. Just as I leaned to thread the curtain through the rod, something on the counter caught my eye.

My heart near jumped clean outta my chest.

There it was a big pretty box from Dimmick supplies, perfect for makin' Frances her very own dollhouse. I lit up, grinnin' so wide I could feel it in my cheeks. Soon as I get done with these curtains, I'm gonna unpack that box and save it for her.

Then I spotted somethin' else. To the left of the box lay an advertising flyer from LeBlanc's Fashion & Fabrics oh, my stars, they had the prettiest cut-out patterns. Right beside it was another paper from Fontenot Furniture. My heart skipped a beat. I could cut out tiny dresses and even paper clippings of chairs or somethin' for Frances. I was so excited I nearly forgot I was still on punishment. My hands moved faster, hangin' those curtains like gossip in the streets of Opelousas.

I was deep in my daydream, plannin' Frances's whole little house, when Terricita strolled back into the kitchen like nothin' had happened.

"Momma said when you're done, start cleanin' out the refrigerator," she said, actin' like she was the boss of me. I spun around. "What? That ain't fair!"

I threw a glance out the window and whispered to myself, "I can't wait to go to Ma"Mu's house."

I stepped down from the ladder. The kitchen felt cold all of a sudden. The whole house was quiet; you could hear pin drop. The air had changed, and I couldn't explain why. Something about it just felt... off.

"Mom?" I hollered. No answer.

I walked over to the sink, grabbed the bucket, and started filling it with water. Reaching under the cabinet for a sponge, I barely had time to register what happened next. The cabinet door slammed shut BAM! loud and hard, right by my hand. I jumped, heart skipping.

A thin layer of sweat broke out across my forehead. It had gone from cold to hot in just a matter of seconds.

I picked up the bucket with my left hand and carried it over to the refrigerator. Slowly, I pulled the door open. A puff of cold frost hit me square in the face and with it, a strange, sour smell. My eyes blinked quick, and my nose crinkled up tight. I covered my face with my hand.

"Whew," I whispered to myself, trying not to gag.

The fridge light beamed in my eyes, sharp and blinding. I reached in and started wiping it out fast as I could, scrubbing through the stink. But then... the light started to dim. Slowly, like someone was turning down a dial. I paused. Glanced around. Did I break something? The house was still. Not a sound.

I tilted my head, listening.

Just as I started to close the fridge door, a white hand big, wide, pale came reaching out from behind it. Fingers stretched open, ready to grab me.

I froze. I couldn't scream. Couldn't cry. Couldn't even move.

My heart was pounding so hard, I felt it in my cheeks.

Then the hand moved through me. It didn't just touch me; it passed through me. My body jerked back, like it hit the very center of my soul.

Mouth wide open, I tried to scream, but no sound came. The kitchen lights flickered and then.

"AAAAAAAHHHHHHHHHHHH!"

A scream tore from deep in my gut. A scream from hell itself.

Footsteps thundered down the hallway, the sound of bare feet slapping against wood.

"What? What happened?" Daddy called out, running into the kitchen.

"Something, something touched me!" I cried, shaking.

"What touched you?" he asked, looking over me.

"I don't know it was a hand! It, it came from behind the fridge!"

Daddy's eyes went wide. Mom looked at him, then back at me, trying to keep her voice calm.

"Alright now, take a deep breath, baby," she said gently. She looked at Daddy. "Raymond, if it's alright with you, I'm gonna send 'em over to Ma'Mu's for a bit. This day's been too much I need a break… and a cold beer."

Daddy rubbed his face and nodded. "Yeah… me too."

Mom turned back to us kids. "Y'all go on and get ready. I'm taking' you to your grandmother's house."

We hurried down the hallway to our room, not daring to look back.

Terrie and I went straight to the mahogany-colored dresser the one with the old glass knobs and the thin cracks running across the top drawer like an old mans crusty foot. We yanked it open and started digging through it fast, our hands moving in a silent frenzy.

Not a single word passed between us.

We each threw on clothes in a rush, trying to wear something opposite of each other. Mom had a habit of dressing us like twins even though we were two years apart. We hated it. Today, we needed to feel different, separate. Like our own selves.

The air in the room felt strange, like it was holding its breath right along with us.

Bodie, Terricita, and I took off running toward the front door. We stood there, shoulder to shoulder, waiting for Mama and Daddy to come out.

As we stood there waiting, their voices carried through the wall muffled and heated, just loud enough to make us nervous.

"They're arguin' again," Terricita whispered.

I nodded but didn't say a word. The muffled sound echoed through the sheetrock like it was bouncing off the black wood that graced the walls. We just stood still, listening, trying not to let it shake us.

Then, the door creaked open. Mama and Daddy stepped out, both of 'em wearin' fake smiles like nothin' had just happened.

"Alright," Daddy said, clappin' his hands once. "We'll take the Jeep today."

"Yeah!" we all shouted at once, the tension breakin' like a snapped twig. We started skippin' and hoppin' in place like it was the best news we'd heard all week.

Daddy opened the door for us, and we shoved the screen door open with one big push.

"Last one in is a rotten egg!" Bodie hollered.

We laughed and raced out of the house, jumpin' into the Jeep like it was a ride at the rodeo.

It was a beautiful day, warm and breezy, the kind of day that made you feel alive. We were finally outside, riding in Daddy's light-blue Jeep with the top off, wind cutting through the still air like laughter on a Sunday afternoon.

Terricita stood behind Daddy with her arms wrapped around his neck, grinning like she ain't had a care in the world. Bode sat next to her, legs dangling and eyes wide, taking it all in. I was squished between Momma and Daddy in the front seat, feelin' the sun on my arms and the road rumbling beneath us.

The Jeep was nice, really nice. Daddy kept it clean, and with the top off, it felt like freedom. We were laughin' and talkin', carryin' on like everything was fine. But I could still feel that quiet tension stretching between Momma and Daddy like a thin wire. They weren't saying a word to each other.

I looked up at Terrie. Her smile was so bright, and the wind danced through her fine Creole hair as we rolled down those old country roads in Louisiana. I turned my head toward Bode, then glanced at Momma sittin' still in the passenger seat beside me, eyes fixed straight ahead.

We made a left onto Railroad, then a right onto Jefferson.

That's when it happened.

We hit a bump hard right on the tracks. The Jeep jolted, and the next thing I knew, Momma popped up outta her seat like toast from a toaster and went flyin' right out the side of the truck.

It all happened so fast.

I whipped my head around, and there she was tumbling down the street like a dandelion in the wind, her black curls rollin' with her, round and round, dust risin' up all around her like she was part of the land.

"Daddy!" I hollered. "Momma's gone!"

He just kept drivin', smilin', not hearin' a thing.

"Daddy! Momma gone!"

He still didn't catch it.

I leaned forward, my voice sharper this time. "Daddy!"

"What?" he finally said.

"Momma's gone, she fell out the truck!"

His eyes shot over to the empty seat beside me, then up to the rearview mirror.

"Oh damn. Oh shit!"

He yanked the wheel so hard the Jeep tipped up on two wheels we all went leanin' to the left like rag dolls then it dropped back down, tires hittin' hard. He spun it around and gunned it back up the road.

We all held our breath as he slammed the brakes and jumped out. From inside the truck, we watched him run to her.

Momma was layin' still for a second, just lyin' in the dust. My heart dropped.

But then she moved, slow at first then sat up, lookin' stunned but alive.

Daddy scooped her up, wrapped his arms around her like she was the most precious thing he'd ever held.

"I'm so sorry, baby. You, okay?" he asked, his voice soft and real shaken.

Momma just nodded, still dazed. She didn't say much, but she let him help her up. He brushed the dirt off her dress, held her hand like he wasn't ever lettin' go again.

When they got back to the truck, Daddy opened the door for her, He helped her get in gently, like she might break. He lifted her legs in one by one, then leaned down and kissed her on the forehead.

She had scratches on her arms and legs, little cuts here and there. But not a single mark on her pretty face.

We made a beeline straight back home. Daddy had changed his mind 'bout takin' us to Ma'Mu's house. Instead, he swung by the corner store, grabbed Mama her favorite beer, a link of hot boudin, and a brown paper sack of cracklins. Then we headed on back.

When we pulled into the driveway, he helped Mama out the truck. She moved real slow, wincin' with every step as she made her way to the porch. Bode hurried up and swung the door open for her.

"Terricita, go get your mama some Tylenol," Daddy said, steadyin' her by the arm. "Betty, bring me some peroxide and gauze."

Mama eased herself down onto the couch with a soft sigh. I handed Daddy the supplies, and we all stood around watchin' as he gently cleaned her scraped-up knees. Her face crinkled with pain, but she didn't say nothin'. Just breathed through it.

Terricita came back and gave her the Tylenol, and after a moment, Daddy sat down at the old upright piano in the corner. His fingers started to dance over the keys soft and familiar tunes Mama always loved.

She leaned back, sippin' her beer, a little smile peekin' through the ache. That boudin sat warm in her lap, and for a while, everything in the house got real quiet except for that music.

I went into the kitchen, pulled out the box and the paper I'd seen earlier that day, and started cuttin' out paper dolls, little outfits, and a shoebox dollhouse for Frances. Meanwhile, Terrie and Bode sat cross-legged on the rug playin' checkers, whisperin' and gigglin' like nothin had happened at all.

The only thing I hoped for was to never see that hand again,

Thirteen

FEARLESS

Pearl aka Ma'mu

*I*ntelligent
    alone
broken
But resilient

The alarm was goin' off, loud as a freight train, and all I wanted to do was smack that bell and roll back under the covers.

"August, wake up, baby," I whispered, leanin' close. "It's time for work. I got your lunch packed already it's in the icebox."

I laid my hand gently on his chest, lettin' my fingers rest there a moment to remind him I still loved him whether he felt it or not. His skin, that warm red-gold color, smooth as cane syrup, and his straight brown hair fell across his forehead just so. His body, lean and wiry, was all I needed back then. At least, it felt like enough... at one time.

Truth be told, some days I couldn't stand him, and the Lord knows, he couldn't stand me either. But there was a time when we loved each other really deeply. We'd play this silly little game, spankin' each other and chasin' through the house, laughin' like two kids. I don't even know why we did that, but I sure do remember how happy we used to be.

"August, baby, wake up now," I said again, a little firmer this time.

He groaned and finally cracked open his sleepy, droopy brown eyes.

"What time is it?" he mumbled.

"It's six-thirty," I said, pullin' back the covers. "You ain't hear the alarm? Or the chicken's raisin' all that ruckus out back?"

"Yeah, whatever," he muttered, swingin' his legs off the bed and rubbin' his face.

I watched him, wonderin' how we'd gotten here two people still married, still in the same house, but somethin' between us had gone quiet over the years. Maybe he was still mad about things I couldn't fix. Maybe I was too. I didn't even know anymore.

But every mornin', I got up and tried to be the best version of myself. I was still a good daughter, mother, and now a faithful wife. And I was still the smartest woman on this side of town, whether anybody said so or not. Funny thing is, one of our boys ain't even his by blood, but he treats that child better than the others sometimes. We got three girls Velma, Theresa, and Ophelia and five boys Clifton, Walter, Bobby, Author, and little David. And Lord, he loves them all. I know somewhere deep down; he still loves me too.

As he sat on the edge of the bed stretchin' and yawnin', I swung my legs over my side and touched my feet to the cold wood floor. I slipped on my satin flowered robe and slippers, tied the sash tight, and headed to the kitchen to make his coffee.

It's so cold in this house, I thought, pullin' my arms close.

I boiled the water, poured it over the coffee grounds, and filled his thermos nice and full. I could hear August movin' around in the bathroom, finishin' up. When that door creaked open, my heart thumped hard in my chest part worry, part hope.

I met him in the hallway.

"Here's your coffee, babe... and your lunch." I held it out with both hands.

He reached for it, and I took the chance to hold his hand just a second longer than I needed to. He looked me in the eye, and there was somethin' there was sadness, maybe... or maybe only tired of love.

"Thank you," he said low.

Then he turned quickly and headed for the door.

I followed behind him, quietly.

He and his brother Eli both worked for Daly Motors. They were mechanics and part-time salesmen too. My husband, August, is a good man quiet, steady, not the type to run the roads or raise his voice.

I stood out on the front porch, watchin' him make his way past Momma and Daddy's house, which sat just in front of ours. He walked across the thick green grass, stepped through the old metal gate that framed the yard, and headed off to work. The front gullies were filled with water from the rain last night, and mosquitoes were already startin' to rise in the morning heat.

We live here on Park Street, all of us together in the same lot. My mom, Amelia LeBlanc, and my daddy, Ernest Guidry, stay in the front house. As the oldest child, I've always helped care for them. Daddy still works for the garbage company, tough as ever even with the years catchin' up to him. Momma, she is staying home now. She was born September 12, 1891, and she's gettin' on in age, barely able to walk these days. Daddy was born in 1881, ten years her senior.

Momma married young so young, in fact, her parents had to sign the marriage license for her. Her folks were Elie LeBlanc and Celesie Pelloquin. Funny thing is, they didn't have Momma until they were 41 and 31 themselves. I guess back then, things just went the way they went.

Now here we are, livin' right behind Momma and Daddy, and I'm the only one helpin' them day in and day out. With all the sisters and brothers I got, you'd think somebody'd come lend a hand. But I guess since we're right here in the back house, it's just assumed I'll do everything. Maybe 'cause I'm the oldest out of the eight of us. It's me, then my brother Wallace, Celeste, Yvonne, Lorena, John, Hilton, and little Vertie Guidry, the baby of the bunch.

I snapped out of my thoughts, Ophelia, my baby girl, was comin' over today. We had plans to do a little shoppin' at the Piggly Wiggly, and she said she'd help me cook supper for Momma Amelia.

I stepped back inside the house, the screen door closin' soft behind me with a slow creak and click. I started tidyin' up a bit, wiping down the counters, sweepin' the floor, gettin' things just right before company showed up.

Not too long after, I heard a knock at the door.

I opened it, and there she was my baby, Ophelia.

"Well look at you! Come in here, my Fefe," I smiled, reaching for the door wider.

"Hey Momma," Ophelia grinned, swattin' at her arms, "you gon' let me in or just leave me standin' out here gettin' ate up by these mosquitoes?"

"Girl, hush and get in this house,"

She stepped in, lookin' every bit like my momma. That big, round nose and that bright, beautiful smile I swear she favored Old Amelia Le Blanc more every year. Her hair was short, fine, and curly, different from her sisters Velma and Theresa. Those two had long, straight, thick hair, silky like their Native American grandma. But Ophelia's curls danced when she walked.

She had three children with that dark-skinned man, Raymond. His momma, Miss Octavia, and my momma, Amelia, were thick as sittin' grits back in the day.

"Mom, you not even ready to go!" Ophelia called from the front room.

"Give me a few seconds to comb my hair and throw some clothes on," I hollered back.

I stood in front of the mirror, draggin' the comb through my hair with quick strokes, my heart liftin' a little. I was excited Ophelia was here to help out today. I ran the grocery list through my mind cornmeal for the hush puppies, some more flour for the dumplings. Momma loved them dumplings. Said they reminded her of when she was a girl.

When I walked back into the front room, Ophelia was sittin' cross-legged on the floor, flippin' through one of our old family photo albums.

"Momma, what's goin' on with your sisters and brothers?" she asked, not lookin' up from the book. "I know Uncle Wallace left for the war, but ain't he back now?"

"I'll tell you on the way to the store," I said, grabbin' my purse. "Come on, let's go."

We opened the screen door, and we went out. I laughed watchin' Ophelia try to tiptoe around the ant piles and shook off the mosquitoes all at once.

We hopped into her car. I slid into the passenger seat a green Pontiac with white-wall tires that still shined like Sunday shoes.

"Ophelia," I asked, side-eying her with a grin, "you got a driver's license?"

"No, Momma, 'course not," she laughed, crankin' the engine.

"Oh Lord, I hope we don't get stopped. There's only one Black sheriff in all of Opelousas, Sheriff Wallace. And he can't do much to help us, far as I can tell."

"We'll be okay, Momma," Ophelia said, easin' the car onto the road.

As we drove toward the store, she rested her hand on top of the steering wheel, and that's when I saw her arm. "Ophelia!" I hollered. "What happened to your arm?"

"Nothin', Momma," she said quick, lookin straight ahead.

I reached over and grabbed her wrist, firm but gentle. That's when I noticed the larger scrape on her knee too. "Something happened, and you gon' tell me right now. Did somebody put their hands on you?"

Ophelia yanked her arm back. "No, Momma. Ain't nobody put hands on me."

"Then what happened to you?"

"I fell out the Jeep yesterday," she mumbled.

I narrowed my eyes. "How in the hell you just fall out of a truck?"

"I don't know, Momma... I just did."

I sat back in my seat, my jaw twisted, my heart poundin' like a drum. The thought of some man hurtin' my baby girl made my blood boil.

"I swear," I said mumbling and firm, "if I find out that man laid even a finger on you, he gon' have hell to pay."

"Momma, Raymond's a good man, just like Daddy. He didn't put no hands on me calm down," Ophelia said, glancin' over at me. "Anyway, tell me what's goin' on with you and Celeste, Lorena, and them?"

I sighed, lookin' out the window at the road ahead.

"I don't know, baby. Somewhere along the way, I became the black sheep of the family. They don't invite me to no family parties or nothin'. So, I just keep to myself."

Ophelia nodded, her fingers tappin' on the wheel.

"You know Lorena can pass for white," I continued. "She moved off to Texas and hardly ever comes to visit. Can you blame her? And when she does come see Momma, she acts so mean lookin' down her nose at everybody like we dirt on her shoes."

"Celeste is sweet," I added, "but she stays up under Wallace. She don't come see me or Momma, and she sure never lets me know when she's in town."

I shook my head, a bit of heat in my chest.

"They had a big party the other day you could hear Hilton's fool self crowin' like a rooster from a mile away." Ophelia burst out laughin'. "Momma, why does he do that?"

"Baby, I have no idea. For some reason, he thinks it's funny. I heard John and Wallace got on drugs after the war, so maybe that's why they don't visit or call. Who knows?"

"I still talk to Yvonne and Vertie," I said, softenin' my voice. "But even they be over at them parties too. At least they don't treat me different like the others."

I paused, then looked at her.

"Ever since I started drinkin' a little more and tryin' to enjoy life while still takin' care of Momma and Daddy they started judgin' me. Gossippin' behind my back like I don't hear things."

"They don't understand I helped raised them", theres nine of us children, while I was pregnat for your sister Velma and your brother Clifton , momma was pregnant for Hilton and Vertie Lee. "Do you have any idea how hard it is to care for your own children and your siblings"? Daddy sick, I don't know how long he is going to last.

I straightened up a bit.

"But let me tell you somethin', baby. My sisters and brothers don't have no heaven or hell to put me in. My brother need to focus on fixin' that cocked eye of his 'fore he talk about me."

Ophelia chuckled, eyes on the road.

"They just busy with their own families, I guess," I said with a shrug. "I don't mind bein' alone, Fefe. I enjoy my peace. Besides, I got enough on my plate with your brother and sister to be worried about which one of mine don't like me."

"Are you really okay with that, Momma?" Ophelia asked gently.

"Absolutely, baby," I said, smiling. "My days are filled with workin' at the church, and now I'm helpin' your daddy with his side jobs."

"Oh Lord," Ophelia laughed, "that's why you been drinkin' a little more helpin' Daddy!"

We both cracked up, laughin' so hard the car swerved just a little, but our hearts felt lighter ridin' down that road together.

We pulled up to the Piggly Wiggly and jumped out of the car, grabbin' our purses and shoppin' list.

"Momma, I need you to teach me some more recipes," Ophelia said, slamming the door shut behind her.

"I'll try to write 'em down for you, baby," I replied. "One of these days, you'll be cookin' circles 'round me." We laughed a little as we made our way through the store, pickin' up everything we needed cornmeal, flour, onions, smoked sausage. Thank the Lord, the store wasn't too busy that day.

"Good," I muttered under my breath. "Won't be here all day."

Ophelia and I sat on the bench near the front, our basket full, waitin' for the white folks to get checked out first. That's just how it was we knew the routine.

After what felt like forever, it was finally our turn. We pushed the basket forward toward the counter, ready to pay and head on home. But just then, a white lady in a big pink hat came strutting in like she owned the place. She shoved her cart in front of ours, damn near knockin' ours back, and stood there like she ain't done nothin' wrong.

She looked us up and down with that pinched-up nose of hers, and said in a high, arrogant voice, "Now, now… y'all know better, don't you? You colored folks gotta sit back and wait your turn. Let the rest of us get checked out first."

I just stared at her, my blood runnin' hot but my body frozen still.

Ophelia's mouth flew open, ready to let that woman have it right there in the Piggly Wiggly. Before she could say a word, I reached over and gently covered her mouth with my hand.

I turned to the lady, smiled as politely as I could, and said, "Yes ma'am. Absolutely."

The clerk, who was white too, looked like her hands were shakin'. She didn't say nothin', just kept her eyes low. The lady in the pink hat leaned in close to her and said loud enough for us to hear, "Don't lose your job not tellin' these colored folks the rules, y'hear?"

The poor cashier just smiled and nodded like her life depended on it.

Ophelia was bouncin' on her heels, still tryin' to talk with my hand over her mouth. That child's fire couldn't be tamed. When the woman finally paid for her groceries and left, I slowly removed my hand.

"Momma," Ophelia snapped, "why didn't you let me tell her off?"

"Baby, you gotta pick and choose your battles," I said, my voice low. "These white folks'll have you under the jail over a slice of bread."

Right then, the cashier, looked at us with sad eyes.

"I'm so sorry," Ms.Pearl, she said quietly.

"No need to apologize," I told her. "Let's just make these groceries and get on outta here."

Ophelia shook her head, still mad. "Momma, they can't keep doin' that. There's this man, Dr. Martin Luther King. He's the same age as me, and he's fightin' for our rights."

"I hope he succeeds, baby," I said, sighing deep. "I surely do. But for now, let's get home."

We drove home in silence. The car was quiet the whole way,Ophelia didn't say nothin', and neither did I. I didn't want some hateful woman's evil spirit to ruin what was supposed to be a good day with my baby girl. As we pulled up in front of the house, I let out a deep sigh.

"Ophelia, I'm sorry," I said gently, my hand still on the gear shift.

"It's okay, Momma. I understand," she replied, reaching over and squeezin' my hand. "We better get inside quick. Look at the sky."

I glanced up through the windshield. The skies were growin' darker by the second, thick gray clouds rollin' in fast and heavy.

"Oh, Lord," I mumbled. "Storm's comin'."

"Yep," Ophelia said, "and it looks like it's comin' quick too."

We both jumped out the car, rushin' to grab the grocery bags. But before we could even make it to the second trip, the rain let loose. It didn't just sprinkle it poured.

"Aw, hell!" I shouted, squinting up at the sky like it could hear me.

We ran back and forth from the car to the porch, arms full of groceries, laughin' the whole time as the rain soaked us through to the bone. Our hair stuck to our foreheads, our dresses clung to our legs, and the paper bags started to sag and tear.

"Girl, we look like two wet hens!" I hollered through the rain, slappin' my knee.

Ophelia laughed so hard she nearly dropped the bread.

By the time we got everything inside, we were drenched and breathless, standin' in the kitchen lookin' like we'd been baptized in a thunderstorm.

"Whew!" Ophelia said, wringin' the water out her shirt. "That was somethin' else."

"Yes, it was," I said, smilin' as I looked at her. "But we made it, baby. We made it."

I looked over at Daddy. He was sittin' in his usual chair in the corner, the one farthest from the windows. The lights flickered off and on, casting long, jumpy shadows across the room. His face looked tight, like he was holdin' back worry.

"Daddy?" I said gently. "What's wrong?"

Grandpa Ernest didn't say nothin' at first. Just puffed slow on his cigar, the orange tip glowin' in the dark like a little eye watchin' us.

Ophelia stepped closer. "Grandpa Ernest, is everything okay?"

He exhaled, his voice low and steady. "It happened again."

"What happened again?" I asked, feelin' the chill of the storm now deep in my bones. "The storm?"

Thunder cracked loud above the roof, shakin' the whole house. I jumped, heart skippin'.

"Daddy, when have you ever been scared of thunder?"

He pointed his cigar toward the other room. "She's in there," he said, voice even lower.

"Who? Momma?" I asked.

He nodded.

I looked at Ophelia, and she looked right back at me. We didn't say a word, but we both knew—neither of us wanted to walk in that room. Not alone.

"Grandma Amelia?" Ophelia called out softly.

"Yes," came a shaky voice. "I'm here."

We stepped into the bedroom. The air felt heavier, colder. Grandma sat on the edge of the bed, her nightgown bunched in her lap, her eyes swollen and teary.

I sat beside her. Ophelia took the other side.

"Momma, what's wrong?" I asked, brushing a curl from her cheek.

She looked straight ahead, voice barely above a whisper. "The poltergeist is here."

"Momma... poltergeists are just restless spirits. They move things, make noise but they can't hurt anybody." She turned her head and stared at me, tears streamin' down her cheeks. "They hurt Baby Daniel."

"Baby Daniel? When did he get here?"

"Hilton brought him over," she sniffled. "Dropped him off for a few hours. But after what happened... he said he ain't never bringin' his son back here again."

Ophelia and I leaned in closer.

"Tell us what happened," I said.

Grandma squeezed her hands together, knuckles white. "Daniel was layin' on the couch. The house got ice-cold, like winter just rolled in through the front door. We heard footsteps heavy, angry, walking' across the floor. Then... it picked up a coffee cup and threw it right at the baby."

"Oh Lord," Ophelia gasped, coverin' her mouth.

"He screamed. Poor thing was shakin' all over. I looked up, and there was a shadow... a tall, dark shadow stretchin' across the wall. Same one I been seein' for months now."

"What'd it do?" I asked.

Her lips trembled. "It said, in a low growl GET OUT."

"Sweet Jesus," I whispered.

"Your daddy," she went on, "he stood up, yelled back 'This is our house, and we ain't leavin'.'"

I nodded. That sounded like Daddy.

"But then," she said, voice crackin', "a woman's voice, real wicked-soundin', answered him: 'Well then, during the next storm, everything around you will be destroyed.' And now look at this... a storm we didn't expect, right overhead."

Her shoulders shook, and she cried harder. I reached out and wrapped my arms around her, pullin' her into me. Her thick, curly cotton-soft hair brushed against my face, her tears and snot dampenin' my shoulder.

Ophelia hugged her from the other side. We held her for a moment in silence, thunder rumblin' low outside like the sky was grindin' its teeth.

"Momma, don't you worry," I whispered. "God is bigger than any poltergeist, demon, or spirit. We're covered." She nodded slow, but the fear didn't leave her eyes.

"Come on," I said to Ophelia. "Let's get started on dinner before this weather gets any worse. You gotta get home to your three babies soon."

"I'll help with the dumplings" Ophelia said, squeezin' Grandma's hand one last time.

"It's gonna be okay," I said, kissin' Momma on the cheek. "I promise. Let's just pray about it."

Ophelia and I walked back into the kitchen and started cooking.

"Momma, I believe her," Ophelia said.

"You do?" I responded, glancing over at her.

"Yes, in fact, I think that house we just moved into is haunted. We ain't even been there three days, and so far, Bode's been attacked by rats, Betty swears she saw a hand, and there's this weird fireplace. It's big, gray, made of stone or maybe marble. It's different," she said, her voice laced with concern.

I wiped my hands on a dish towel and raised an eyebrow. "I've heard rumors about that house. Look, let me finish this for Momma and Daddy. You need to get on home to your husband and your haunted house," I said with a chuckle.

Ophelia smiled and swatted me on the arm with the towel. "Okay, Momma," she said, shaking her head. "I guess you're right. I'll call you when I get home."

She leaned in, gave me a kiss on the cheek, and walked out the door

I finished up dinner and fed Momma and Daddy, cleaned up the kitchen, and reassured them both that everything was gonna be just fine. I left Daddy sittin' in his chair and helped Momma into bed.

As I walked to the front door, I couldn't shake the feelin' that somethin' was followin' me. It was an odd energy somethin' I couldn't quite describe, like the air had thickened behind me. I locked the wooden front door and pulled the screen door shut behind me, then made my way out the back door.

The rain had left big puddles across the yard, and my shoes got soaked as I stepped through the wet grass. I was carryin' food to take home enough to serve August when he got off work.

When I stepped inside the house, I went straight to the kitchen and set the food on the stove. But as I turned to clean up the water trackin' from my shoes, I froze.

There was another set of footprints.

They weren't mine.

They were much larger.

A man's print deep, heavy, and fresh trailing right behind my own.

A chill ran down my spine. My heart thudded hard in my chest. I grabbed the mop with trembling hands and started wipin' up the prints fast as I could.

That's when August walked through the door.

I looked up at him, bracin' myself for that usual disappointed look he always seemed to wear. But not tonight. Tonight, there was a smile on his face.

"Hey, how was your day, love?" I asked, tryin' to keep my voice steady.

He didn't say a word at first just walked straight over and wrapped his arms around my waist, pullin' me close.

"It was wonderful," he said, and planted the biggest kiss right on my lips.

Then he sniffed the air. "I smell food. What did you cook tonight?"

He headed toward the kitchen, grinnin'.

I stood there for a moment, stunned and happy all at the same time.

"Chicken and dumplin's with hot water cornbread," I said, followin' after him. "Can I fix you a plate?"

"Yes, ma'am! I sure hope so, woman," he teased, makin' me laugh.

I looked at him, my heart overflowing with joy, and started fillin' up his plate. I handed him a cold glass of ice water, and we sat down and ate together, just the two of us.

Whatever kind of day he had at work, it must've been a good one.

And whatever that was followin' me earlier... I decided, for tonight at least, to let it be.

We took a bath together that night, laughin' and talkin' like two people fallin' in love for the first time. All the heaviness of the day seemed to wash down the drain.

Later, we crawled into bed, wrapped up in each other like old quilts on a cold night.

The thunder rolled louder as we started to drift off. The rain beat hard against the windows, hittin' the glass like it was tryin' to break in. The lightning cracked so bright it lit up the whole room in flashes.

But August? He slept through every bit of it, breathin' slow and steady beside me.

Just as I started dozin' off, a smell pulled me back sharp, bitter... smoke.

Then came the bang.

A deafening clap of thunder shook the house, followed by a blinding bolt of lightning that struck the light pole out front. My heart jumped into my throat.

And then I saw it smoke thick in the room, curling through the air.

The house was on fire.

I looked toward the far side of the room, eyes strugglin' to focus through the haze. That's when I saw it—a tall, dark figure movin' through the smoke. Slow, silent, and eerie. It turned toward the doorway and disappeared down the hall.

"August!" I screamed, shakin' him hard. "Baby, wake up! Wake up, the house is on fire!"

He shot up, eyes wide. "Oh Lord Pearl!"

He didn't waste a second. He grabbed my hand, and we ran.

We burst through the front door and out into the storm, the cold rain hittin' our skin like needles. August pulled a wrinkled newspaper from the porch bench and held it over our heads as we stood there, bare feet on wet grass, watchin' it all.

Our home, the one we loved, fought in, dreamed of was burnin' right before our eyes.

The flames danced against the dark sky, eatin' up everything we owned. The heat poured out into the rain, and all we could do was hold each other, shiverin' under that thin piece of paper, watchin' it fall.

Burned clear down to the ground.

Pearl Guidry-Guillory was born in 1911 and died in August 1966, buried at St Landry cemetery next to the Holy Ghost catholic church in Opelousas, Louisiana. She was only fifty-five years old when she died.

Her mother was Amelia Le-Blanc-Guidry and was born Sept. 12th 1891 and died April 10th, 1969, her father was Ernest Guidry born Aug.15th 1881 and died December 8th, 1952.

Pearls grandparents are Elie Leblanc (1850-1903), and Celizee Pelloquin Their race was classified as Octoroon. one-eighth African and seven eighths European.

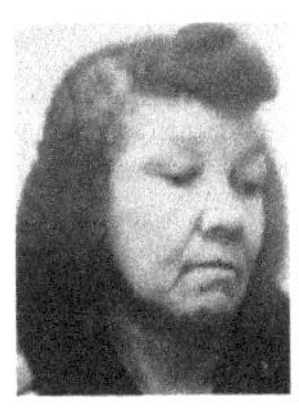

Fourteen

WHAT'S INSIDE

Ophelia aka Fefe

The road was dark. The sky flashed with lightning, and the thunder felt as if it rambled the car.

I could barely see out the window; the water drenched the windshield. The car slid, swirled, as the wind pushed against it. I hit a pothole, bam! ,the car jolted me outta my seat.

My heart was poundin'. All I wanted to do was get home to my children and husband.

The window was foggin' up, which made it even more difficult to see. I used a napkin, tryin' to wipe the condensation off the window.

I turned down our street and pulled up in front of the house. I turned off the ignition and sat there for a moment.

I took a breath and thanked God; This '56 Chevy got me home safe, I thought to myself.

I reached for the door handle and attempted to push it down to open the car door.

"Is it stuck?" I said to myself.

I tried again. I rattled it and heard the clicks, but it wasn't openin'. My heart started to pound again. Suddenly, the night sky lit up again with lightning and thunder. The sound and light caught my attention I glanced at the night sky in fear.

I tried again, with no success. I looked over towards the house, my mouth dropped open.

Who is that... in the upstairs attic window? It's damn sure not the children... or Raymond.

My eyes blinked again. I moved over to the passenger seat, wipin' the window with the sleeve of my shirt,starin' up at that window.

I tried to open the door on that side. It too was stuck.

My eyes were stuck on this woman. She walked back and forth with cups in her hands, appearin' to pour something' out.

Suddenly, the curtains on each side caught fire yet she continued.

In her white, nurse, lookin' uniform, she walked calmly, pourin' out some kinda substance from her cup. Her face was bare and straight, with no expression of fear or worry.

I screamed as loud as I could.

"Oh my God! Oh my GOD!"

I started shakin' the handle of the car frantically. I was outta breath and couldn't scream no more.   The sky stood still. The air quiet and silent. I could only hear my own breathin'...

Then suddenly

I heard a noise. Ka-Chik, Ka-Chik. The sound startled me.

I quickly turned to the driver's seat and the locks popped.

I had no time to be scared. I turned, grabbed the handle once more, and fled the car runnin' towards the front door to save my kids and husband.

I ran as fast as I could through puddles of mud and water. The ground felt like it was tryin' to swallow my feet with every step.

My clothes were soaked clean through, and my hair clung to my face, heavy with rain. I grabbed the door handle and fumbled to get the key in the lock, my hand shakin' like a leaf.

Just then, the wind kicked up behind me, and before I knew it, it shoved me clean through the doorway. The front door slammed hard against the wall.

I stumbled inside, breathin' heavy, heart poundin' out my chest. I stood right there in the doorway, water drippin' from every inch of me, and hollered,

"Raymond!"

The house was quiet as a moth on a cotton ball.

Then I heard a thud. Raymond came runnin' out the hallway, barefoot and in nothin' but his underwear, lookin' half-crazy and half-asleep.

"Lord, Ophelia! You tryin' to bring the storm inside with you?" he said, rubbin' his eyes and squintin'. "What in the hell done happened to you?",

"What's wrong with you women? Can't you see everyone sleeping, and why are you coming home late in all this rain? Where have you been?"

"Raymond, the house is on fire. There is a woman upstairs."

With a look of frustration on my face, I pushed him out of the way and ran upstairs to the attic, tracking mud and water everywhere.

"You're tracking water everywhere! There's no fire, Ophelia!" Raymond yelled.

As I approached the door, an eerie stillness followed me. I stopped and listened, placing my ear against the door, I sniffed the doorway to smell smoke, but nothing was there no sounds, no smoke. I opened the door slowly; the hinges creaked. I stepped inside. There was nothing. The curtains were still hanging, never touched.

I picked the curtain up with my hand, looking at it. I dropped it back down. My heart sank.

What did I see? Why did I see that? I thought to myself.

I turned back around and walked quickly to the door. Raymond stood at the bottom of the stairs.

"Did you find the lady in the fire?" he said sarcastically, then laughed.

"Screw you, Raymond," I snapped brushing pass him.

"Well, can't be mad at me. Come on, get showered up and come to bed," Raymond said.

I stepped into the bathroom, lettin' my soaked clothes fall to the floor with a plop, then climbed into the tub. The warm water hugged my skin like a soft blanket, and little by little, the knot in my chest started to loosen. I could finally breathe again.

I leaned back, lettin' my head rest against the cool porcelain. The house was quiet, Terrie, Bode, and Betty were still sleepin'. Thank the Lord, I thought. Glad I didn't wake 'em.

But my mind kept spinnin'.

What did I see? I tried to shake it, but the memory held tight like a burr on a Sunday dress. I was locked in that car. I know I was. I ain't crazy.

I closed my eyes, lettin' the water lap softly against my shoulders. Raymond did good findin' us this place. It's cleaner, quieter. Still... there's somethin' about it. Somethin' that doesn't sit right in my spirit.

I sat there in that tub longer than I meant to, thinkin' and thinkin', tryin' to make sense of it all.

I guess I better drag myself on outta here, clean up that mess, and crawl into bed. Lord knows I'm worn out. Didn't take me long to drift off once my head hit that pillow.

The morning sun peeked through the curtain, casting a warm glow across my face. The storm had passed, and it was a brand-new day. I could already hear the kids in the next room, gigglin' and carryin' on, their laughter bouncin' off the walls like little sparks of joy.

Raymond was up too, clankin' around in the kitchen, probably gettin' ready for a day out huntin'.

He walked into the room and looked at me with a question already waitin' on his lips.

"So where were you all day yesterday?" he asked, his tone low and concerned.

I blinked, taken aback. "I was with Ma'Mu," I said, sittin' up in bed. "I told you she needed my help. I wanted to spend some time with my mama; she's been feelin' a little down lately."

I paused, heart beatin' just a tad faster now.

"I can't believe you even askin' me that, Raymond. Especially with all these rumors floatin' 'round town... about you."

Raymond rolled his eyes and crossed his arms, tuckin' one hand up under his armpit like he always did when he was annoyed.

"Yeah, well, you go on and believe what these crazy folks say about me if you want to," he said flatly.

Before either of us could say another word, the phone rang, cuttin' through the tension like a sharp blade.

"Ain't you gonna answer that?" I asked, my voice still laced with frustration.

He looked at me, shook his head slowly, and picked up the receiver.

"Hello?... Hey Ma'mu. Naw, not much, just gettin' ready to go huntin'..."

He paused.

"What?... When?... No, she.

The sudden shift in his voice made me turn around quickly. His face had gone pale; brows furrowed deep with worry.

"What is it?" I asked, my chest tightenin'. "Raymond, what's wrong?"

He held up one finger, signalin' for me to wait as he listened intently. Then finally, he nodded slowly.

"Okay... yeah. I'll let her know."

He hung up and turned to me.

"What?" I asked again, tryin' not to sound too panicked.

He took a deep breath.

"Your grandma Amelia just called. She said Potoon and Ma-Mu's house... it burned down last night."

My mouth fell open. "Oh my God..."

My heart started poundin' like thunder all over again. Grandma Amelia. The stories she told about that evil spirit in the house... the one that attacked Daniel. The storm. The fire I seen last night in my mind...

This was no coincidence. I knew, deep in my bones Somethin' evil was lurkin'.

"I'll get the kids and the truck, and we can head over there," Raymond said.

I grabbed my purse, and we headed out the door. I didn't want to say nothin' about the spirits at Grandma Amelia's house, I didn't want to frighten the children.

"We're gonna have to really pray in church tomorrow," I whispered more to myself than anyone else. This ain't just no evil spirit. This here is a poltergeist.

Only a poltergeist can burn a house down. Spirits, they're usually peaceful loving even. They like talkin' and communication'. Ghosts though... they ain't always sure what to do. Some don't even know they're dead, so they'll show up and scare the hell outta you, not even meaning to.

All them thoughts swirled through my mind as we traveled down the road. The sun was out, but the streets were still wet. Steam rose up off the pavement, dancin' in the heat as we drove on in silence.

We pulled up to the house, Raymond driving, me sittin' in the passenger seat, starin' out the window at Grandma Amelia's place. The property where Ma'mu and Potoons house once stood directly behind. My parent's home burned down to the ground, Lord, my heart sank all over again.

As I opened the door, I noticed water pooling deep in the gutter below.

"Raymond, can you pull up just a bit? This side's flooded," I said, noddin' at the curb.

He cranked the engine and rolled forward a little. I jumped down from the truck, swung open the rusted metal gate surroundin' the house, and ran up to the door.

"Ma'Mu! Patoon!" I hollered as I stepped inside.

"We're back here, Ophelia," Ma'Mu called from the rear of the house.

I hurried to the back room. Theresa and Duke were already there. The sight of Ma'Mu and Patoon sittin' together brought tears to my eyes.

"Oh my God… Ma'Mu, Patoon! Are y'all okay? You should've called me!"

Ma'Mu smiled gently. "Baby, I didn't wanna disturb you so early. Wasn't nothin' you could've done nohow." Theresa stood in the doorway beside Duke, arms folded, face tight.

I turned to Duke. "Is the insurance gonna cover this, Duke? You the insurance man in this town, please tell me you put a policy on their home?"

Theresa didn't say a word, just stared like she'd seen a ghost.

Duke rubbed the back of his neck. "Well… no. I didn't put no fire insurance on it. I just wrote up a life insurance policy."

"You didn't do no homeowner's policy?" My voice rose without even meanin' to. "Come on, Duke!" Raymond, leanin' in the corner with his hands in his pockets and chest puffed out, chimed in, "I bet I know who the beneficiaries on them policies are."

"Okay now don't start nothin' in here," Ma'mu cut in, her voice calm but firm. "It was a mistake. Life happens."

"It was the devil that started that fire it didn't just happen, Pearl," Grandma Amelia said, step-pin' in like she'd been waitin' her turn. "I told you last night... told you somethin' awful was comin'."

Theresa frowned and looked at me. "What's she talkin' about, Ophelia?"

"Nothin'," I muttered, avoidin' her eyes.

"Well, she talkin' about somethin'," Theresa pressed.

Just then, the screen door slammed hard behind us, and we all jumped.

It was Velma, stormin' in with all her children: Linda, Herman, Fernando, Lolita, and Cindy Janice trailin' behind her.

"Y'all alright in here, baby?" Velma asked.

"We're okay," Ma'Mu answered.

"Alright then, go on outside and play with your cousins," Velma told the kids.

The little ones ran off to join Terrie, Bode, and Betty in the front yard.

The room got quiet again, but the tension didn't stop. It thickened when Velma and Raymond locked eyes. If looks could start fires, we'd all be runnin' for water.

"Raymond let's go outside and take a look at the property," I said quickly, tryin' to ease the heat.

"I'll go with y'all," Patoon offered.

"Okay then, come on, Daddy."

We stepped out onto the porch. The air was thick and muggy, and the sun hit us like a slap. I could feel the sweat bead up on my neck in seconds.

Then, in the distance, we heard the rumble of an engine comin' down the road low and steady. The heat shimmered off the pavement, wavy like water, before we could even see what was comin'.

As the truck rolled up, I notice Pearl and Patoon's boys: Cliff, Walter, Bobby, Author, and David, all packed in the back like they were headin' to war.

"We're here to the rescue!" Walter shouted, grinnin' big.

They all hopped down with shovels and tools slung over their shoulders, ready to work.

I stood quietly, watching the men work and the children play. Velma and Theresa stood beside me, chattering away, but my mind was elsewhere.

All I could think about were Grampa Amelia and Ernest's words from last night. The woman in the window... the burning curtains inside the house... my doors not opening... the rats that attacked Bode... and that hand that touched Betty.

Their voices, Velma's and Theresa's, faded to a distant murmur in my ears, like I was underwater. Then suddenly,

A loud scream.

A sharp cry.

I was jolted out of my daze as the children came running toward us, panic in their eyes.

"Bode's hurt!" one of them shouted.

His face was streaked with tears, and his left eye was swollen shut.

"What happened?" I yelled, heart pounding.

Bode was crying too hard to speak.

Herman stepped forward, fidgeting. "Janice hit him in the eye… with a metal pipe."

I looked over at Janice. The look on her face was pure fear.

Velma turned toward her, eyes flashing.

Girl, what in the hell is wrong with you? Go on and get me a switch! I'm gon' tear that little tail up!"

Janice took off, sniffling.

I scooped Bode into my arms and rushed him inside.

Ma'Mu took one look at his face and didn't say a word, just moved. She pulled a wash rag from the sink, ran cold water, and gently wiped his swollen eye.

"Grab me some salt meat out the refrigerator. Quick."

I fumbled with the fridge, found it, and handed it to her.

Ma'Mu laid the cold slab of meat gently across Bode's eye.

"Hold it here for fifteen minutes, you hear me, boy? It's gon' be okay."

His little body trembled, but he nodded. The crying slowed, then stopped.

Theresa and I stood on either side of him, watching, waiting for salt meat to work magic.

Outside, the work continued in the yard. The other children ran back to their games, laughter returning slowly to the air.

Then came the sharp, familiar crack of a switch from the back room, followed by Janice's yelps echoing through the house. Velma was giving her spanking.

Theresa sighed. "Where are your kids today?" I asked, glancing over at her.

"We left them at home. Karl's old enough to watch them. We weren't even planning to come by just saw the house on our way to the store." She rubbed her stomach. "I need a ginger ale. My stomach's torn up... I'm pregnant again."

"Oh, Lord, again? "I replied, half-shocked, half-laughing.

She looked at me. "I might be too," I said.

We both burst out laughing.

"Don't say anything," she whispered.

"I won't if you won't," I said, still smiling.

Just then, Ma'Mu paused in the doorway on her way out, hand on the screen.

She looked back over her shoulder with that knowing look she always had.

"I heard what y'all said," she said, calm and firm. "I knew you was pregnant."

Then she turned her voice toward the back. "And Velma stop spankin' that baby! It was a accident."

"Okay, Mama!" Velma hollered from the other room.

Theresa and I just stood there, shakin' our heads, hands on our hips with her still holdin' that stomach like it had a secret itching to be told.

Fifteen

 COUSINS AT PLAY

Lolita

The joy of playing in the yard just made us all wanna play longer. We hadn't even seen Aunt Ophelia and Uncle Raymond's house yet, and all our cousins were buzzing to go over there. They had the biggest house in all of Opelousas.

I darted inside, nearly tripping over my own feet. I wore my cute black flats with a single strap across, white socks pulled just a touch above my ankles, and a white dress scattered with pink flowers. The collar came all the way up to my neck. My hat sat neat on top of my head, sitting right over my big Shirley Temple curls.

"Aunt Ophelia! Can we all come to y'all's house today and play?" I asked, breathless with excitement.

She looked over her glasses and smiled warmly. "Well, baby, you gotta ask your mama first and I need to make sure Raymond's okay with it too."

I nodded and jumped with excitement. I turned to Auntie Theresa and asked, "Auntie Theresa! Can you drop off Karla, Margo, and Karen so they can come play too?"

She laughed and said, "Of course, baby. I'll bring 'em over after lunch."

I didn't waste a second. I ran back outside and hollered like my feet were on fire, "We goin' to Auntie Ophelia and Uncle Raymond's house!"

Later that day, we pulled up in the car, all of us smooshed against the windows with wide eyes and wild smiles. "Wow," I whispered, staring at that big ol' house like it was a castle. "This is crazy."

Uncle Duke and Auntie Theresa pulled up right behind us. As soon as the car stopped, the door flew open.

"Last one to the porch is a rotten egg!" someone hollered, and we all went flying toward the front door, arms flailing, shoes kicking up dust.

Bode opened the door just as we reached it. His eye looked so much better already Grandma Pearl's salt meat cure had worked a miracle.

"Come on in here, y'all!" Auntie Ophelia called from behind him, waving us in with that familiar grin. "Don't be standin' in that doorway like y'all don't know better."

Mama Velma stood on the sidewalk a moment longer, waving at Auntie Ophelia. They shared a silent goodbye with just their hands, the kind mamas use when they know the kids are too excited to notice much else.

The door closed behind us, and we were off running through that big ol' house like wild ponies let loose, laughter echoing down the hallways.

"Fernando, did you see the piano?" I asked, eyes wide with excitement.

"No... where is it?" he said, lookin' around, curious.

"Right in the front room," I whispered, grinnin'. "Come on, let's go see it!"

We started headin' that way, but before we could take two steps, Auntie Ophelia popped around the corner like she'd been watchin' the whole time.

"Uh-uh! No, y'all can't play with that piano, baby," she said, waggin' her finger. "Raymond gon' be mad if y'all mess with it."

We froze in our tracks.

"As a matter of fact," she said, shiftin' her apron and reachin' for her purse, "I'm fixin' to send y'all to the store to get some treats instead. Then y'all can go on outside and play. Sound good?"

"Okay," I said, tryin' not to sound too disappointed.

She handed me a few nickles and gave us that don't-make-me-come-get-you look.

"Now don't take all day, and don't be buyin' nothin' silly."

"Yes ma'am," we said in unison, already turnin' for the door.

Terrie and Bode came runnin' up with that look in their eyes.

"Let's walk to Mesh's store on Bullock Street!" Terrie said, already bouncing with excitement. "We can go and get some gingerbread cakes".

"YEAHHH!" We all hollered, jumpin' around like we'd just won gingerbread cakes for the year.

"Is Linda comin' with us?" Bode asked, squintin' toward the porch.

"Nah," I said with a grin. "She's stayin' here. Wanna be with her new boyfriend... Alvin-n-n-n, "I teased, stretching his name out real long.

We all cracked up laughin'.

The sun was high and hot as we made our way down the dusty road. By the time we headed back, our shirts were stickin' to our backs. We stopped at a house on the way and bought some cold cups, bright red, blue, and purple ones that stained our tongues and teeth. We sat out on Auntie Ophelia's wide ol' porch, legs swingin' off the edge, eatin' them in silence except for the occasional slurp.

"Here comes Patrick," Terrie said, pointing down the road. "And Cathy too."

"Oh cool! That's my friend from school!" I said, standin' up to wave.

"You know them?" Terrie asked.

"Yeah!"

Patrick was already callin' out. "You ready to play some marbles, Fernando?"

"Yeah, I'm ready!" Fernando shouted back.

The boys dropped to the ground and started drawin' a circle in the dirt with a stick. They got their bags of marbles ready like it was a serious tournament. We watched for a little while, gigglin' and whisperin', then Cathy tugged on my arm.

"Let's play hopscotch," she said.

Margo grabbed a rock and went first, hoppin' through the boxes like a pro. Then it was my turn. I bent down, tossed my rock, and started jumpin'.

Just then, Brenda and Ann came strollin' up the sidewalk, hands on their hips and big grins on their faces.

"Hey y'all!" Brenda called out. "We came to play too!"

Brenda and Ann were Uncle Raymond's nieces, and they fit right in like they'd been there all day. By now, we had at least twelve of us in that yard, playin' games, laughin', shoutin', and singin' songs between turns.

"Miss Lucy had a baby, she named him Tiny Tim, she put him in the bathtub to see if he could swim!" We sang loud and proud, the hopscotch squares dusty and well-worn by evening.

The sun started to dip low, and that Southern heat finally softened into a warm breeze. Crickets chirped loud in the grass, and the smell of dinner drifted through the air.

Auntie Ophelia stepped out onto the porch, hands on her hips.

"Time to come on in, y'all!" she hollered. "Get washed up! Dinner and bedtime!"

"Aww man," Joanne groaned, dragging her feet toward the porch. "Do we hafta, Auntie Ophelia?"

"Yes, baby, it's time," she said, smiling gently. "Go on now."

"Okay," Joanne sighed, already unbucklin' her shoes.

We all shuffled inside, tired and happy, feet dirty, bellies rumblin', and hearts full.

Auntie Ophelia had made us pallets on the floor. We laughed and giggled ourselves silly 'til sleep finally took us one by one.

But around two in the mornin', I jolted up, swattin' at my face like something was crawlin' on me. My heart was poundin'. I sat straight up, lookin' around the room. Everyone else was still asleep, breathin' slow and steady like nothing was wrong.

It's cold in here, I thought, shiverin' as I wrapped my arms tight across my chest. A puff of fog came outta my mouth with every breath.

That ain't right.

I stood up and crept toward the thermostat on the wall.

"Seventy-eight degrees?" I whispered, eyebrows pulled tight. "That can't be…"

I turned and looked at the wallpaper those birds… Lord, it felt like their painted eyes were watchin' me, starin' dead-on, like they knew something I didn't. The air gripped me. Still and heavy and unwelcoming.

I could feel it somethin' behind me.

A shadow? No… maybe not.

I blinked fast. I wasn't sure if I really saw anything in that corner or if my eyes were playin' tricks.

Then I heard it.

The piano.

It started playing, soft at first, like somebody pressing just a few keys.

Thank God. Uncle Raymond must still be up, I thought.

I tiptoed down the hallway, the hardwood floor creaking beneath my bare feet.

"Uncle Raymond?" I called out in a whisper.

No answer.

I reached the front room and gently pushed the door open. The light was off. The room had just the shadow of the moon beaming through.

"Uncle Raymond?" I said again, a little louder now.

He wasn't there.

But the piano... it was still playin'.

I felt the hair on my arms stand up as I stepped inside.

A chill ran through me.

I walked slowly toward the piano. The music had no rhythm, just random notes, as if a child or ghost were bangin' on it with no sense of tune. I stood right over it and froze.

Ain't nobody there.

But the keys...

They were movin'.

Up and down pressin' like invisible fingers were dancin' across 'em.

What in the world...?

My knees got weak.

My heart pounded so hard I could hear it in my ears. The sound from the piano grew louder, sharper, turning from eerie to painful.

Then came the screamin' in my head.

A high-pitched screech from the piano rang out so loud it pierced my eardrums. I clutched both sides of my head and cried out in pain.

"No! Stop! Please stop!"

Tears fell fast from my eyes. My breath came short.

The room got colder.

I turned to run, but just as I reached the door it slammed shut right in my face.

I grabbed the knob and yanked.

Locked.

"No, no, no! Let me out!"

I beat on the door with my fists, panic risin' in my throat.

"Help me!" I screamed. "Auntie Ophelia! Uncle Raymond! Please!"

My voice cracked and faded as the piano got louder and louder. I turned back toward it—shakin', sobbin', barely able to breathe.

And that's when I saw it.

Somethin' was sittin' on the bench.

No... not sittin'. Perched.

It turned its head slow, like an owl in the dark searching for prey. And smiled.

Its teeth were yellow and jagged, twisted like old corn kernels.

"Oh my God," I whimpered, stumbling backward.

I spun around and banged on the door even harder. "UNCLE RAYMOND! PLEASE! IT'S IN HERE!" Suddenly the door flung open, and I collapsed into Auntie Ophelia's arms, bawlin'.

"It's okay, Lolita baby, it's okay," she whispered, rockin' me gently. "Shhh... You safe now."

"What happened?" Uncle Raymond asked, steppin' into the hall, lookin' half-dressed and mad.

"You weren't in there playin' the piano?" he asked, Uncle Raymond looked at me with a scrutinizing stare. "Girl, it's two in the mornin'. I felt breathless, eyes wide and wet with tears. No, I wasn't playin' no piano."

"I thought... I thought it was you. But the keys were pressin' down on their own," I stammered, shakin'. "Then the door locked, and somethin' something' was sittin' there watchin' me. Smilin' at me."

My chest was heavy. I couldn't stop crying. I couldn't calm down if I tried.

Uncle Raymond frowned and walked into the room. He grabbed his gun off the shelf on his way.

"There ain't nobody in here," he called out after a moment. "You kids need to stop lettin' your imaginations run wild."

He didn't believe me.

But I knew what I saw.

He sent me back to bed like I'd just had a bad dream. I walked slowly. Everyone else was up now, sittin' with wide eyes and tangled blankets, watchin' me like they'd heard everything.

The room was dead silent.

Then Betty, still curled up on the pallet, spoke without lookin'.

"You ain't supposed to touch that piano."

She pulled her blanket back over her shoulders and laid back down.

I swallowed hard and climbed into my spot on the floor. My body was still shakin'. My hands wouldn't stop tremblin'.

We laid down. But not a single sound came from anybody else.

Not for the rest of that night.

This page is dedicated to Fernando Morris, a beloved father, brother, twin, and dear cousin. The life of every party. May you rest in heaven for eternity. (Departed November 2024)

I also dedicate this page to my sister Janice and Joanne. Until we meet again.

Sixteen

Sitting and scared

Octavia White-Chatman (Maw"ma)

I've seen a lot in my time. I've buried loved ones. I've given birth during storms, with no lights in the house, just my prayers and courage. I've prayed through war and held on through loss.

But what's in this house?

This ain't human. And it sure ain't nothin' livin'.

This is like nothing I've ever known.

I got up early, like I always do, but this morning felt different.

The house was quiet. Louis had already gone off to work. Brenda and Ann were over at Raymond and Ophelia's place.

For once, I had the whole house to myself.

I sat up in bed, stretched real good, then pulled the scarf off my head and set it on the nightstand. The house was cool and still. The sun hadn't even made its way up yet.

Mmm. "This is gonna be a good day," I whispered to myself, smiling.

I slid down to my knees beside the bed and said a quiet prayer just me and the Lord, like old times. I thought about the little joys ahead: getting the bathroom all to myself, drinkin' my coffee on the porch, watchin' the sun rise in peace and silence.

I brushed my teeth, washed my face, then stood there lookin' at myself in the mirror runnin' my fingers over the soft folds of my now-wrinkled skin.

Where did the time go? I wondered.

I made my way to the kitchen to fix a little breakfast, reminding myself to cook just enough for one. That's still hard some days. I've spent so many years caring for others raised seven children and now, here I am raising two grandbabies: Brenda and Ann.

As I stood there, lost in thought, the phone rang. I already knew who it was.

"Hey Amelia," I said, picking up.

"Hey Octavia," she replied, her voice warm and familiar. "Just callin' to say good mornin'."

"Good mornin'. How's Pearl and August doin' after that fire?"

"They doin' good. On their way to look at that house up on the hill."

"Already? That soon?" I said, surprised. "That's great news."

"Yeah, well, everybody need their own space, you know."

I smiled, holding the phone close. "Well, I got some quiet time right now, so I'm gonna sit out on the porch and enjoy it while it lasts. Can I call you back in a bit?"

"Sure, sugar," Amelia said. "You enjoy your peace."

I hung up the phone, poured my coffee into my favorite cup, then grabbed the tea kettle and filled it with hot water.

Next, I walked over to the fridge, grabbed that can of Pet milk, and added two teaspoons of sugar, just how I like it. I gave it a good stir and took a small sip.

"Mmm... perfect," I whispered, smiling to myself as I made my way to the back porch.

I stepped outside and sat down, watching as the sun rose over the trees. The light spilled across the yard like honey on warm biscuits.

It's so beautiful.

Our garden looked like a little piece of heaven. Louis had planted a whole mess of corn, along with other vegetables. That man worked hard. Between his long hours at the railroad and tending to the yard, I don't know how he did it. I always figured gardening was his quiet time, his way of praying without words.

I glanced to the left, over at the old chicken coop, the same one where Raymond got trapped all of them years ago as a little boy.

The memory washed over me like it was yesterday. That was the same day he saw that head floatin' in the canal.

Lord have mercy, I was sure that thing would haunt him forever. But he never spoke about it again. I reckon he's made his peace with it.

Maybe I'll get out there today, gather some eggs from the hens, and pick a few ears of corn and some tomatoes. I could make Louis a good ol' pot of succotash for dinner. He always loved that.

I sat there humming my gospel songs same ones my mama used to rockin' gently in my chair, lost in a soft daze of morning thoughts, just as the sun fully broke over the cornfield.

Then suddenly, the phone rang again.

It startled me.

Now who could that be? I wondered.

Amelia's the only one who calls me this early... and I already spoke to her.

I got up outta my comfortable rocking chair and headed back inside to answer the phone. The receiver was that same old heavy black one hangin' on the wall.

Lord, I wish they'd come up with something better, I thought, lifting it to my ear.

"Hello?" I said.

"Hi, Maw'Ma, it's Ophelia."

I could hear the strain in her voice.

"What's wrong? The girls givin' you a tough time?" I asked.

There was a pause, then she said it, the words that ended my quiet morning at once.

"Maw'Ma, I'm bringin' Brenda and Ann back... but can you babysit Terrie, Bode, and Betty for me? I gotta work today, and Raymond went huntin'."

I sighed, one hand on my hip, lookin' around at my peaceful house the porch still warm from my coffee and quiet.

"I s'pose I can," I said, slow and a little reluctant, but meanin' it all the same.

"Thank you, Maw'Ma! We'll be there shortly," she said, her voice perking up.

I stayed on the line a second longer, then added, "You know what, Ophelia? I'll come to y'all instead. I haven't seen the new place yet, and truth be told, it'd do me good to get out the house."

"Really?" she asked, surprised.

"Yes, absolutely. Just give me a minute to get myself together."

"Okay!" Ophelia replied, sounding downright relieved.

I slipped on my light blue dress, tied my dark blue apron around my waist, pulled up my long socks, and stepped into my black Mary Jane shoes. I grabbed my purse and headed toward the door.

Just before locking it, I paused. I suppose I should leave Louis a note, I thought, in case he got home early.

I tore off a little piece of paper and left it tucked right under the phone: *"Dear Louis, I will be at Raymond and Ophelia place for a few hours. I will be back in time to cook but if not there's some left-over chicken in the refrigerator, Love you Octavia".*

I shut the door gently, locked it behind me, then pulled the old thin tin screen door closed. It creaked like it always did, a noisy thing that told all your business to the street.

I made my way down the sidewalk, walkin' fast before the heat set in.

As I walked, my mind wandered to my sisters, all four of 'em. They do this kind of work every single day, takin' care of other folks' children over on the south side, across the tracks. White folks, mostly.

That's why everyone calls them by their "nanny" names: Nanny White, Nanny Pat, Nanny Bay, and Nanny Shine.

Lord, no one better not call me "Nanny."

And I still can't believe John; Louis's brother got my sister workin' like that in the first place.

Matter of fact, I still shake my head that both me and my sister ended up marryin' the Chatman brothers.

I had six sisters and seven brothers growin' up. I have a favorite brother, folks called him Uncle Rock, but his real name was Betholem Lord White. Louis and his people never did take to him, but he's still my blood and always will be.

I kept on walkin', my feet hittin' the pavement and my thoughts rollin' with each step. Hope Raymond's kids are behave today, I thought, sighin'.

That little boy of his is somethin' else spoiled rotten. One time he stuffed a whole punch of trash down in the radiator, said he was "workin' on the car."

I turned the corner onto Freeman Street. That must be the house over there.

I smiled as I walked closer to the house. It was a beautiful house big, bold, and proud.

"Good job, son," I thought to myself.

I walked up a little closer and opened the old metal gate. Right then, a gust of wind swept through and kicked up a cloud of dust, nearly blinding me. My face scrunched up as I waved my hand in front of it, tryin' to clear the air.

Lord, have mercy, I thought, steadyin' myself as I made my way up the front steps.

The wood creaked loud beneath my feet sounded like their planks were fixin' to give way at any moment. I took a breath, got ready to knock, and before I could even raise my hand, the front door flew open all on its own. BANG!

It slammed hard against the wall behind it.

I stood there, frozen.

Ain't nobody in sight.

Just then, I heard quick footsteps, and here came Ophelia runnin' from the back of the house. Her face lit up when she saw me.

"Maw'ma! You're here!" she said, breathless. "I ain't hear you knock."

I raised my eyebrows. "Yeah... well, I didn't have to. That door swung open all by itself. You might wanna have Raymond come fix that."

"Yes ma'am," she said, glancin' toward the door like she was already second guessin' what she just heard.

"Come on in. Thank you for watchin' the children. I'm runnin' late. I'll see you later. They already ate," she added quickly.

She leaned in, gave me a hug, and ran out before I could say another word.

I stepped inside, my eyes drawn to the olive-green walls. They were faded, dull like they hadn't been touched in years. I ran my fingers gently across them, feeling the cracked paint beneath my skin.

A chill passed through me. A quiet stillness hung in the air, too quiet.

My heart started to thump heavy, I think it already knew something my mind hadn't caught up with yet.

What kind of place is this? I thought, my eyes scanning up, down, and all around the room. The air felt thick, like it was trying to smother me and pull me under. There was a coldness deep in my bones, something unnatural. I could feel it... like my soul was slowly being sucked into the house.

And then, just like that, the silence broke.

"Maw'Ma!" five little voices shouted, nearly in unison.

I turned, startled, and saw the children come runnin' toward me, arms open wide. They wrapped themselves around my waist like they hadn't seen me in years.

"Hi, my babies," I said, tryin' to force a smile as I leaned down and hugged them close. Their warmth was a comfort, but my eyes drifted past them, and that's when I noticed more little ones, some cousins, laid out on blankets in the back room. Leftovers from the night before.

I frowned. Ophelia didn't say nothin' 'bout no extra company.

"I ain't watchin' all these damn kids," I muttered to myself. I know that might sound mean, I thought, but the Lord knows I wasn't prepared for all this.

I straightened up. "Will your momma be pickin' y'all up soon?"

"Yes ma'am," Linda answered, polite as ever. She was the oldest, nine or ten, and always tried to play the little mama when nobody else would.

"Good," I said, letting out a soft sigh. "Well, all y'all go on to the park and play for a while. Make sure you stay on the north side, you hear me?"

"Yes ma'am," they all echoed, already halfway out the door.

I watched them go, their little feet pounding down those rickety steps like they'd done it a thousand times. But as the screen door slammed shut behind them, the stillness crept back in.

And the house... Well, it didn't feel empty.

I tried to ignore it.

Lord knows I did.

Instead, I started cleanin' up behind the mess the children left. Toys scattered everywhere, crumbs in the corners, blankets thrown across the floor like tumbleweed. I hoped I wasn't comin' off mean. See, I'm the one who does the discipline in this house.

Louis? He hardly raises his voice. Never laid a hand on our babies not once. Just threatens 'em a lot with that deep voice of his. Me? I'm firm, but I ain't my momma, Mae Temple. Now she was a whole other level. Raymond still brings up the time he and Perry fell outta that pecan tree. I was mad at Momma that day too. She had called and told me they didn't cut the limbs and pick the pecans like they was told. So when they got home, I spanked 'em both and made 'em march back out there in the heat.

Sun was beatin' down hard that day. They climbed back up that big tree, sweat drippin' from their little faces while Mae Temple stood at her kitchen window, watchin' like a warden.

Then it happened.

The top branch cracked SNAP! and both boys came crashin' down, fallin' toward the deep well she had sittin' right there in her yard.

Raymond hit the side and bounced off, but Perry... Perry was holdin' on for dear life, legs danglin' over the edge. Raymond, thank God, jumped up and grabbed his brother's hand, pullin' him out.

After that? I never let 'em go back to Momma's house again. Her mean ways almost got my babies killed. Moma Mae Temple... lawd, she was well respected. Not just 'round here, but all across the state with that Baptist convention. She worked right alongside the president. She was aslo a midwife, smart and highly educated, 'specially for a Black woman born in 1870 down South.

They called her mama Sunshine. Mmm-hmm. Just before she passed in '48, she asked to see Jules my boy, old Rat we call him. I didn't know how in the world I was gon' make that happen, with him being off in the military. But God... He worked it out. She laid eyes on him one last time.

I hope her spirit's here now. Watchin' me. Protectin' me in this ol' scary house.

I shook off the memory and picked up the last blanket, startin' to fold it. That's when I heard it.

A giggle outside the window.

I froze.

Now I know good and well them children are supposed to be at the park,

I walked to the window and peeked out nothin' but still air and silence. "Terrie?" I called. "Bode?"

Suddenly, I heard another giggle behind me.

I spun around so fast my heart near jumped outta my chest. "Y'all better stop playin' in this house!" I yelled. My voice trembled.

I wanted it to be them. Lord, I hoped it was just the kids. But deep inside, I knew it wasn't.

I stuffed the folded blankets into the closet quick, breathin' heavy. My eyes were drawn toward the bathroom door. That old door had a little glass window built into it, and just then, a dark shadow passed behind it.

My mouth went dry as paper.

"Hello?" I called out, barely above a whisper. No answer. No movement.

My knees buckled with fear, but I didn't run.

I dropped to my knees right there in the hallway.

"Father God, cover me," I whispered. "Yea, though I walk through the valley of the shadow of death, I will fear no evil..."

The air turned ice cold. The whole room became a freezer. I started shiverin'. My fingers were numb. I couldn't move.

But I kept prayin'.

I've seen a lot. I've been through storms. I'm a strong, courageous woman. I'll be damned if I let a demonic spirit run me out my son's house.

My voice grew louder. Stronger.

"I rebuke this spirit in the name of Jesus. God promised He'd never leave me nor forsake me."

Suddenly, the temperature shifted. Just like that.

The cold was gone.

The air went still again.

I stood up, still tremblin', and made my way to the front door. I flung it open, gaspin' for air like I'd just come outta deep water. I bent over on the porch, one hand barely holdin' on to the post, tryin' to catch my breath. Then I heard it the sound of a truck rumblin' up the drive.

It was Raymond.

He jumped out before the truck had even come to a full stop.

"Mama, you alright?"

"Yes, son... I'm fine," I replied, still breathless.

"What happened? Where are the kids?"

"They're at the park," I said, lookin' him dead in the eye. "I don't know what just happened in there."

"Come sit down," he said, reachin' for my arm.

"Oh no," I shook my head, firm. "I'm not goin' back in that house. Ever again."

Raymond blinked. "Mama..."

"You need a pastor or a priest to come bless that house," I told him. "It's gonna destroy you if you don't. That chipped paint on the wall something came through it. I felt it with my own two hands."

"Mama... I just painted this whole house," he said, confused. "There's no chipped paint. Everything in there is brand new."

I looked him square in the face. He saw it whatever I had seen was still in my eyes.

He ran inside to check. I stood on that porch and waited.

He came back a minute later, brows furrowed.

"Mama... the walls look fine."

I shook my head.

"Your home, son... it's got somethin' evil in it. Please, for the love of God, get that house blessed before it's too late."

Raymond rubbed the back of his head. "If you ain't comin' back in, can I at least drive you home? Or get you a beer or somethin'?"

I looked at him sideways. "Now you know I don't drink. Just get my purse. I'll walk."

"Mama, I can't let you walk home."

"Watch me," I said, snatching the purse from his hands. I made my way through that gate, slowly and steady, with my chin held high.

"And don't forget to call the priest!" I yelled back over my shoulder.

I walked the whole way home this time with no fear, no questions, no voices in my head. Just one thought repeatedly.

Thank God for savin' me.

This chapter is dedicated to, my great, great grandmother born enslaved, Circa Glaze, my great grandmother Mae Temple Glaze,and grandmother Octavia White Chatman our Nanny Tee. She and her sister, Nanny Pat, whose given name was Elnora White Chatman, married two brothers: my grandfather, Louis Chatman, and his brother, John.

On August 31, 1968, right at twelve noon, Octavia slipped away in her sleep while taking a nap. Folks say that later that very day, her spirit left this world and traveled straight to her sister's house. Not long after, Nanny Pat was gone too. Opelousas had never seen the likes of it before the first double funeral in town. The two sisters were laid to rest side by side at Little Zion Baptist Church cemetery.

Some say Nanny Pat's heart gave out when she saw her sister standing there in her room. Others whisper it was something deeper, something beyond what our eyes can see. Either way, the story still lingers... a shadow passed down through the family.

And sometimes, when the house is quiet, it feels like they still walk together.

Seventeen

The Shell That Shall

Raymond Sr.

I stood out on the porch, the sun beatin' down on my head like a frog leg over the firepit. My nose scrunched up from the heat, and I squinted down the street, watchin' Maw'ma shuffle along in that slow, steady way of hers. Now, I don't know if I believe in ghosts or not, but with everything that's been goin' on lately... well, she just might be right. Maybe I oughta call a priest or somethin'. But that'd have to wait.

I'd only come back home to grab my Rabbit backpack my lucky green one, and head back out huntin'. Probably oughta swing by North Park and check on the kids while I'm at it.

I made my way down the porch steps, passed through the squeaky gate, and turned the opposite direction Ma'Mau had gone. The heat hung in the air like thick Karla syrup.

When I got to the park, all the kids were runnin' around, hollerin', laughin', just bein' kids. That big ol' Spanish moss tree stretched over the field like it was tryin' to protect 'em from the sun. The swings creaked with every push old and worn, paint flakin' off like sunburnt skin. The baseball field and backstop looked like they were holdin' on for dear life leanin', rustin', barely standin'.

I spotted Bo-Scott out there, tryin' his best to play baseball. Or somethin' close to it.

"What in the world is he doin'?" I mumbled under my breath.

He was standin' in the field, glove hangin' limp at his side, lettin' balls sail right past him like he was swattin' flies.

I walked over and hollered, "Boy, let me show you how to catch a ball, now. Come on."

He looked up, all wide-eyed. "Okay, Daddy."

"Alight now, Take your glove and stand over there, about ten feet or so. Gimme the ball."

He handed it to me, and I stepped back, winding up.

"Now listen, son. When I pitch it to you, hold your glove up at an angle, alright? Make sure you protect your face. Got it?"

"Alright, Daddy!"

I tossed the ball. Not too hard just a clean pitch, right toward him.

"Catch it!" I called out.

Bo-Scott looked up, eyes squintin' against the sun. The ball came down fast real fast.

Pop!

Right on the nose.

He dropped his glove and started cryin' big old tears, hands coverin' his face. The other kids burst out laughin', not mean, just caught in the moment.

I ran over. "Lord have mercy, Bo-Scott! I told you to catch it, not headbutt it!"

As I bent down to check his nose, I heard a car pull up. I looked up and saw Theresa gettin' out, keys janglin' in her hand.

"Hey, Raymond," she called, glancin' at the commotion.

"Hey, Theresa."

She glanced at Bo-Scott snifflin' and shook her head, smilin' just a little. "I'm takin' the kids on home. I'll drop Velma's little ones at her place too, alright?"

"Appreciate it," I said, standin' up and brushin' off my jeans.

She gave me a nod, gathering the children like a mama duck, and just like that, the park started clearin' out. looked back at Bo-Scott, who still had a little dirt on his face from that pop fly.

"Well," I said, patting him on the back, "you sure can't play ball, but you do know how to hunt. Ready to go?" He nodded, still sniffin' a little but tryin' to be tough.

"Alright then. Get your sisters."

We walked on down the street toward the house, his little boots kickin' up dust with every step.

"Terricita, Betty,"," y'all wanna go huntin' with me and Bo-Scott?"

Terrie shook her head quickly. "No, Daddy, we'll stay home."

"I don't like killin' rabbits, Daddy," Betty added, her little arms crossed like she meant it.

I chuckled. "But you sho do like eatin' 'em."

They both looked away, tryin' not to smile.

We got to the house, and I had Bo-Scott grab the rest of the huntin' gear from the closet.

"Girls, y'all go on upstairs and lock the door. Don't open it for nobody 'til your momma gets home, you hear?" "Yes, Daddy," they said in unison, headin' up the stairs.

Me and Bo-Scott loaded into the truck. The seat squeaked when we sat down, and the old engine grumbled like a tired hound dog.

"I'm gonna pick up my cousins Willie, Francis, and Charles" I told him as we pulled out the driveway. "You're gonna have to sit in the back with Charles."

Bo-Scott's face twisted up. "But Daddy... He's got twelve fingers. I'm scared."

I let out a big old laugh, he was being honest.

"Well, then you can sit in the back with Black instead. Did you bring his leash?"

He nodded, relieved.

"Now that's my real hunting' buddy," I said, smilin'. "That dog can retrieve any wild animal out here. Quicker than you can blink."

We rumbled down that dusty old country road, the sun hangin' low and hot, dust risin' up like smoke in the side mirrors. My hands were gripped tight 'round the big ol' steering wheel, and them tires bounced like a bronco over every dip and rut. Felt like the road was tryin' to shake us loose like a bag of popcorn on the stove.

I slowed down and made a sharp left near Landry Street, pullin' up in front of Willie's house. Gave the horn two quick taps.

Outran Willie, Charles and Francis, gear slung over their shoulders, rifles in hand, ready like they'd been born for it.

"Hop in, fellas! Let's roll!" I hollered.

They tossed their rifles and bags in the back and climbed in, slammin' the doors behind 'em.

"How you doin', lil' cousin?" Francis said, reachin' over to shake Bo-Scott's hand. He gave him that big old grin, but Bo-Scott just froze.

I glanced up in the rearview mirror and nearly choked laughin'.

Bo-Scott's eyes were big as biscuits. He was starin' down at Charles's hand like it done grown extra limbs. Truth be told, Charles had them extra fingers born with 'em and Bo-Scott hadn't seen nothin' like that in his young life.

We all bust out laughin', couldn't help ourselves.

"You oughta see your face, boy!" Willie hollered, slappin' his knee.

Bo-Scott sunk down in his seat, still wide-eyed. "I ain't never seen a hand like that in my life..."

"Don't worry, he don't bite," I chuckled, easin' back into the road.

A few minutes later, Willie leaned up from the back seat. "So how's that new house of yours?"

"It's a beautiful place, man," I said. "You know I worked hard for it. But my woman and some of my family swear it's haunted. They been hearin' strange sounds, seein' shadows, feelin' things that ain't there."

Willie nodded slow. "Well, now... you know that house got a reputation."

"A reputation?" I raised my eyebrow.

"Yep. Lotta bodies been carried through that place. After folks got electrocuted down at the courthouse, they say a doctor used to meet 'em there to pronounce 'em dead."

"Where you hear that from?" I asked, glancin' at him sideways.

"It was in the paper, some years back," Willie said. "Remember that case? Two Black boys saw a white couple foolin' around on the railroad tracks. Word is, they killed the white fella and had their way with the girl. She got away and called the police. They caught the boys not long after and fried 'em right there at the courthouse. Took the bodies straight over to that house on Freeman Street."

I shook my head. "Lord, have mercy. That's heavy. But who knows what's true anymore."

Charles chimed in, "I heard it was a brothel back in the day. One night, some fool didn't pay what he owed, and all hell broke loose. Folks got shot. Blood everywhere."

"I heard a little girl died there," he added after a pause. "Fell right into the fireplace. They say she was only seven. Folks say somethin' pushed her in."

I looked at them both, tryin' to piece it together. "Where y'all hear all this from?"

Willie shrugged. "It's just stories, man. Rumors. Stuff folks whisper 'bout when the lights go out."

Charles nodded. "Yeah. Neighborhood folklore. Might be true. Might just be ghosts of gossip."

I didn't say nothin' for a minute. Just let the silence ride with us while as stared out the window in deep thought. But deep down, I knew somethin' about that house felt... off. And now I was startin' to wonder what I was going to do.

"So, if ghosts and spirits really do exist… and this house of mine is haunted what the hell am I supposed to do about it?" I asked, squintin' through the sun as it hit me straight in the face.

Willie leaned forward from the back seat. "I can take you by Miss Rousseau's place 'fore we head out huntin'. She can give you somethin' for protection."

"I don't know, man," I muttered.

"Serious, it's on the way. "Won't take but a minute," Willie said, already convincing me.

I looked in the rearview mirror at Bo-Scott and Black, our old hound, sittin' quiet in the back seat. Bo-Scott's eyes were still big from earlier, starin' at me like he was readin' my thoughts. The sun made my eyes squinch up as I drove on in silence.

"A'ight," I said finally. "What street should I turn on?"

"Holy Ghost Lane," Willie said, like that was just an everyday name. "It's comin' up soon. Right here slow down."

I eased the truck off the main road and onto the narrow dirt lane. Big mossy oaks lined the left side, their arms stretchin' out like they were tryin' to wrap us up. To the right, there was nothin' but open field, browned by heat, scattered with rusted junk and a saggin' scarecrow that looked more haunted than anything in my house. Up ahead, a little house sat far down a gravel driveway full of potholes big enough to swallow a tire. I hit every last one of 'em. The truck rocked side to side, our bodies jerkin' along with it.

"Damn, Willie, what kinda place is this?" I asked, tryin' to keep my frustration in check.

"It's good, man. Keep goin'. She's real," he said, noddin' like this was just another Tuesday.

I shot him a look half curiosity, half regret.

We pulled up slow. Miss Rousseau was already outside, feedin' chickens in a patch of dry grass near a messy garden. Chicken feet and, wind chimes danglin' from the porch roof and clangin' out a haunted little tune. The house was wood, white once, now faded and fallin' apart like it was holdin' on to time by the last nail.

She looked to be 'bout ninety years old. Pale skin, deep wrinkles like the bark of an old cypress, her back hunched just enough to make her head hang low. She had on old Jesus looking sandals with striped orange and red socks., movin' slow but steady.

Willie jumped out first and called, "Hello, Miss Rousseau!"

The sun was in her eyes, so she squinted, then smiled wide at what was left of her yellowed and jagged teeth. Willie stepped in closer, lettin' her see him better. "Brought a friend needs some help."

He waved us out the truck.

"This here's Charles, Raymond, his boy Bo-Scott, and that's our dog, Black," he said, pointin' as we stepped out one by one.

"Nice to meet you, ma'am," we each said, shakin' her hand her skin was soft but cold like creek water.

Black just sat and let out a long whine, then started barkin', uneasy.

"Black, hush!" Bo-Scott scolded, tryin' to calm him down.

Miss Rousseau turned her eyes straight to me. "You... you must be the one needs help," she said, her voice raspy but sure.

She stepped closer and gently rubbed my face with her fingers, like she was feelin' my soul.

"I seen you the other day," she said.

"You... seen me?" I asked, brows furrowed.

I looked back at Willie and Charles, confused. "No ma'am. You didn't see me I wasn't here."

She chuckled, soft and eerie. "Come around back," she said, then turned and shuffled toward the side of the house.

I hesitated.

Willie nodded at me. "Go on. Me and Charles'll stay with the boy and the dog."

I gave 'em a look half scared, half annoyed then followed her through tall grass, steppin' over rusted tools, cracked flowerpots, and one mean-ass rooster that chased me halfway 'round the yard.

She stopped at a half-buried wooden box, picked up some old pliers, and broke the rusted lock clean off. From inside, she pulled out a big sea shell white and pink, large enough to fill both her hands.

"You remember this?" she asked, holdin' it out to me.

"No, ma'am. I ain't never seen that before," I said, starin' at it. "I've never even been to the ocean."

She gave a little "hmm," and nodded. "Well... take it. Place it at your front door right there at the threshold. It'll protect you."

"Protect me how?" I asked, cautious.

"This here shell'll catch every evil force and dark thing tryin' to come in or go out. You got spirits in that house, Raymond. Some live there. Some just pass through. This shell catches 'em all. Traps 'em."

She looked me dead in my eyes, her pale face sharp with warning. "Now listen to me. Never break it. Never give it back. If taken never let it return to your family, and when you move' cause someday you will, bury it right there at that house. You understand?"

I swallowed, feelin' a chill crawl down my spine. "Yes, ma'am. I understand."

"Good," she said, more to herself than to me. "Now come over here. I'm gon' anoint you with some oil."

I followed her to another patch of the yard, this one full of roses, daisies, and a stone fountain drippin' with water like it was cryin'. She dipped her fingers in oil and touched my forehead.

But then she paused.

She stared at my face, brows pulled tight. "Raymond... you real sure you never seen that shell?"

I shook my head. "No, ma'am. I don't recall it."

She gave me a long, worried look, then finally nodded. "Alright, then. If you're a hundred percent sure, take it home. Let it do what it's meant to do."

I thanked her, my voice low, still unsure what I was holdin'.

We walked back to the truck slowly. Her head stayed low, bent from age, and I walked beside her, ready to catch her if she fell.

Willie, Charles, and Bo-Scott were already inside, eyes wide with curiosity. Willie was chewin' his gum fast, real fast.

Bo-Scott lit up when he saw me. "You okay, Daddy?"

I nodded and smiled at him. "Yeah, I'm good."

The shell felt heavy in my hands, heavier than it should've been. I climbed in and carefully tucked it behind the back seat like it was a precious stone.

The truck rumbled to life. We waved goodbye as we pulled off, and Miss Rousseau stood there, still as a shadow, watchin' us drive away

"So what was that she gave you, Daddy?" Bo-Scott asked, his voice curious and innocent from the back seat. "Oh, just a little gift for the house," I said, glancin' at him in the rearview mirror. "Don't go tellin' your momma we stopped by Miss Rousseau's, though."

Bo-Scott nodded, grinnin'. "Okay, Dad. I won't."

We rumbled down that long country road, laughin' and talkin' the way we always do when we're out huntin' for next week's supper. I love deer meat. Love rabbit too. Some days, we kill and clean the deer right there in the field, not botherin' to wait 'til we get home.

"Y'all remember last time?" I asked, glancin' over at Charles and Willie. "Bullet hit that stop sign and Sheriff thought we done lost our minds."

Willie busted out laughin'. "Boy, yeah he pulled us over so fast I thought the truck was gonna lift off the ground."

"The sheriff asked, 'Who shot that stop sign?'" I said, smilin'.

"I did it," I told him.

Then Willie cut in, "Nah, I did it."

And Charles piped up, grinnin', "No sir, I did it."

The sheriff pushed up his gun belt, stepped high on his toes, then crushed his cigarette under his boot. "Alright, boys," he said, squintin'. "Who really did it?"

He turned to Bo-Scott, dead serious.

Bo-Scott pointed straight at us. "They all did it," he said, wide-eyed.

The sheriff looked mad for a second then shook his head and said, "Y'all be careful with them guns," and walked off back to his cruiser.

We hollered laughin' the whole rest of the way.

When we got to the woods, we jumped out the truck, dressed in our gear. Each of us stepped light, quiet like shadows in the brush.

"You eat what you catch, son," I told Bo-Scott. "You don't catch nothin' you don't eat nothin'."

We crept through the brush, eyes sharp.

Suddenly, I spotted somethin' movin'.

"There's one," I whispered. "Okay, son, there he is. Get your gun ready."

Bo-Scott cocked the rifle slowly, pointed at it just as the rabbit turned and locked eyes with us big old marble eyes, wide with fear. In a flash, it bolted across the open field.

"Go get him, Black!" I hollered.

Black our good old dog took off like a rocket.

"Go, Black, go!" Bo-Scott yelled, cheerin' him on.

The rabbit zipped under the gate of some old, abandoned farm, where two scrappy dogs came outta nowhere and pounced. They grabbed at the rabbit, pullin' it apart, but Black knew that was our dinner.

He leapt clean over that gate, snapped that rabbit right outta their jaws, and came trottin' back proud.

"Good boy, Black," I said, patting his head. "Now... let's go get ourselves a deer."

We moved slowly through the trees, stayin' low. The woods were still, like the whole place was holdin' its breath. Then, crack!

Bo-Scott's shot echoed through the trees.

We all took off runnin'.

Willie ran ahead, laughin', his boots thumpin' against the roots and pine needles. "He got him! He got a big one, Raymond!"

We reached the deer, and Lord have mercy, it was huge.

"Whew," I said, bendin' down beside it. "We got dinner for months with this one. Let's clean him up and hang him to dry."

"I'm good with that," Charles said, noddin' as he wiped his brow.

Bo-Scott stood nearby, grinnin' from ear to ear.

"Alright," I said. "Grab his hind legs, let's get him up on the wagon. On the count of three, one, two, three!" We all grunted, liftin' that heavy buck and settin' him down on the cart. The rabbits were already tucked in their sacks.

We hauled everything out of the forest, across the dry field, and loaded it all in the back of the truck.

Once we were back on the road, tired and satisfied, everyone slowly drifted off to sleep Willie snoring', Charles mumblin', and Bo-Scott curled up with Black. That gave me some quiet time to think. My mind drifted back to that shell... and that haunted house.

When we got home, I wasted no time. I followed Miss Rousseau's instructions to the tea and set that shell right at the doorway. Didn't rush it, didn't speak a word. Just placed it gently and stepped back.

After that, we unloaded the truck, cleaned the deer and rabbits, and called it a day. We were bone tired but our families. They were gonna eat good for the next few weeks. And just maybe, that house might finally be at peace.

Eighteen

THE GRAVEYARD

Terricita aka Tot–tee

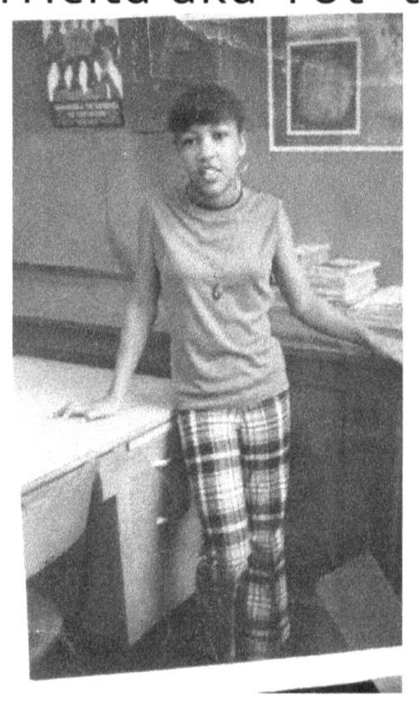

F righten
   Breathe
Inhale, exhale

I jumped clean outta a deep sleep, hands shakin' like I'd seen a ghost.

I sat up quick, pressin' both palms to my face. My dreams had turned to pure nightmares lately, and this one lawd, this one was somethin' else.

I dreamt Daddy had me clean one of the rabbits he caught huntin'. But when I opened it up, tucked deep inside was a nest of tiny, unborn babies soft, limp, barely breathin'. I knew the mama rabbit was gonna be tonight's supper. My stomach twisted as I reached in and started pullin' 'em out, one by one. Tears poured from my eyes. Suddenly, a nurse came stridin' straight through the bathroom door connected to our room.

In the dream, I could see her comin' through the glass of the bathroom door. The glass that I mentioned was shaped like them old ladyfinger cookies. She had on the whole old-time nurse outfit: But it was dirty. Most nurses wear a crisp white dress, stockings, squeaky white shoes, and one of those starched little hats pinned to their head. Her skin looked dusty and pale gray like ash and she moved fast, too fast like lightning.

I looked up just as she got close. The left side of her face was burnt bad, pink flesh twisted and bubbled, and her teeth jutted out like they were tryin' to fall out. Her gums were dark, pink and showin', and she looked madder than the time Auntie Velma slapped dad while he played the piano.

But strange thing was... I felt safe.

She reached down, scooped up them baby rabbits, and stuffed 'em back in the bloody hunting sack Daddy left on the floor. She pivoted sharply and stormed out of the room, towards the bathroom like she had someplace urgent to be.

That's when I woke up.

My hands dropped from my face, and I looked around, breathin' heavy.

My eyes landed on Betty. She was sittin' straight up on her twin bed, back turned to me, her hands restin' in her lap like she'd been prayin'. She had on her fuzzy lime green pajamas with small pink flowers she loved so much, and her hair was tied up in two thick ponytails parted heavy down the center.

"Betty?" I called out, my voice hoarse. "What are you doin', girl?"

She didn't answer.

Just stared at the bathroom door... like maybe she'd seen what I just saw in my dream.

"Betty?" I said again, a little louder this time.

She finally responded, her voice flat. "What?"

"What are you doin'?"

She had a long neck already, but right then it looked longer than ever. She slowly turned her head halfway back toward me, her eyes low and glassy.

"Nothing," she said real soft.

Then she turned back around.

The room went still. So still, I could hear my own heartbeat.

Betty stood up, stiff as a board, and started walkin' toward the bathroom without lookin' at me again.

As she passed, I heard her mumble under her breath, "Don't forget... we got catechism this mornin'."

I sat there starin' at her until I couldn't see her no more. My heart was still poundin', and I swallowed hard, tryin' to get hold of that unwanted fear that had crept in me like a shadow in the dark.

Pushing myself to the edge of the bed, I sat for a second before getting ready for church, The Holy Ghost Catholic Church. The graveyard sits to the left of it. Every Sunday after catechism, Mama makes us walk through it to "visit our people" and pay our respects. Today wouldn't be no different.

I stood up and felt a sudden gush of blood slide down my leg.

"Oh, great," I muttered to myself. "Now my period done started. What awful timing."

Then it hit me if mine just started, that means Mama's probably started too. We always went on at the same time, every month.

I only knew this 'cause Mama had this… ritual. She'd store our used pads in a grocery bag, then hide 'em in the back of the bathroom cabinet for thirty days. She believed if we threw our saturated maxi pads outside in the garbage, somebody could dig 'em out and use 'em for voodoo to put a curse on us.

I don't know how true that is, but I sure ain't tryin' to find out the hard way.

Still, I hated the smell of our old pads sittin' in a tied-up bag in that cabinet. It stunk up the whole room by the end of the month. After thirty days, Mama would pull that bag out, walk outside, and burn the entire bag. Said it was the only way to protect us.

The wood floor creaked beneath my feet as I moved toward the dresser. Yellow blankets lay wrinkled at the foot of my bed, and the green-painted walls glowed faint in the early morning light.

Another Sunday.

Another graveyard visit.

And now, another bad dream I hoped too never have again.

I walked toward the bathroom, the floor creakin' beneath me.

Just as I reached for the knob, a quick shadow passed across the small window in the door.

I froze.

That can't be Betty, I thought. She ain't tall enough.

Something stirred in me half fear, half fire. I got bold, even angry.

"Forget this," I whispered, fists ballin' up tight at my sides.

I swung the door open hard BAM! ready to fight whatever it was. My heart was thumpin', my breath felt tight and heavy pressing into my chest.

But when I looked inside, there was nothin'. No Betty. No shadow. Just steam clingin' to the mirror and silence. I let out a long breath and whispered, "Thank God."

I brushed my teeth, showered, and got dressed. The sound of laughter drifted in from the kitchen just our usual Sunday morning noise. Familiar, funny, and warm.

When I walked in, Mama barely looked up from the stove.

"Terricita, grab you a bowl of Corn Flakes and milk so we can get to church," she said, her voice sharp but steady. I pulled out my chair, grabbed the cereal box, and ate fast, spoon clinkin' against the bowl.

We always dressed nicely for church. I'm not sure why Mama insisted on dressing Betty and me alike, it's not like we were twins or anything. But there we were, every Sunday, in our patent black leather shoes and matching yellow plaid dresses.

Our hair was thick not soft and wavy like Mama's so no matter how she tried, it always puffed up in the front like we had a tiny afro sittin' right on top our heads. Daddy wouldn't let her hot comb it. Said he didn't want us "fryin' our crowns."

We all piled into the car, Mama's hair lookin' especially cute that day cut short with big bangs swoopin' across her forehead. She always looked like she stepped out of a magazine, even on her worst days.

When we got to the Holy Ghost Catholic Church, we walked in quiet, the big wooden doors creakin' behind us. We stopped just inside to dip our fingers in the Holy Water, makin' the sign of the cross before headin' to our pews.

Ma'Mu and Potoon sat on the left side, like always. Papa sat on the right. We waved to them before kneelin' down in our spot.

The priest stepped forward, his voice calm but strong as he prayed: To the church throughout the world. May she be a beacon of hope and love.

The choir and congregation answered in perfect harmony: Lord hear our prayers.

We didn't get to take communion yet, not until we finished catechism class.

Potton leaned over from across the aisle and gave us a slight nod. That was our signal.

Time to go to class.

We sat in class listening well, mostly having fun, teasing each other and passing candy around when the teacher wasn't looking. The church nuns taught us the importance of repentance and fasting for one hour before taking communion. We had all been christened here at the church. The whole purpose of catechism was to teach us the Bible and how to live by it.

We'd kneel down near the Blessed Mother statue, surrounded by glowing candles, whispering our prayers until we were released from class. The same way we walked in blessing ourselves with Holy Water we walked out, making the sign of the cross again.

Now it was time to pay our respects to our loved ones in the graveyard.

"Why we gotta go to the graveyard all the time?" Bode groaned, swinging his arms with his head down, kicking rocks along the gravel path.

"I don't know," I said. "Let's just do it and get it over with."

Betty, quiet as ever, didn't say a word. She just kept walking; her eyes focused on the graves as we passed.

"Let's cut through here," I said, pointing to the old fence. "It's a shorter route."

"Okay," they replied collectively.

We crawled through the hole in the broken fence. One part was a tight squeeze somebody's grave sat right there, a tall white concrete slab. We made our way behind the stone.

Betty was the smallest, so she went first, then Bode, then me.

By the time I came around the corner of the above-ground grave, Betty and Bode were standing still, eyes locked on the big red maple tree to the left of the cemetery.

They looked scared, their eyes were big and wide.

Bode moved his head back and forth like he was trying to see if something was still there.

"What are y'all lookin' at?" I asked.

"There's somethin' over there," Bode said.

"I think it's a man," Betty added, her voice trembling. "But he looks... strange."

"You guys are so scary," I said. "I don't see nothin'. Come on, let's go."

Betty stood frozen. "No!" she yelled back.

"Girl, if you don't get over here". I responded.

I grabbed her by the arm, and we started walking. I could hear them both breathing hard, the leaves crunching under our feet. I held their hands tightly. I always felt like it was my job to take care of them.

Then we heard a loud thump.

I froze, eyes scanning the graveyard. My heart pounded in my chest, palms slick and clammy with sweat. There it was a black flash. A figure darted from behind the tree to the next grave.

We were stuck standing right there in the middle of the graveyard, unable to move or speak.

I'm scared to breathe.

My clammy hands squeezed theirs tighter.

Suddenly, the figure appeared again.

We saw a black, fog-like form rise from the ground. There was a low growl deep and heavy. We stood frozen. It was huge. I couldn't make out its face, but I held on tight to Bode and Betty.

Betty screamed, "Aaaaahhh!"

"I'm gonna tell my daddy!" Bode shouted, his voice shaking. "He gon' shoot you!"

He said it like he was trying to be brave, but it came out weak.

"My dad is Raymond Chatman!" he yelled.

Suddenly, the shadow vanished, and a chilly wind blew right through us pushing us back.

We looked around, then ran as fast as we could.

I was ahead of them both. Betty was to my left, Bode to my right behind me.

"Run!" I yelled.

Their faces were tight, lips tucked in, eyes widened. They were running as fast as they could.

Then we suddenly stopped, we could not go any further.

There was a long stretch of dirt in front of us like a dirt barrier.

We approached it fast, our heels tilting digging into the ground, arms out to catch our balance to prevent us from falling forward.

Bode slid in right behind me, feet barely touching the dirt. Betty slowed down just enough to stop beside us, breathing hard bent foward with her hands on her knees, she looked up,

"What is this?" she asked.

"I don't know," I replied.

We stepped closer.

There were three graves freshly dug, neat and square.

Right above each one was a headstone:

Terricita Chatman, Raymond Chatman Jr. , Betty Ann Chatman

We stood silent.

Scared.

Our hearts thudding in our ears.

"It's gonna kill us!" Bode yelled.

"It already has our graves dug", "Run!"

We turned and bolted.

The weeds scratched at our legs. We jumped over raised tombstones, ducked tree branches.

The faster we ran, the darker the sky grew.

It started raining hard and fast.

It felt like forever before we made it out of that graveyard.

But something was there. Something guiding us. Protecting us.

All I could hear was our breathing Huuu... huuu... huuu and the splashes of our feet against the muddy ground. The back door to the church was open.

We ran straight in.

I fell to my knees in front of the Blessed Mother statue.

"Thank you, God," I whispered. "Please help us. I don't understand why we just saw our own graves. Are we all gon' die together, Lord? Please... have mercy on my soul." I cried out.

Momma walked in to pick us up, "Terricita what's wrong?" momma asked with a look of concern on her face. I was scared to tell her we never got to visit the graves; I just looked at her and then Betty. Betty was still shaky and crying, Bode ran to mom and hugged her around her waist, she hugged him back, Lets go home, you can tell me what happen when we get home.

The drive back home was quiet. So quiet you could hear the gas in our stomachs bubbling. We were all still shaken from the graveyard incident.

"Where's Daddy at, Momma?" I asked, trying to sound casual, though my voice cracked a little.

"Oh, he went to help Ma'mu and Potoon move into their new house over on 734 Melancon Street. It's right on the hill," she answered with a soft smile, her voice trying to lighten the mood.

"Oh wonderful, can we see it?" I asked, sitting up a little straighter.

"Yes, baby. We're going to stop by and bring some food to cook. Just need to swing by the house first, grab Ma'mu pot and get out of these church clothes," Momma said, eyes focused on the road.

"I can't wait to see it!" I grinned.

We were all excited to visit our grandparents, Ma'mu and Po-toon, and see their new house. As we pulled into our driveway, the air seemed to shift again heavier now. Momma leaned over and peered through her window, staring up at the second floor before opening her door.

I watched her. She was looking for something.

Or maybe... someone.

She was still haunted just like the rest of us by what she saw in the window that night: the figure of a woman standing upstairs, behind curtains that appeared to be on fire.

We sat still.

Then, "Come on," Momma said briskly, pulling herself togeth-er.

We all jumped out of the car and headed for the front door.

"Last one to the door's a rotten egg!" I yelled, and we all took off running.

Momma beat us there and laughed as she dug deep into her purse for the house keys.

"Come on, Momma," Bode said, fanning himself. "It's hot out here."

"Oh hush, boy," she replied, still searching. That's when the phone inside began to ring.

"Oh, shucks," Momma muttered.

"Last one to the phone's a rotten egg!" Betty squealed.

The phone kept ringing.

"It must be important it's still ringing!" I said, now more curious than playful.

"Ah! Found them!" Momma said, finally pulling out the keys.

She unlocked the door with a twist of the old brass knob. It clicked open with a groan.

We raced inside, running down the hallway, laughing as we all tried to get to the phone first.

But we stopped dead in our tracks.

The laughter vanished.

The hallway felt cold and unnaturally cold. The phone was no longer resting on its cradle.

It was floating. Suspended in the air.

We all stood there, frozen, staring with wide eyes and trembling legs. I could hear my own heartbeat thudding like a drum in my ears.

The sound of slow, shallow breathing filled the room though none of us were speaking.

The air turned icy. The hair on my arms stood straight up.

"Oh my God... what is in this house?" Momma whispered, her voice shaky.

Slowly, she stepped forward, cautious, her feet making the old wooden floorboards creak under her weight.

"Momma, don't answer it!" Bode cried.

But she didn't listen.

With steady hands, she reached for the floating black phone. It was heavy and cold to the touch too cold. She raised it to her ear.

"...Hello?" she said, barely above a whisper. "Is anyone there?"

We could all hear the voice through the receiver. Clear and very loud.

It was a woman.

Friendly, almost cheerful.

"Hello? Is Carol there?"

Momma turned to us, her eyes wide with worry.

"You have the wrong number," she said firmly, then slammed the receiver back into its cradle.

Silence crept back in worse than it was in the car.

She looked at us all, her face pale.

"Let's get out of these clothes... and get the hell outta here. Quick."

Nineteen

My house on the hill

August Guillory aka Potoon

L ift 1,2,3

Heavy

Turn it

"Come on, Duke! You gotta lift it higher than that!" I hollered, wiping the sweat from my brow. "Y'all Norman boys act like the only thing you can lift is a pen and some paper over at them insurance offices."

Duke snapped his head around fast, eyes wide. "What'd you just say?"

Raymond chimed in and chuckled low. "I think he said you talk too fast."

Duke shot back, raspy, and sharp, "you talk too damn slow! "!". "I can't even understand you, sounding like a damn Frenchie!"

"I ain't got time for your hunkies," Duke grumbled. "Let's just get this couch inside." I laughed at Duke; he was a great son-in-law regardless of what people around town said about him. I turned my attention to Raymond. "Raymond, you got the other side?" I asked, already crouching to lift.

"I sure do," he replied, squatting with me.

"Alright now on the count of three. One... two... three Lift!"

"HMMM!" We all grunted together, straining under the weight.

I was already sweating buckets. My red-toned skin was taking a beating from that Louisiana sun.

"Don't you drop my couch, Patton!" Pearl yelled from the doorway, hands on her hips.

"I ain't gon' drop your couch, Pearl!" I hollered back. "We got it!"

We maneuvered the heavy thing inside and set it down right by the front window. The sun beamed in on the cushions as if it were sending us a message that this home would be our final resting place.

"I gotta go," Duke said, brushing dust off his hands. "I'll be back later."

"Alright," I muttered, watching him dart out the door and down the four steps, disappearing fast like a bat out of hell.

"He ain't comin' back," I told Raymond.

"That's okay," Raymond said with a smirk. "He won't be gettin' none of this beer I just made and sure as hell not any of my Sunday super daddy herbs," he laughed.

"Potton, you still makin' beer and... all of them potions for the men?"

"Of course I am Raymond," I said, waving to him to follow me to the back. "Come on, lemme show you." We walked through the kitchen and out to the shed behind the house.

"See what I do is," I began, "I get my big ol' pot, boil some water, throw in some rice. Sometimes your daddy gives me corn. I crush it all up, boil it down until it's mushy. Then I add sugar cane... little yeast. Let that fermentate for a week. By the time Sunday rolls 'round, folks lined up outside waitin' for a bottle."

Raymond laughed, shaking his head. "Man, what about that special herb you make? The one that helps a man... well, you know..."

"Get a better rise?" I finished for him with a wink. "Yeah, I know what you mean."

"I'd be rich if you taught me that one," Raymond said.

"Naw, see, I can't teach you that," I said, grinning. "That's my secret. Matter fact, I gotta get this batch ready. Got some men comin' by later, promising their women a whole lot tonight!"

Raymond laughed till his eyes watered. "Potton, why do you make all this stuff? You work at Daly Motors. You and Eli have been there for years. Don't they pay y'all decent?"

I looked at him, then down at my hands. "Well... our hair might be straight enough and our skin light enough to fool folks into givin' us a decent job… but we still colored. We get less than what the white folks get, and that's just how it is,"

Raymond nodded his head with his hand resting on his top lip.

"I'm just tryin' to figure out how I'm gon' pay for all this," I said, waving my arms around our new house. "I put everything I had down on this place. We couldn't live with Amelia forever. And Ernest just died." Raymond's eyes went wide. "What? Does Ophelia know?"

"Not yet," I said quietly. "Anyway, I need to bring in a little extra money. So, I'm doin' what I know how."

"I can lend you the money, Patton. Just let me know."

"Thanks, Raymond. I appreciate that."

"As a matter of fact," he said, "why don't you come work at Daly Motors full-time? I can get you in. They need somebody to sweep the floors. It pays good."

Raymond raised an eyebrow. "Sweep the floors, huh?"

"I know you got your pride," I replied, "but hey…"

"I just might do that," Raymond said, thinking on it. "Do I gotta dress like you every day?"

"Dress like me?" I laughed. "Man, what's wrong with how I dress?"

"You got on a yellow button-down shirt and some faded Dickies. Look like you stepped out a catalog from three years ago."

I grinned. "I like how I dress, Raymond."

We walked back toward the porch. The house was small, with just two bedrooms, but it was me and Pearls.

"Man, look at this place," I said. "I like how soon as you walk in, the living rooms right there. Kitchen in the back. The backdoor leads right out to the yard. Porch big enough for me and Pearl to sit all night and look up at the stars."

"How's you and Ophelia house feel?" I asked Raymond. "I ain't seen it yet."

"I don't know," he said slowly. "I feel like... like the house is changin' me. Strange things been goin' on. I need someone to bless it."

"That ain't good," I said, rubbing my chin. "I'll call the priest from Holy Ghost catholic Rev. Francis he has been there a long while. He'll come and bless the house."

I walked over to the phone and stuck my finger through the dial holes, turning each number slow and steady. 337-942-2732

Brrr... Brrr...

"Hello? Rev. Francis? This August Guillory."

"Hey, how are you?"

"I'm alright, sir. Listen, I need someone to bless my daughter and son-in-law's house. It's on Freeman Street." "Hello?"

"...Father, you there? The phone went quiet; I raised an eyebrow, a puzzled look on my face and pulled it away from my ear. I glanced at the receiver, then quickly brought it back up to my ear." Hello, Father," I said, again. I could hear a slight grunting through the phone. "Thought I lost you for a minute"." You got quiet".

"Yes, sir. I'm here. Freeman Street, you said? "Father replied.

"Yes. 1010 Freeman Street. "Can you make it?" Wonderful!

"I looked at Raymond, one hand over the speaker part of the phone".

He said he could come after church next Sunday.

"Thank you, Father. I'm grateful."

I hung up the phone and turned back to Raymond.

"I hate to say this about the Reverend," I muttered, "but he acted like he didn't wanna do it. Could've just been static, but... for a minute there, I couldn't hear nothin'."

Raymond looked scared and puzzled. "Well... I suppose the house might already be tryin' to run him out.

This chapter is dedicated to my grandfather August Guillory. His mother's name was Ophelia Durousseau and his father Auguste Guillory. My great-great grandmother Clara V. Durousseau and my great-great grandfather Augustin Durousseau were born 1852-1893. He spoke broken English and was a creole man, Spanish, French, and native American a tribe from Texas.

My grandfather August Guillory died in 1970. He had four brothers and three sisters.

His great -great grandfather fought in the Spanish war and was honored by his plaque in a wall in Austin Texas to this present day, Trinadad Ramon.

My mother Ophelia Chatman was name after her Grandmother Ophelia Durousseau, she died in 1939 right as my mother was being born.

"It is said, that when one soul exhales its last breath, another quietly inhales its first".

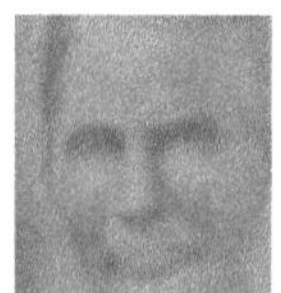

Twenty

CURVE BALL

Bode

"Bases are loaded. Terrie's at bat! Y'all get back you know she swings hard!" I hollered, my voice cutting through the thick Louisiana air.

Betty scooped her hands around her mouth and screamed, "Black's gonna catch the ball don't worry! He always does!"

We had driven over to Ma-maw and Potton's house that afternoon after church. Momma was inside, cooking up a storm with Ma-maw, while Daddy and Potton were busy shifting furniture around the house, trying to get everything in its right place.

Meanwhile, Terrie, Betty, and I were out back, playing baseball with our dog, Black. The backyard was a huge wide, open stretch of grass with a few crooked trees lining the old metal fence. The air smelled of fried okra and cornbread drifting from the kitchen window, and the sun beat down on our heads like fried cracklings.

I gripped the ball tight, eyeing Tot-Tea, that was our nickname for Terecita. I hurled it up and threw it fast and hard, hoping she'd miss.

Whapp! The crack of the bat echoed across the yard.

"Oh, Lord!" I shouted.

The ball shot through the air like lightning. Tot-Tea took off, first base, second, third, then home. She was grinning the whole way. Black barked and bolted after the ball, tail wagging, his black coat flashing in the sun. That dog could hunt rabbits and retrieve anything, we always said he was better than any boy in the neighborhood.

I shaded my eyes with my hand, squinting toward the trees. "C'mon, Black!" I called. "Bring it on back!"

But instead of returning, Black was pacing back and forth, nose to the ground, letting out little whimpers.

I turned to Tot-Tea. "Dang, girl! You hit that ball clean to the other side of the parish. Even Black can't find it!" "I didn't mean to!" she hollered back, shrugging.

Betty put her hands on her hips. "I'll help him," she said, already walking toward the end of the yard.

We stood and waited. Betty and Black searched for what felt like ten minutes, ducking behind bushes, peaking under the trees. Finally, they both came back, empty-handed.

"We can't find it," Betty said, brushing her hands on her shorts. "Guess we'll have to play something else." We trudged to the front yard, brushing sweat off our forehead and still giggling about Tot-Tea's home run. That's when we noticed a line of men walking up the road most of them in boots and hats, some holding paper sacks.

"Are they all coming to help Daddy and Potton move furniture?" I asked, watching them slow down in front of the house.

Terrie squinted, then shook her head. "Nah. I think they're here for that special juice Potton makes."

Betty wrinkled her nose. "What special juice?"

"I don't know," Terrie said, shrugging. "Momma won't tell me. She just said, 'stay away from it and stay in a child's place.'"

We looked at each other wide-eyed, wondering what in the world was in that juice. But none of us dared ask again.

"I wonder if Daddy'll take us to get some ice cream at the Dairy Queen," I said, wiping sweat from my brow. "It's hotter than a skillet on Sunday."

"Let's go ask him!" Betty shouted.

We took off running, tennis shoes slapping against the dirt and porch steps. We went around the side of the house, then up onto the front porch where Daddy and our grandfather, Potton, were sitting, their chairs tilted back, eyes half-closed in the heat.

"Daddy!" I called out. "Can we go get some ice cream? Please?"

"Pretty please with sprinkles on top!" Betty added, grinning wide.

Potton glanced over at Daddy, then gave a little nod. "Go on, son. Take the kids to get some ice cream. Might do 'em some good in this heat and you are too. This line here's gettin' a bit long, if you know what I mean."

Daddy looked confused. "What line?"

Potton leaned in, lowering his voice with a sly grin. "The line of folks waitin' for that 'special juice.' You know the kind of Kool-aid that don't go in a child's glass."

Daddy chuckled under his breath. "Ahh... that line."

Potton waved his hand toward the road to make the men aware he was ready to serve them. "Besides, Pearl's brothers Wallace, Hilton, and John they're supposed to be here soon to help move some things. My brothers Joseph and Eli too. Might get crowded round here quick."

Daddy stood up and stretched, his shirt sticking to his back. "Alright, y'all. Hop in the truck. Let's go cool off with some cold cups and ice cream."

We skipped and cheered all the way to the truck, smiling from ear to ear with the promise of cold cups and vanilla ice cream cones. Even the cicadas seemed happy, buzzing loud in the trees like they were getting ice cream too.

As we reached the truck, Momma came running out the house.

"Don't forget about me!" she hollered, hurrying with her high hell Mary Janes ,across the porch and down the steps. She climbed in, rubbing her belly with a soft smile.

Little did I know, Momma was craving ice cream for a reason.

We jumped in and started singing our family nursery rhyme, all off-key but full of pride.

"There was a little mouse that lived on the hill, hm hm, there was little mouse that lived on the hill, He was tough and rough like Buffalo Bill,hm hm..."

The Dairy Queen was packed, but we stood and waited, still full of excitement.

I watched Momma. She rubbed her belly again, her eyes soft and far away.

"Tot-Tea, Betty, Bo Scott come get your ice cream cone," Daddy called from the window.

"Thanks, Daddy!" I said, my voice sticky with sweetness.

"Yeah, thank you!" Tot-Tea and Betty echoed.

Momma just stood there smiling, still rubbing her belly.

"Let's head on home," Daddy said. "Try not to get ice cream on the seats, you hear?"

"Okay, Daddy," we all chimed in unison.

As we drove down the street, I noticed a group of men staring hard at us. I didn't think much of it. Just kept licking my cone.

Then suddenly, Daddy stopped at the stop sign, and that same car we passed earlier came speeding around the corner. It swerved, nearly sideswiping us.

Daddy jerked the wheel to the right, hugging the curb.

In the back seat, Terrie, Betty, and I looked at Daddy's eyes through the rearview mirror. What we saw wasn't Daddy.

There was fire in his eyes, darkness I had never seen before.

"Oh my God," Momma yelled. "What the hell is wrong with people?"

Daddy extended his left arm out the window. He stared into the side mirror.

We followed his gaze.

A man was stepping out of the car, a pipe in his hand. He was yelling loudly, his voice full of hate.

"You colored boy I'll teach you!"

Daddy always kept a shotgun under his seat.

As the man stormed toward us, Daddy threw open his door, grabbed the gun, and cocked it.

Clank-CLACK.

Tot-Tea, Betty, and I dropped to our knees, peeking out the back window. Our eyes were wide, hearts pounding. Ice cream cones wobbling in our hands. Tot-Tea was still licking hers, even while breathing hard.

Daddy stepped forward and fired.

POW!

The man stumbled, dropped the pipe, and backed away.

Two more men jumped out from the car. One stayed inside.

"Daddy gon' get killed," I whispered, frozen.

My ice cream started to melt and dripping down my fingers.

Clack! Another round chambered.

One of the men ran for the pipe. Daddy fired again.

POW!

That's when we heard the car door slam.

It was Momma.

"Raymond, STOP!" she screamed, running toward him. She grabbed his arm, trying to pull him back.

Daddy was too far gone. He swung his arm back, yelling at her to get away.

Momma fell to the ground.

The second man lunged toward Daddy.

Another shot rang out.

POW!

Momma scrambled back to the car, her nose bleeding, her eyes full of panic. She yanked the door open and slammed it shut.

Daddy kept firing.

The driver screamed, "Get in, fellas!"

One man jumped back in the car. The last one took off running, his feet slapping the pavement.

The car slowed just enough for him to leap into the back seat. The door slammed, and they sped off down the street.

But Daddy, Daddy's a hunter. If he had wanted them dead... they'd be dead.

Daddy walked back to the truck, fists tight, the shotgun resting over his shoulder. He opened the truck door, placed the shotgun back on the floorboard behind the seat, then climbed into the driver's seat without a word. All three of us kids quickly turned around in our seats sitting up straight, facing forward, quiet as church mice. Our hearts still pounded and melted ice cream ran down our hands.

Daddy looked at us in the rearview mirror. His eyes were blank. Hollow.

We didn't dare cry but deep down, I was screaming:

That's my daddy. Brave. Protector of his family.

He turned to look at Momma. Her face was so sad, her nose still bleeding. You could see it in his face, he felt horrible.

There was a different kind of sorrow in his eyes when he looked at her.

Without saying a word, he reached over, gently wiped the blood from her nose with his thumb, and smeared it onto the leg of his pants. That was Daddy's way of saying, I'm sorry.

He turned back to the road, checked his side mirror one more time, took a long deep breath, then started the truck.

We drove down the road in silence.

When we got home, Black, our dog, jumped out of the truck first, tail wagging like nothing had happened. Then the three of us climbed out, followed by Momma.

I turned around and waited for Daddy. He was still sitting in the truck, picking at his chin something he always did when he was stressed out.

We ran up the wooden steps and opened the front door. I looked down at the seashell by the threshold and thought to myself:

The protection of this shell follows us everywhere.

Inside, Tot-Tea followed Momma to the bathroom to get cleaned up. Betty and I plopped down in front of the TV and turned on Gunsmoke.

A few minutes later, Momma and Tot-Tea came out and joined us. We all curled up together on the bed, the TV flickering shadows on our faces.

Then we heard the front door open, followed by footsteps in the kitchen.

Here came Daddy, carrying his favorite snack: a bowl of vanilla ice cream and a handful of oatmeal cookies. He walked into the room, set the bowl down, and without a word, crawled into bed with us.

We passed around the cookies, scooping ice cream on top, our fingers still a little sticky from earlier.

It had been a crazy day.

I didn't know if we were more shaken by what happened out on the road, the graveyard... or by the strange noises that always lingered in this old house.

But one thing I did know.

I felt protected.

Twenty-One

THE RETURN OF EVERYTHING THAT SHOULDN'T

Betty

S till
  Dirty

frighten

Tot-Tee stood in the hallway still.

She stared directly at me, her pink pajamas dirty and clinging to her legs, her hair tangled and full of spiderwebs. The dogs were barking outside, loud and restless.

"Tot-Tee?" I called out softly. "What are you doing?"

She didn't answer. Just kept standing there.

I took a cautious step closer, trying to make sure it was really her. The hallway light felt dimmer than usual. Heavy and scary.

"Where's Momma and Daddy?" I asked.

She slowly tilted her head to the side and shrugged. Then, with dirty fingernails, she lifted her arm and held something out in her hand. I couldn't see what it was yet.

Just then, Bode ran up behind me, his breath hot and stank on my neck.

"What's wrong with her?" he whispered.

"I don't know," I whispered back. "Where's Momma and Daddy?"

"They left for work already."

"What should we do?"

"I don't know," he said again, quieter this time.

His bright yellow pajamas glowed like a sunflower in the dark hall.

"Go turn on the hallway light," I told him.

Bode ran over and flipped the switch up and down.

Nothing. The light wouldn't come on.

Tot-Tee started walking toward us slowly, her hair swinging across her face, her steps light, faster but chilling. Her face was flat, expressionless, as she kept holding out that object like she wanted us to take it.

We stood frozen. Too scared to move.

"Should I go get the shell?" Bode asked. "The old lady said it would protect us."

"What? No!" I hissed. "Maw'Ma don't like us messing with stuff like that."

Then Tot-Tee spoke.

"Here is the ball. I found it." "Take it", she spoke.

Her voice was raspy. Eerie.

"The ball? The one we lost yesterday?" I asked.

"Yes," she said. "You have it now."

I reached my held my hand out and she slowly placed in the palm of my hand, my eyes followed.

"How'd you find it?" I asked. "We searched all over the woods yesterday"

"Why does it matter?" she said flatly, walking right past us without even blinking. "By the way, Momma's pregnant."

"What?" I said in shock, looking at Bode.

"She is, she's pregnant" Tot-Tee repeated. "Her bloody pads ain't in the cabinet this month."

Then she turned and looked straight at us her eyes dark and strange.

I looked down at the ball in my hand. My fingers trembled.

It was the same one. The same ball we used yesterday. Same scuff on the side.

I quickly shoved it into Bode's hands.

"I don't want it!" he cried. "Where did she find it? How did she even get here? She walked through the woods to Granddaddy's house alone?"

"She's not right," I whispered. "She's not herself."

Tot-Tee turned and headed to the bathroom. The door slammed shut behind her, and a moment later we heard the water running.

Bode turned and sprinted to the fireplace. He threw the ball in hard.

"We need to burn it," he said. "Just like Momma does her pads every month."

"What?! That's ridiculous!" I snapped.

But before we could argue even more, we heard something behind us.

Clink. Clunk.

The sound of the fireplace coming to life.

We spun around.

But there was no fire.

Just the ball bouncing gently back out of the fireplace.

Bode screamed.

I stepped back, my mouth dry.

"I'm callin' Maw'Ma," I said. "I'm going to her house for the rest of the week. I don't care what Momma say. I'm not stayin' here."

I was too scared to use the phone after seeing it rise on its own the other day. But I had to call.

I picked it up with shaky hands and dialed the number by heart.

Ring... Ring...

"Hello?"

"Maw'Ma," I said, already crying. "It's Bean Face Betty. Can I come to your house?"

"You can come on Wednesday," she replied gently. "What's wrong, baby? Why you cryin'?"

"This house is haunted!" I sobbed. "Something ain't right in here..."

"Stop that cryin' now," she said, firm but loving. "Just pray, you hear me? Pray over that house. You can come Wednesday. Everything gon' be alright."

"...Okay."

I hung up, still sniffling.

Bode and I headed to the kitchen.

"I guess we gotta fix our own breakfast this mornin'," he muttered.

I opened the refrigerator and grabbed the milk. Bode dragged the little wooden step stool across the floor to reach the cereal on top of the fridge.

We sat at the table, trying to calm down, still jumpy from what we'd seen.

I poured our cereal, splashing some milk into the bowls. We started eating quietly, chewing slow, like every sound might wake something up.

Then suddenly Tot-Tea walked into the kitchen.

Happy.

Smiling.

Like nothin' had ever happened.

Our spoons froze in mid-air, jaws dropped wide open.

"Look who's growin' up!" she said, grinning. "I'm proud of y'all."

Bode and I just stared at her.

If I had gotten in trouble for saying a bad word, I would've dropped the F-word right then and there. Tot-Tea sat at the table and started pouring cereal and milk for herself

I heard Mom and Dad talking last night.

"They said we're goin' to Galveston this weekend," Tot-Tea announced over breakfast. "Little vacation before school starts."

"Oh... okay," I replied, lifting my spoon slowly and cautiously to my mouth.

"Hey," Bode cut in, looking sideways at her. "You said Momma was pregnant. How you know that?"

Tot-tee leaned in, her voice full of sass and surety. "Because Momma and I usually start our period at the same time every month same day. I started… she didn't. Besides, didn't y'all see how she kept rubbin' on her stomach? And all that ice cream she been eatin'?"

We all paused, thinkin'.

Then we laughed.

" I did notice that "I said, eyes wide. "If it's a girl, I think her name should be Sandra."

"Sandra Marie," Tot-Tee added.

"Yeah," Bode grinned, "and we can call her Sandy."

We sat around the table, full of giggles cracking jokes, the morning sun pouring through the kitchen window as we enjoyed our breakfast. After breafast, we spent the day cleanin' sweepin' up, moppin', and takin' care of Grey Boney, our cat and our dogs. Bode complained about doing the challenging work, but we all chipped in he needs to shut up sometimes.

"Y'all better clean that cat pan good," Terrie warned, holding her nose yelling from across the room. I just ignored her while cutting my eyes.

While cleaning out the hall closet, I stumbled across something' strange, odd tools, things that didn't belong in a house. Not just old junk. Medical stuff.

"Hey," I called out, pulling out a worn, dusty doctor's bag. "Y'all come look at this."

Inside was an old-timey stethoscope, antique lookin'. along with a small bottle labeled Holy Water.

"Ooooh Lord," Terrie said, snatching the stethoscope. "Come here, little girl. Let me check your heart."

"She doesn't have a heart," Bode teased. "We gon' hear the devil in her!"

He grabbed the bottle of holy water and started flingin' it at me, yellin' in a deep preacher voice, "Be gone, Satan!"

We laughed so hard our stomachs hurt, rollin' on the floor. None of us wanted to admit it, but there was somethin' uneasy 'bout that bag.

Later, we realized we forgot to feed the dogs. We rushed out into the heat thick and heavy like syrup. Bode turned on the water hose while I held the bowls, lettin' the cold water splash over my hands.

Before we knew it, Mom and Dad pulled back up from work.

"Daddy," Terrie said, wiping her forehead, "can you please paint the windows on the bathroom door?"

Dad raised an eyebrow. "Why?"

"Because... I keep seein' something pass by 'em at night."

He squinted at her, then looked over at all of us. "Okay, Puput and the gang. Can I get in the house good first?" "Where's your momma?" he asked, stepping through the back door.

"I think she said she was stoppin' by one of the meat markets," I said, trying to remember. "She named a few Century Meats... Meat Mountain that's Joe Malick's place. Maybe Mesh's."

He grunted. "Why's she doin' that? I got all that meat I hunted with Francis Louis, already cleaned and packed in the freezer."

I just shrugged. "I dunno, Daddy."

He didn't say nothin' else just walked out back, grabbed the gallon of black paint, came back in, and started paintin' the bathroom windows. We stood behind him and watched.

It only took him ten minutes. By the end, the lady-finger windows were solid black. Couldn't see nothin' through them.

Wednesday finally came. The house had been quiet since Daddy painted those windows. Felt calmer, like whatever used to pass by had moved on.

That morning, Momma dropped me off at Ma'Mu's house just like she promised.

Now, Maw'Ma's house was always spotless. You could eat off her porch if you had to. She made everything herself our dresses, our blankets, even our curtains. I always wanted to call her by her real name, Octavia, but I knew better.

"Don't try me," she'd say with one raised brow. "I will snatch the black off ya."

Maw'Ma was short, with thick legs and a soft belly, but she stood taller than most like her thick shoes added a foot to her height. She said her mama, Mae Temple, and Auntie Sally were both tiny, even smaller than her.

That day, we went window shoppin'. Maw'Ma had an eye for fabric. She spotted some wool, let out a little "Ooh, child," and marched straight into the store.

"I'm takin' this to the only Black tailor left in Opelousas," she said.

As we were leavin' the shop, I saw it. A tall, lean, black figure with no face just standin' near the fabric rolls, starin' right at me.

My heart started poundin'. Sweat trickled down my back even though the store had a fan. I stared back, frozen. My hand in Maw'Mas, she was leadin' me out, her handbag swingin' on her arm. Just as we reached the door. SLAM.

I cried out. My finger had got caught in the door.

"Oh, baby!" Maw'Ma gasped.

Blood was already tricklin' down my hand, my finger throbbin' and swellin' up like a red sausage in the sun. We walked home in the heat, Maw'Ma hummin' and singing like usual. I followed beside her, my finger dripping blood down the sidewalk. Folks stared but said nothin'. Her hummin' got stronger the closer we got to the house.

As soon as we stepped inside, she dropped the shopping bag and headed straight for the fridge.

"Sit down, baby."

She came back with a chunk of salt meat. Cold and wet.

She wrapped it around my finger, held it firm, and began hummin' again low and slow. The kind of hum that ain't just music, but medicine.

When the humming stopped, she got quiet. Her eyes closed. I stood there with my big almond-shaped eyes, watchin'.

Then she opened her eyes, smiled, and unwrapped the meat.

My fingers were clean. Healed. No blood. No swelling. No mark at all.

I stared at it in shock.

"Let's get ready for Bible study," she said, casually.

I nodded, still speechless.

"You know your Papa and I take Brenda and Ann every Wednesday night."

We went to Little Zion Baptist Church. The old wooden one with the red carpet and creaky pews. The graveyard was attached to this church as well. Mae Temple Glaze White is buried there. She died in 1948.I enjoy going to church with Maw"ma.

Daddy picked me up after service, the porch light flickering as we walked to the car.

Something had changed in me that day. I'd seen a shadow. Got healed by hands that hummed with love. I didn't know what it all meant yet but I felt it. Deep in my heart.

As the days went by, the hauntings at 1010 Freeman Street didn't stop. They just became... routine. Strange as it sounds, I was honestly beginning to get used to it.

That is until our family vacation in Galveston.

Daddy and Mama had packed us up for a trip down to the coast. I remember it clear as day: my hair was styled into three little pigtails, two in the front, one in the back each tied neatly with white ribbons. I wore my favorite dark blue jumper with white lace around the waist. I thought I was too cute.

As soon as we arrived, excitement exploded inside us. There were big roller coasters, water everywhere, boats and ships lining the docks. Me, Tot-Tee, and Bode rode the roller coaster and laughed until our bellies hurt. We stuffed ourselves with cotton candy and corn dogs while the Texas sun tanned our faces.

Then Daddy had the idea that we should take a boat ride just the family.

He helped Mama climb down into a small creaky boat, the kind that rocks even when you breathe. "Y'all be careful now," he said, steadying the side while we all clambered in. Once we were aboard, we laughed and sang silly songs as we floated over the deep brown water.

That's when I thought I had seen something.

A hand.

Yes, a hand, sticking straight up out the water. It was grayish-green, the skin soggy and sagging, like it had been soaking in acid or had been in the ocean for centries. Patches of blood and slough clung to the wrist like old rags. The fingers didn't move... but somehow, it felt like they wanted to.

I stared, frozen. Everyone else was still singing, still laughing, still rocking the boat gently with joy.

I was in a different world. A quiet one. The air got cold. Distant. I could hear Mama's voice, but it sounded far away like she was calling from a tunnel.

"Ooh, look at that crab in the water!" she said. "We could catch some fresh ones and make us some gumbo!"

I blinked, snapping out of my daze.

Suddenly, crabs were everywhere.

Tiny, angry things started crawling into the boat, dozens of them. They scuttled across the floor and up my leg. Before I could holler, one had made its way up into my romper.

And pinched me.

Right on my noon.

I screamed so loud the seagulls flew away.

"Daddy! Daddy!" I shrieked, running in place and flailing my arms. "It got my noon! It got my noon!"

Daddy turned, confused and half-laughing. "What got your what?!"

"The crab! It got my noon!"

I was jumping and spinning in the boat like a wild child. Everyone started laughing, everyone but me.

"Take it off! Get it off!" I cried, tears pouring now.

Daddy shouted, "Uh uh! I ain't takin' no crab off your noon! Go to your mama!"

I ran to Mama, shaking and squealing. She pulled me to the side, trying not to laugh as she untied my romper. "Hold still now," she said gently, pulling the fabric down. She spotted the one little crab and plucked it off like it was lint. "There. You're fine, baby."

But here's the thing...

Nobody else saw the other crabs.

Not one.

Just me.

That ride started out sweet and silly... but it ended with me embarrassed, angry, and real scared. Because deep down, I knew it wasn't just a crab. It was that spirit. That evil presence that kept showing up no matter where we went.

Even on vacation.

Twenty-Two

THE BLESSING

Theresa Guillory-Norman

"Duke! I'm headin' over to Ophelia's house after church. You gon' have to watch Karla and them! "I hollered from inside the shower. The steam was fogging up my pink and peach bathroom, which was covered in flowers from the floor tiles to the little lace curtains on the window.

Duke cracked the door open, sticking his head through the steam like a curious cat. His voice came fast and raspy like always.

"Say what now?"

"I said I'm goin' to Ophelia's after church!" I repeated. "Potoon our daddy he asked me to meet the priest over there. They gon' bless the house."

Duke groaned. "Theresa, I got them insurance documents to finish today. Can't you ask your sister Velma to go instead?"

I rolled my eyes, rinsing soap off my shoulder. "Now you know damn well Raymond and Velma don't get along. We tryin' to bless the house not stir up the devil."

Duke laughed under his breath. "Alright then. But don't be long."

I stepped out the shower, wrapped a white towel around my head, and used the edge to wipe steam from the mirror. That's when I froze into place.

Something was standing behind me.

My heart dropped straight to my feet. I couldn't see its face, just the outline. A spirit still and dark.

I started praying without delay. "Jesus, Jesus, Jesus..."

Whatever it was... vanished. Gone. Like it was never there.

I snatched open the door and bolted out the bathroom like my tail was on fire. I got dressed quickly and skipped church altogether. I headed straight for Ophelia's house with my prayer books stacked in the back seat.

I pulled up to the house and sat for a moment, staring up at it. The place looked mean. Like it was holding its breath while fighting the devil. I was nervous, yes, but I also know I'm covered in the blood of Jesus.

I grabbed my prayers, opened the car door, and walked up the steps. Each one creaked under my feet like it was warning me. The front door stood open, but the screen was locked tight.

"Ophelia? Raymond?" I called through the screen.

Ophelia came shuffling down the hallway in her house shoes.

"Theresa? Girl, what you doin' here so early? You, okay?" she asked as she unlatched the screen.

"I'm alright," I said, stepping inside. "But listen... Ophelia, I need to tell you somethin'."

"Well, come on in here, Sha," Ophelia said, waving her hand to usher me inside.

The screen door creaked as I stepped in, but just as I took a step forward, my foot bumped into something hard.

Thunk!

"Ouch! What in the world is this, Ophelia?" I asked, bending down.

She glanced over her shoulder, completely unfazed. "It's a seashell. Raymond brought it in here for protection." "A seashell?" I blinked at her, brushing off the top with my foot. "Lord, have mercy, Ophelia. We don't need no seashell we need that priest in here today."

"He comin'," she said, already walking back toward the kitchen. "Just leave that shell where it's at and come on in. It's workin' for now."

I looked down at the shell again. It was large, ridged, and sat perfectly centered in the at the front door like it was the most common place for a seashell.

I stepped over it carefully and followed her down the hall.

Ophelia was in the kitchen stirring grits in a pot. She turned, wiping her hands on a towel.

"What is it, Sha?"

"This mornin', I seen somethin' in the mirror. When I was lookin', there was something', someone."

She raised her eyebrows and chuckled. "You see yourself, baby. That's what happen when you look in a mirror!"

I gave her a look. "Ophelia, don't play. I ain't jokin'. I seen something standing behind me. First, I was scared… but now, I think it was a warning. A warning from the Lord."

Ophelia's smile faded just a little. She looked me in the eyes.

"You are sure that thing ain't already followed you here?"

I paused… hand still clutching my prayer books.

"I don't know," I responded. "But we gon' find out."

The smell of chicory coffee filled my sister's kitchen, floating through the air like it was trying to comfort me. The morning light shined through the lace curtains, soft reminding me that God is still in control. Who or what should I fear, surely not a haunted house.

"Well, Theresa, I think we should go to church and pray on this first," Ophelia said, motioning toward the table. "Sit down and have some breakfast with us."

"I'll take a cup of coffee, baby," I replied, easing into the chair.

As I reached for my cup, my eyes caught something unusual. My brows furrowed. "Ophelia… is that ,are you pregnant?"

She smirked, resting a hand on her belly. "What does it look like, Theresa?"

"Oh, Lord. How far along are you?"

"Far enough," she said with a little laugh.

I leaned in, lowering my voice. "Okay… well, I'm sure you heard the latest gossip that your husband, Raymond, got that lady across town pregnant. I think she just had the baby. A boy."

Ophelia didn't even flinch. "Theresa, I don't care. Raymond is my husband, and he's good to me. I'm sure it's just a rumor. You know how jealous folks can be in Opelousas."

I sighed, shaking my head. "Well, I guess we should pray on that as well."

"Yes, we should," she said, sipping her coffee.

"So, what do you think boy or girl?" I asked, nodding toward her belly.

"I think it's another girl. The children want me to name her Sandra Marie. Isn't that cute?"

"I like that name. It's pretty."

"Well, let me get on outta here, sha," I said, pushing back my chair. "I'll see you after church with the priest." "Sounds good, Theresa. I'll see you soon."

It seemed like it took forever for me to get to church. There are only two stoplights on Union Street, and I managed to get caught at both.

I glanced up at the sky. Dark clouds had started gathering, heavy and low, like they were in a hurry to empty themselves. By the time I reached the church, fat raindrops were splattering against my windshield.

It was a good thing I hadn't done much to my hair that morning. Normally, I'd wet-set it with my big pink hard rollers, but today I'd let it be. My outfit was just right for the weather too a light brown, long-sleeved blouse with little flowers stitched across the front, a black skirt, and my brown Mary Jane shoes.

Still, the rain found me. By the time I ran from my car to the church doors, my thick, long black hair was damp and clinging to my face. Lord, by the time I walked inside, I looked like I was ready to have an exorcism performed on me.

I looked around the sanctuary. No sign of Mommy and Daddy just Papa, Raymond's father, sitting tall in his usual spot. Lord knows that man never missed a Sunday. I gave him a small wave and slid into a pew.

During communion, I caught the priest's attention and quietly confirmed that he would be coming to Ophelia's place later. He nodded. "Yes, I haven't forgotten," he said with a gentle smile.

I broke my bread and placed the dry wafer on my tongue. The taste clung there for a moment before I lifted the chalice and drank the warm wine. It slid down my throat, sharp and sweet.

Slipping out the side aisle, I dipped my fingers into the front. The cool holy water touched my forehead, chest, and shoulders as I made the sign of the cross. Then I pushed open the heavy church doors and stepped back into the rain.

The humid Louisiana air wrapped itself around me like a wet blanket. My skirt clung to my legs, my blouse sticking against my skin. Thank goodness I brought a change of clothes, I thought.

Driving back toward Ophelia and Raymond's house, I turned onto Hirman Street. Out of the corner of my eye, I noticed Chatman Memorial Mortuary. The parking lot was crowded.

Lord, I wonder who died, I thought to myself. That place belonged to Charles Chatman Sr., Papa's brother, and I never liked that it sat just around the corner from Ophelia's home.

Pulling up in front of her house, I killed the engine and bowed my head in prayer. The clouds above were still dark, only a thin strip of sun breaking through.

I can't wait to get home, drink a cold beer, and get out of these church clothes, I thought. And I guess now that Ophelia's pregnant, we won't be able to go dancing next week. Maybe I'll ask Velma if she wants to go.

I looked up just in time to see the priest's silver car turning onto the street. Waving my hand out the driver's side window, I flagged him down.

He pulled alongside me.

"This is it," I called. "Ophelia left me a key. We can just go on in."

He nodded, then parked. I climbed out of my car, waiting as he gathered himself. He sat for a moment, eyes fixed on the house, before finally reaching for his Bible, his rosary beads, and a small vial of holy water. When he stepped out, the priest stood tall in his long robe. He glanced toward the house once more, then lifted his hand and made the sign of the cross.

"Let's go inside," he said firmly. "Have faith. Don't doubt."

I swallowed hard, my mouth dry. My heart was racing. He seemed fearless, but the Lord knows I wasn't.

We walked side by side toward the porch. The sky was still gray and quiet, like it was holding its breath. The milkman had already made his stop; two glass bottles sat by the door, beads of condensation running down their sides.

I slid the key into the knob, the priest standing just to my right. Suddenly, a crack of thunder split the sky. The priest startled, jerking back. He nearly tripped over the hem of his robe, but instead the fabric swept against the bottles. Three of them toppled, shattering across the porch. Milk splattered everywhere, soaking the bottom of his robe.

"Oh, Father in heaven, please forgive me!" he gasped.

"It's okay, Father Apple," I said quickly, reaching for the door. "I'll get something to clean it up."

I pushed the door open, the hinges groaning. "Step inside, Father. Oh watch the shell," I said quickly.

He glanced down at the conch shell by the doorway, his face twisting into a strange, unreadable expression. He looked away and scanned the room, his eyes moving slow and cautious. Raising his hand, he made the sign of the cross again before pulling open his Bible. He didn't even notice the milk still soaking the hem of his robe. "Stay here," he said firmly. "I'll go alone."

"Are you sure, Father Apple? I mean the Bible says where two or more are gathered, there he will be," I whispered.

He shook his head. "You can't do this with me, Sister Theresa. It's too dangerous. I can hear the spirits in this house." His voice trembled, though he tried to hide it.

I stood stuck in place, watching as he moved toward the staircase. His breathing was heavy, each step creaking beneath his weight. He paused at the foot of the stairs, staring upward as though something was waiting for him. Then, quickly, he climbed up.

I followed a few steps behind, stopping at the bottom, my hand gripping the rail. He disappeared into the upstairs room. A cold breeze drifted down the stairwell, prickling my skin. He looked back at me, shook his head once, and then.

SLAM!

The door shut hard behind him.

My mouth dropped open, and I covered it with both hands. Tears stung my eyes. "Father? Father, are you alright?" My voice cracked as I yelled out.

Then I heard an unfamiliar voice.

A voice loud, deep, and demonic close to my ear. I could feel the presence of something in my face.

"Sit down. It's just me... and the Father."

Suddenly, a force shoved me backward into a chair. The wind had been knocked out of me and my feet slid as the wood rattled beneath me. A low moan came from upstairs, carrying down the stairwell like something not of this world.

I jumped to my feet. "I will fear no evil!" I cried, my voice shaking but strong. I ran up the steps two at a time and grabbed the doorknob. Before I could turn it, the door swung open with a violent crack, slamming into the wall.

"Father Apple!" I called, stepping into the room.

He stood motionless, facing the window. Flies buzzed in a thick cloud around him, crawling across the glass, landing on his robe, clinging to his sleeves. My heart pounded so hard I could feel it in my throat.

"Father Apple... you okay, sir?" I whispered. No answer.

His prayer beads hung heavy around his neck, the cross turned backward against his back. The Bible lay on the floor at his feet, its pages torn, scattered across the room like dead leaves.

"Father, please answer me," I begged, getting closer.

I walked around him, forcing myself to meet his face. Tears streaked his cheeks. He didn't look terrified he looked broken, sorrow written in every line of his face.

"Father?"

Slowly, he turned his eyes on me, and the sadness there made my stomach twist in knots. Then he looked back out the window, where rain was now pouring down in a torrential downpour.

Through the storm, I saw Ophelia, Raymond, and the children pulling up outside.

Father Apple's voice broke as he spoke, soft but sharp with finality. "Don't ever ask me to come back here again."

He walked past me, his robe brushing my arm. As he stepped out of the room, the flies vanished gone in an instant, like they had never been there.

I ran down the stairs behind him, my heart still racing. "But Father, what happened?" I called out.

Just then, Raymond opened the front door. "Hello, Father," he greeted.

Father Apple didn't stop, didn't smile. He walked straight past Raymond; his eyes fixed on the ground. The only words he left behind were cold and haunting:

"That shell will not save you… or your family."

We stood there, frozen, watching him climb into his car.

Raymond turned to me. "What happened?"

"I, I don't know," I stammered. "He went upstairs to bless the house, and then… there were flies. Everywhere." "Flies?" Raymond frowned. "Theresa, you should've just waited for us to get home."

Ophelia hurried over, placing her hand on my shoulder. "Are you okay?"

"I don't know," I admitted, my voice trembling.

Terricita, Betty, and Bode just stood there, their wide eyes full of fear.

"Go on to your rooms, babies," Ophelia said gently. "Let me take care of your Auntie."

The children scurried off, their footsteps quick and nervous. Raymond sank onto the porch, staring out into the storm, while Ophelia stayed by my side, her hand warm against my back doing her best to comfort me.

Twenty-Three

Remincing, past, present...

Raymond Sr.

I want to stop and take a moment to reflect on how we made it so far in this house of evil. If you think at some point we must have found some peace, you're mistaken. We were attacked financially, spiritually, and physically every single day.

Once our third daughter, Sandy, legal name Sandra Marie was born, we became poor overnight. I must wonder... was I cursed after experiencing the head in the canal, or was this some kind of generational curse? Or was it just the house itself?

Our parents and grandparents prayed for us, but their prayers could only do so much. Spiritually, I was shaken to my core, questioning God's very presence in my life. Physically, the attacks weighed heavy. My children are starting to suffer and Ophelia, her left leg, has been hurting for months, doctors can't figure out what's wrong. This must stop. But I'm too poor to move. High-paying jobs for colored folks don't exist here. Dimmick's supply refused to give me a raise, although the federal Equal right acts just passed. I reported it but nothing happened. Now I'm working seven days a week and hearing ghost stories when I get home.

The house turned us into different people. Ophelia became distant, quiet, smoking cigarettes and drinking beer like she was fading away. I grew angry. Terricita turned mean, fighting at school, beating up every child in her path, and stealing. Raymond Junior, my son, started collecting junk like piling it up in his room. Old Betty stayed shut away in her room, reading books and staring off into space. And this new baby, all she does is cry and eat.

Though we carried on, the spiritual warfare in the house continued. Getting the house blessed only made things worse. The unknown screams, the shadows, the faces on the walls... it was like the house was alive.

It boiled over like a hot pot of gumbo left too long on the stove three days old, rotting, bubbling, stinking up the whole place.

And I knew in my heart it was only the beginning.

Twenty–Four

THE WALLS HELD SECRETS

Raymond and Ophelia

I woke to the sound of Sandy crying. I sat up quickly, pulling my knees to my chest and rubbing my left leg. The pain shot through my calf and shin sharp, not like a Charlie horse this is different.

"What's wrong, Sandy? I just fed you," I whispered.

Raymond rolled over, still snoring, tugging the covers with him. I swung my legs off the side of the bed, but before I could stand, the air turned bitter cold. My flannel mo-mo gown did nothing to keep the chill off me. That's why she's crying, I thought. It's freezing in here.

The room was dark, pitch dark. I tried to be quiet, knowing Raymond had work in the morning. Slowly, I tiptoed to her brown wooden crib. The floorboards creaked beneath me, each groan loud in the stillness of the room. My breath came out in white fog. Crossing my arms, I rubbed them, desperate to warm them up.

"What's wrong, baby?" I whispered as I leaned over the crib.

My heart dropped. I gasped. My throat clenched, I couldn't scream. My legs trembled beneath me.

A large gray-black cloud swirled above Sandy's bed, twisting, writhing, until it shaped itself into something almost human. The figure formed into a doctor, his face pale and hollow, eyes nothing but two dark pits that bled shadow. His mouth stretched too wide, curling into a grin that wasn't human at all.

Beside him stood a nurse, her worn cap tilted on her head, but her skin was gray, stretched tight over large, deformed cheekbones. She looked at him, then at me, her lips parting into a smile, slow and wicked, it made my stomach turn.

The room became darker and colder. The nurse stretched her arms, her fingers long and bone thin, reaching into the crib for Sandy.

"Leave my baby alone!" I screamed, darting forward. I ripped Sandy from the crib, holding her close to my chest.

Raymond jerked awake, his voice thick with panic. "What, what happened? Who's in here?"

He grabbed his rifle, eyes wild as he searched the corners of the room.

I clutched Sandy, both of us crying, my words breaking in gasps. "I, I don't know. I seen a doctor... and a nurse. But they weren't real. Lord, they weren't real."

Sandy cried louder. I bounced her up and down, whispering prayers through my tears, my own heart palpating through my chest, like it might give out. Although the ghost had vanished, it felt like they were still there, the cold clung to the room... heavy, watching, waiting.

Raymond searched the rest of the house. The noise had woken Terrecita, Betty, and Bode. They stood in the doorway, drowsy and rubbing their eyes.

"What's going on, Momma?" Bode asked, his voice groggy as he dragged his little hand across his face.

"Nothing, y'all. Just go back to bed," I whispered, trying to sound steady.

Terrecita slanted her head, eyes wide. "You seen it, didn't you?"

I couldn't even speak. I just nodded, and the tears came all over again.

All three of them rushed to me, wrapping their arms tight around me as I clutched Sandy to my chest.

"It's going to be okay, Momma," Betty said softly.

"I know, baby. I know," I muttered out.

Raymond came back into the room, his face tight. "Ain't nothing here. Y'all go on back to bed. First day of school's tomorrow, and you gotta be up in just a few hours."

"Yes, Daddy," they answered sadly, dragging their feet down the hall.

Sandy finally started to calm down. Lord, she was growing so fast. I crawled back into bed, still holding her close against my chest. My eyes met Raymond's in the dim light.

"Raymond," I whispered, my voice trembling, "we gotta find out what's in this house. We can't keep living like this, pretending it doesn't exist. After the kids go to school, we need to go down to the library, do some research." He sighed heavily. "I got to work today. Money's tight, and you keep gettin' pregnant"

I snapped. My whole body was fueled with anger. "Oh, like I got myself pregnant, Raymond? Tell me this are we broke because of Sandy, or because of that little fling you been havin' across town?" My voice rose sharp enough to cut through a turtle shell.

"What!" he shouted back, eyes big like a deer caught in a taillight. "What are you even talkin' about? You done lost your mind, believin' what folks around here say?"

We went back and forth, voices loud, words flying like daggers. My chest heaved as I stared at him right in the eye.

"You comin' with me, or do I need to find somebody else that's willin'?" I said sassy and firmly.

Raymond stared at me, anger in his eyes. Finally, he said low and steady, his head moving up and down, sucking in his bottom lip, "We'll go. But we gotta make it quick. Then I'm headin' to work."

We laid back down, trying to get some rest. I never told Raymond I was pregnant before Sandy came. I had lost the baby. I cried in silence for months.

Sleep pulled me under, and soon I was dreaming.

In the dream, I was pregnant again carrying the child I thought I had lost before Sandy. I could see myself lying there in that very room, wide awake. A doctor and a nurse stepped toward me, their smiles crooked and wicked. I could barely make out their faces, blurred like .

They whispered to one another. I couldn't hear most of it, but then the doctor's voice came sharp and clear:

"Destroy him."

He lifted my shirt, and I realized I couldn't move. I was paralyzed. My heart thundered in my chest as he pulled out some strange-looking tool. Then he started to cut my stomach open.

The pain was real. I could feel it tearing through me. I saw the blood.

People I didn't know drifted around the room, watching. Their faces were pale, their eyes empty. I tried to scream, but a hand clamped over my mouth. The weight of it pressed down, and I felt myself suffocating.

In the bed, my body thrashed. My legs kicked as I fought to pull myself out of that nightmare.

And then

I jumped upright, gasping for air. My chest rose and fell fast. It was only a dream.

I swung my legs off the bed and stood. The smell of coffee floated in from the kitchen. Raymond was already up with the children, getting them ready for their first day of school.

When I walked in, he handed me a steaming cup of coffee with cream and sugar. "We're going to the library after they leave," he said.

His voice was soft, his demeanor gentle nothing like the man I argued with a few hours ago.

I looked at him and managed to put on a small smile. "Thank you, Raymond," I said.

I drank my coffee and sat watching the kids laugh, excited about the first day of school. They looked so cute, and of course I had dressed Terrcita and Betty alike. Bode wore a red-and-black plaid shirt with blue jeans, ready for the day.

Each of them kissed me on the cheek before heading out.

After they left for school, I walked back inside and got dressed. I changed Sandy's diaper, cleaned her up, and then we dropped her off at Ma'Mu's house before heading to the library.

I sat in the passenger seat, staring quietly out the window at the tall trees lining the road, my mind wandering about what we might find out at the library.

When we walked inside, Raymond stepped up to the clerk's desk.

"We need to do some research," he told her.

The woman peered over her glasses. Her lipstick was bright red, shining against her pale skin. "You got a library card?" she asked, her tone sharp.

"Yes, I do," Raymond replied.

"Okay then, let me see it."

Raymond patted his back pocket, searching for his wallet. He finally pulled it out. "Here you go."

She looked at the card, then back at him. "Alright then. Colored folks to the right, in the back. Don't touch nothin' outside that area without permission, you hear, boy?"

I could see the frustration rising in Raymond's face. His jaw tightened, and I knew he was about to let her have it. Before he could, I quickly slipped my hand around his arm.

"Yes, ma'am, we understand. " I said softly, trying to ease the tension.

We walked toward the back, Raymond mumbling under his breath the whole way.

Down the aisle, we started pulling books from the shelf's local history, genealogy records, county histories, and the city directory.

Before long, we had a tall stack of books spread out in front of us, ready to dive into.

My eyes stayed glued to the pages, scanning back and forth, flipping one after another.

"Raymond, have you found anything yet?" I asked, not looking up.

"Not really," he muttered.

I lifted my head and squinted toward him. My left eyebrow arched, and my face twisted when I noticed he wasn't even looking at anything related to the house.

"Raymond... what are you looking at?"

He grinned a little, like a boy caught sneakin' candy. "Baby, this some interestin' stuff. Did you know Frank Sinatra and Sammy Davis Junior helped Joe Louis pay off his back taxes to the IRS? This poor man ends up in a wheelchair, fought for this country, and now if he doesn't pay, they gonna lock him up. Did you see that new billboard of him on the Chesterfield cigarette ad? Good Lord, between him and Jackie Robinson, I don't know which one's is my bigger hero."

I slammed my book shut and leaned in. "Raymond!"

He looked at me, eyes fluttering. "What?"

"We ain't here to do research on Jackie Robinson and Joe Louis. We here to do research on 1010 Freeman Street," I said, my voice firm with frustration.

"I'm sorry, baby," Raymond said softly, scooting closer. He slipped one arm around my back and leaned in to look at the books with me. "What you got?"

"Look here it is."

I slid my fingers across the words as I read them aloud. "This property was once a hospital back in the early 1900s. It was used to transport those found guilty of crimes. After they was put to death, their bodies were carried from the courthouse straight to the hospital on Freeman Street, where they was pronounced dead. And because abortions were illegal back then, women came here in secret. Some died durin' the procedures. And those taken from the courthouse... well, they weren't always dead. Some of 'em were tortured, used for medical experiments."

Raymond's face frowned up like bitter taste in his mouth, his hand still behind me embracing my back. "Lord have mercy," he whispered. "That's some dark shit baby."

I moved closer over to the book, the yellowed pages fragile under my index finger. My voice trembled as I read aloud.

"It says here the fireplace was used as a crematorium. And the room to the left of the house those sinks" I swallowed my spit hard, my hands shaking, "that's where they drained the blood from their bodies. "My eyes even bigger".

"Oh, my God," I whispered, a chill ran down my spine.

Raymond's eyes stayed locked on the page, unblinking. He wouldn't even look at me.

"Keep readin'," he said low, his voice firm but muzzled.

"Raymond..." I turned toward him, but he just shook his head, staring at the book.

I forced myself to keep going. "This... this explains why our children's bathroom door got those windows shaped like lady fingers. And why they say they see people walking by."

Raymond finally looked at me then, his face pale as a ghost, his full lips pressed inwards and tight.

I drew in a shaky breath and kept reading. "One late night, six nurses were killed along with three doctors. A woman who was supposed to be dead hanged earlier that day at the courthouse suddenly woke up and murdered the staff. The police searched for her all night, lockin' down the whole town. They were determined to end her life or take her to Pineville a place where they took anyone who had a nervous breakdown. Nobody ever figured out how she escaped the hospital."

The words felt heavy in my mouth, thick as fudge.

"They say the Opelousas police searched every field, every house, but never found her. Rumor was she was demonic. That she killed them... and to this day, her soul lives in that fireplace."

Silence and fear wrapped around us. Even the sound of pages turning made us scared, the library's lights flickered, we looked up at them and then at each other.

Raymond finally spoke, his voice barely above a whisper. "Baby... what kinda house we livin' in?"

"I don't know... did anybody tell you 'bout this before you bought it?" I asked, my voice low and shaky.

"No," Raymond answered, tight and clipped. Then he let out a long breath. "But... there was this story an old lady told me years ago. I just never put the two together."

"What story?" I pressed my hand against my chest fearing what he would say.

"I once asked her why the courthouse windows were all busted out. Furniture thrown everywhere, glass scattered like diamonds on the floor. She said a "Black man had been hung after he was con-victed." His father was there to watch. But the man he wouldn't die. They tried again, but still nothin'. His face turned red and purple, his tongue hangin' out, blood drippin' from his nose yet he was still breathin'."

My stomach knotted up in a ball, but I couldn't stop myself. "Ooh, Lord sha, have mercy... then what?" Raymond's eyes became glossy, his voice dropping low and deep. "His father pulled out a little booklet the Seventh Book of Moses. He walked slow around that courtroom, chantin' loud, his voice echoing off them high walls: *I conjure ye, O ye strong and holy angels of God, in the name of Adonai, Elohim, Saddai, and by the name Jehovah Tetragrammaton, that ye appear in form anointed, and fulfill what I command you in the name of the Most High; by Him who spoke and it was done, by Him who commanded and all things stood fast I conjure ye!'"*

Raymond's voice shaking. "And that's when it started. Windows shattered one by one, glass flyin' across the room like the air itself was mad as hell. Chairs lifted, slammin' against the walls. Papers swirled in the air like a storm had broken loose inside. Folks screamed, runnin' for the doors, but the doors slammed shut on their own. She told me people swore they felt hands brush past them, cold, evil hands that weren't there. That old lady said, right then and there, the man's father sold himself to the devil."

Goosebumps filled my arms. My voice cracked when I asked, "What happened to the man?"

"He died," Raymond said, daring to even say it. "His body was transported to..."

We locked our eyes, both of us frozen, fear sitting heavy in the pit of my chest, throat, and stomach. Together we finished the sentence: "Our house... to confirm his death."

Tears stung my eyes, spilling fast. Raymond reached up, brushing them away with his thumb. His hand lingered on my cheek, calming me.

"Baby," he said, voice steady but low, "we'll get another priest to bless the house again. Let's call on our sisters and brothers. I have always been told where love and unity dwell, evil can't stay."

I nodded, trembling, my breath caught in my throat. "Okay."

We snatched up the books from the table, shoving them back on the shelves any which way. Raymond grabbed my hand, and together we hurried out.

The librarian tried to call after us, her voice sharp. We ignored her and kept moving. Lord knows I wanted to throw up my middle finger at her, but we already had enough trouble hangin' over our heads.

Raymond swung open the car door for me, and I jumped inside. He slid behind the wheel, cranked the engine, and we sped off.

"Can we stop by the house before we pick up Sandy?" I asked, chewing my fingernails to the quick. "I need to grab my phone book so I can start callin' everybody."

"Sure," Raymond said, his eyes fixed on the road, his jaw tight with what we'd just read.

The ride felt longer than it was, the silence heavy between us. By the time we pulled up, we just sat there, starin' at the house.

"You go first," Raymond said laughing, a silly smirk to his smile.

I turned my head quickly toward him. "What? Are you serious? I'll be damned, Raymond."

He chuckled low. "I'm just kiddin'. We'll go together."

We climbed the steps side by side. Raymond unlocked the door, then bent down, slid his foot under the seashell, and propped the door open.

We stepped inside.

I made it to the kitchen before, and I froze right in my tracks. My hand flew up over my mouth. Slowly, I backed out, my heart hammerin'.

"What's wrong?" Raymond shouted, rushing toward me. He stopped short when he looked past me into the kitchen.

Every dish was out of the cabinets; some shattered on the floor. The table was flipped clean upside down. And in the corner our dog lay stiff and cold, his eyes stared wide open his lips pulled back, teeth showing like he'd been grawling and scared.

Raymond's spoke in a low tone yet urgent. "Get your phone book. Grab the kids some clothes. We're leavin'. We ain't comin' back 'til we got a priest."

I dug in the kitchen drawer and grabbed my little black phone book. Raymond stood at the kitchen door waiting on me. We hurried to the kids' room, snatched up some clothes, and packed as fast as we could. That's when I noticed the bathroom door windows were no longer painted over. I looked at Raymond, and he just waved his hand, motioning me to come on. We ran out the house and headed straight to Raymond's mama's place Maw'Ma house.

Twenty-Five

THE GATHERING

Sibby & Sally

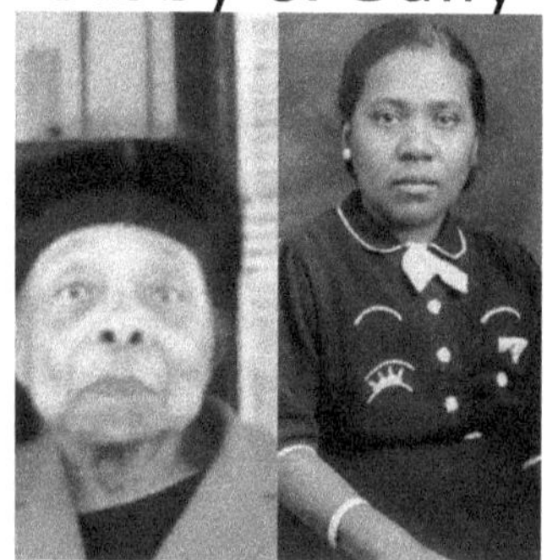

H azel (Sibby) and I come strollin' near the house, laughin' so
hard our sides hurt. We had just come back from Zydeco
dancing.

"Lawd, Hazel, I can't believe Momma want us over here
tonight," I said, shakin' my head.

Hazel grinned and said, "It's aright. I gotta bring something to
Ann anyway". "What does Maw'ma want us to do"?"

"She says she want us to help with the blessing of Raymond and Ophelia house," I replied, as we approached the front door pushing it open.

Soon as we stepped in, I near bout tripped 'cause there sat Raymond, my ugly brother, Ophelia, and all they damn chillum, lined up on the couch like they waitin' on Jesus Christ to walk in.

"What da hell wrong wit' yawl?" I asked, plantin' my hands on my hips.

"We got somethin' in our house," Ophelia hissed, eyes big as hell.

"Oh, cher," I said, bustin' out laughin'. "What yawl s'posed to do go beat da ghost ass?"

"Sally!" Maw'ma snapped, her voice firm and sounding mad "Das enough now! I need yawl to pray wit' us. An' 'fore anybody lay down tonight, y'all best wash ya feet 'fore crawlin' in dat bed. We gotta be clean an' free of sin 'fore steppin' foot back in dat house fo' da blessin'."

I rolled my eyes. "Aw naw, Maw'ma. Ain't no such thang as no ghosts. Yawl just talkin' fool mess."

"Dorothy!" Papa hollered from the back room. "Watch ya mouth!"

"Sorry, Daddy," I said quick, moving my head to see if he was coming. He only calls me Dorothy when he is serious about something.

"So... what we doin' now?" Hazel asked softly, still standin' by the door like she ain't wanna come no closer.

Maw'ma lifted her hand. "I need yawl to call all ya brothers and sisters. Tell 'em meet at Ophelia an' Raymond house Wednesday night right after Bible study. Ophelia, you get on dat phone an' start wit' ya people, you hear me?"

"Yes, ma'am," Ophelia said in a muffled voice.

I snatched up the phone, the cord swingin', and started callin' folks, my jaw twisted with frustration.

"Hazel," I yelled, glancin' over my shoulder, "yo' ass just sittin' there daydreaming'! Sibby, I muttered in frustration under my breath, "you can't respond?" "Lord, gimme patience get the phone book and look up our brothers' numbers."

Sibby fumbled with the book, pages flappin' slow. I tapped my foot hard against the floor. "Start wit' Louis L.J, then Sam Austin the Dot, Jules the Rat, an' George the Perry. Write Raymond's number down too."

Sibby squinted. "Why are we writin' Raymond's number down? He right here."

I slapped my hand against my thigh. "'Cause I don't have his damn number, that's why!"

One by one, I dialed, the numbers my fingers stuck inside the rotary dial on front. "Okay, listen up," I told each one when they answered. "Meet at Raymond an' Ophelia's house Wednesday night, six o'clock sharp, 1010 Freeman Street. We gon' do a blessin'… an' chase some ghost out." My voice dripped sarcasm, every word with a tease and deliberate.

"What?!" each one yelled back through the cracklin' line.

I rolled my eyes hard as I held the phone to my ear. "I'm just tellin' you what Maw'ma said. Don't shoot me over it." I slammed the receiver down with force.

I looked at Ophelia sittin' stiff on the edge of the couch. "Okay, gal it's yo' turn."

She slid over, her hands tremblin' a little as she dialed. I started laughin', foldin' my arms across my chest.

"Lawd have mercy, Ophelia you really scared, huh? Girl, don't you know the Lawd is yo' protector?" Ophelia shot me a crazy look but kept on turnin' that dial, lips squeezed shut. But Ophelia didn't have much lip to squeeze anyway "She called her two sisters and five brothers: Told 'em the time and place."

I stood and walked away from the counter to have a seat, I told Ophelia. "Maw'ma already got a pastor comin' from Little Zion Missionary Church. If there's any evil in that house, he can get rid of it. That church has been around a long time. It was first organized as Opelousas African Baptist Church, I believe, back in June of 1867. Then they bought the land in August of 1869 and held their first service on May 15th, 1871. Folks think we goin' through rough times now. Can you imagine what they went through?"

I then let out a big yawn, my hands restin' in my lap. "Anyway... I guess we should pray. I gotta get home to the kids, make sure Greene ate."

Hazel, quiet as ever, just stood by the window twisting her braids, waiting for us to start prayer. Afterward, she went to the next room to make sure Ann and Brenda had washed the dishes and their feet before going to bed.

"I'll see all of y'all Wednesday," I called over my shoulder.

Home for me was a ten-minute walk.

The moment I stepped inside, all thirteen of my kids came running up to me. Greene, though, just sat in his gray overalls, looking the same as he had that morning.

"You ain't changed your clothes yet?" I asked, staring at him.

"Nope," he said, calm as can be.

"Well, you eaten dinner, or you waitin' on me to fix it?"

He leaned back and grinned. "Oh, come on now, Sally. Where you been?"

"Greene, I'm entitled to some fun," I shot back. "Now don't start fussin' and carryin' on. What you wanna eat?" He shook his head, smiling. "I just don't understand how the smallest woman in all of Opelousas can be so sassy."

I laughed and swatted the air. "Mm-hmm. Keep talkin'." Then I set about cooking him some smothered turkey necks and gravy over rice.

While he ate, I reminded him, "I need to be at Raymond and Ophelia's house on Wednesday. So you best be home on time."

"I'll try," he said. "Depends how many plumbing jobs I got that day."

The next few days went by quick. Life carried on as usual. I cooked, I cleaned, I fed our pet raccoon. I packed Greene's lunch every morning and sent him off to work. Most days, I'd stand on the porch in my pink mo-mo gown, rollers in my hair, and watch him drive off. He'd stick his hand out the truck window to wave goodbye. The kids scattered out to school, happy, laughing as always. Darci always had his instrument slung across his back, and Eric was forever singing.

"Okay, boys, time for y'all to get on outta here! You gon' be late!" I hollered from the porch.

Before I knew it, Wednesday had rolled back around, and it was time for the blessing or exorcism of the house. I fixed dinner, got the kids settled, and sat waiting for Greene to come home.

Where his big ass at? I thought, patting my foot on the floor. I'm gon' be late.

I sat on the couch with my purse in my lap, arms folded, a frown etched clear across my face.

Then I heard the rattle of his loud truck pulling up. I jumped to the window and peeked out. Here come Greene slow ass now.

I swung the front door open and stood there with one hand on my hip, waiting.

He climbed out the truck, walked right past me, and didn't say a word.

"Greene!" I snapped.

"I'm comin', Sally," he mumbled, heading toward the outhouse.

When he finally came back inside, he asked, "You ready?"

I tilted my head back, looking up at all six-foot-six of him, and gave him that look. Then I snatched up my purse.

"I'll see you in the truck," I said, pushing past him.

Freeman Street wasn't but five minutes away. We pulled up in front of the house, and I spotted something right off.

"Whose little girl is that sittin' on the porch?" I asked.

Greene glanced around. "What girl?"

"You don't see that child sittin' right there?" I pointed, leaning forward.

He squinted, shook his head. "No, Sally. I don't see nobody."

I cut my eyes at him. "So not only have you forgotten how to tell time, but you done gone blind too? Lord have mercy." I blurted, still mad at him.

I grabbed my purse, stepped out the car, and shut the door a little harder than I meant to. With my head down, I dug through my bag for some of Sibby's candy, she always had a candy dish set out. I figured I'd offer the little girl a piece.

But when I looked back up at the porch, the girl was gone.

I froze, then turned slowly to look back at Greene. He just waved from the truck like nothing was wrong, then drove off.

I knocked on the door. From inside, I could hear folks talking and laughing. Suddenly, a soft voice behind me made me jump clean out my skin.

I spun around. It was the little girl again.

Whose child is this? I wondered.

Her hair was long, brownish, and straight, falling down her thin shoulders. Her skin was pale, her eyes sunk in with dark circles underneath.

"Oh, it's you again!" I gasped, pressing a hand to my chest. "Lord, you scared me half to death. How you disappear so fast? You one of Betty Ann and Terrcita's little friends?"

She didn't answer. Just stared at me, quiet as a mouse. Then she lifted her finger toward the door.

"Can you move that seashell from the front?" she asked softly. "I don't like it there."

"What shell?" I frowned.

"You'll see when you get inside. Just move it."

I blinked, stood tall as I could for four feet eleven. "Now, hold on. Who you think you talkin' to, little girl?" She didn't say a word, just turned away and sat back down on the wooden porch like she waiting for someone.

The door swung open, and there stood Ophelia.

"Hey, Sally, come on in," she said.

"Ophelia," I whispered, glancing over my shoulder, "who is that little girl sittin' on your porch?"

Ophelia stepped outside, looked around, then back at me. "What girl? I don't see nobody. All the kids are inside playin'."

I threw my hands up. "Well, somebody out here sure enough is! Had the nerve to tell me to move a seashell away from your front door. What in the world is she talkin' about?"

Ophelia's face grew serious. "That wasn't no ordinary little girl, Sally."

"Hell, I know that! I almost slapped her, in her damn mouth" I muttered, shaking my head.

Ophelia chuckled low, then sighed. "You just experienced one of the many things we been dealin' with. "That seashell she's talkin' about". She pointed toward the bottom door. "It's right here. It's supposed to protect us and trap evil spirits that try to come through. That's why she wanted it gone. So she could come in without gettin' caught."

I stared, wide-eyed. "Ophelia... you shittin' me, right?"

"No, I ain't," she said firmly. "Come on, let's meet with the others."

As we walked inside, I noticed her limp. "Ophelia, you still hobblin'? What's wrong with your leg?"

She winced. "Hurts somethin' awful. Doctors can't figure it out."

I shook my head. "Well, we might need to pray over that leg tonight, too.

We walked into the main room of the house. A very old chandelier hung from the ceiling, swaying slightly as though it had been there since the 1800s. Raymond's piano sat close to the window, keys yellowed with age.

"Everybody's here, huh? Cliff, Walter Lord, I ain't seen y'all in a long time."

"Who else we waitin' on, Raymond?" I asked.

"We're waitin' on Perry," he said.

"Oh, hell. He always late for everything."

The room filled with laughter just as I spotted a few more faces. "Well, look at here—Theresa and Velma! David and Bobby too. Ophelia, you sure did make certain all your sisters and brothers came."

"I'm here!" Perry's voice rang out as he stepped inside.

"'Bout time," someone muttered.

So now we had all of Raymond's people gathered, Jules, George, Louis Junior, Austin, Hazel, and me.

"What a blessing," I said. "Our parents too. We gotta do this kind of gathering another time when we ain't tryin' to cast out demons."

Everyone chuckled, but the pastor from Little Zion didn't. He looked scared as sin.

I leaned over to whisper, "I don't even know why Momma picked him. I heard the last time he tried a deliverance; the demon in the daughter chased him clean out the house with a weed-eater. Left thin slices all across the back of his neck."

The double doors opened and he walked in. The wood trim around the frame was beautiful, but my eyes stayed on the pastor. I wasn't sure if I believed in all this ghost talk, but I loved my brother and Ophelia. I'd do anything to help them.

He had us take communion first, then pray together. "Lord, bless this house and cast anything out that's not of You," he said, his voice trembling. We all repeated the words tighter, hands locked in a circle with Raymond, Ophelia, and the kids in the middle. He anointed the house with oil, then touched each of our foreheads.

I cracked one eye open and froze.

That little girl stood behind Velma.

How in the world did she get in here? My chest tightened, my throat knotted, and my heartbeat thundered. She smiled, but I could see the fear in her eyes. She wouldn't step across our circle.

"Close your eyes," the pastor said.

"But...the little girl" I whispered my voice shaky.

"I don't care," he snapped, raising his voice and breaking into tongues.

"Oh shit! Then it happened.

A wasp circled above him. Then another. The more he prayed, the more came. Soon the buzzing roared above us, and before we could move, the swarm dropped onto him.

The pastor screamed as they stung his face, his neck, his arms.

Chaos broke loose.

"Lord have mercy!" somebody shouted.

Children cried, chairs toppled. Everyone scattered, but Potoon and Papa grabbed a spray can and doused the air until the wasps dropped dead.

The pastor's face was swollen, blistered, and bleeding. He clutched his chest, gasping, moaning in pain.

"Call an ambulance!" Papa yelled.

Hazel clung to Momma, both sobbing. Theresa paced, pulling at her hair and praying under her breath. Velma just sat down hard, eyes wide.

Oh, Lord… somebody get me a beer," she mumbled.

Jules didn't move. He sat in the corner, eyes narrowed, deep in thought. Up to something. He was always up to something.

Raymond pulled everyone outside, trying to calm them down. Inside, I knelt by the pastor, pressing a wet cloth against his swollen face. The chandelier light flickered above us, shadows jerking across the walls.

"What's takin' so long?" I said, panicked. "Where's the ambulance?"

"Téléfone té fini," Patoone grumbled.

"What?" I asked, not understanding.

Papa shook his head. His Creole was too thick, too broken for me to follow.

"The phone dead," he explained. "We need the neighbors'."

Papa sent David running. Finally, we heard the distant wail of sirens. The stretcher rolled in, and as they carried the pastor away, we kept on praying.

After it was over, we sat together in the quiet, trying to catch our breath. The children seemed strangely unfazed. Velma's daughter, Cynthia, wanted to stay behind and play with Terricita, Bode, and Betty Ann. She especially liked taking care of her little cousin Sandy.

But for me, the house felt mean and even more angry. That little girl's smile stayed in my mind, chilling me to the bone.

This chapter is dedicated to my Auntie Sally and Sibby; my auntie Sibby was murdered. The sweetest memory I have of her is when she brought me my first tricycle, I honor that love by giving my nieces and grandchildren that same joy.

My auntie Sally was so funny, I remember her saying in her extremely thick southern accent that she was going to beat someone with a weed eater. It was always a blessing to visit her.

Twenty–Six

FINDING OUT THE HARD WAY

Circa

M omma, can I please stay the night with Auntie Ophelia?" I asked, pullin' at her apron, my eyes wide like maybe beggin', would change her mind.

"No, not tonight. Y'all got school in the mornin'," Momma said, cuttin' her eyes at me. "You can come back Friday night. Now, go round up your brothers and sisters and tell Herman and Linda not to forget they coats this time."

I never could figure how Momma told our jackets apart. They was all the same navy blue with brown stitches and gold buttons, stiff from too many washings.

Auntie Ophelia walked us to the porch. The night air was thick, heavy with the smell of magnolia and damp earth. Daddy's old car idled at the curb, headlights glowin' weak yellow against the gravel.

We squeezed inside me, Herman, Linda, Fernando, Lolita, Janice, and Joanne.

"Move over, Janice!" Joanne fussed. "You hoggin' all the seat."

"Don't y'all start nothin' in here," Momma warned from the front, her voice sharp as a whip.

I leaned forward, stuck out my tongue, then laughed when they frowned at me with anger on their faces.

By the time we reached home, the house was quiet and tense. Everybody scattered to their beds. I laid down too, but sleep didn't hold me long. Something had followed us back from Auntie Ophelia's.

They say spirits can cling to you, ride the air like a shadow. During the night, I felt a spirit. First, a burn like red ants dancing across my skin. Then a heaviness pressed down on me, like a large invisible hand sinking into my ribs.

I tossed and turned, breathin' hard. It's hot in here, I thought, though all I had on was my purple and pink night gown. I fumbled with the top buttons, tryin' to ease the tightness across my chest, but the more I pulled, the heavier it felt. The room seemed to swell with heat, hot steam stickin' to my throat.

Then suddenly.

My chest locked. My eyes flew open wide, my legs kicked against the sheets. I tried screaming, the sounds coming out my throat were weak, yet high, a shriek.

"Stop... please let me go... stop!" I gasped, tears spillin', blurring' my sight. My tongue felt thick, my body burnin', lungs inflating and deflating rapidly' for air.

I launch upright, draggin' in a ragged breath. Sweat poured down my back. My hands trembled, clammy as if I'd dipped 'em in ice water.

That's when I felt her. Not evil but watchful. A woman's spirit, close enough it my made the hairs on my arms stand up. She was near, protecting' me, though she remained unseen.

I snatched up my Bible and sat propped against the wall, readin' aloud, prayin' hard till the alarm clock screamed into the dawn.

I got out of bed and headed to the bathroom to wash my face and brush my teeth.

Exhausted, I stumbled to the closet. "What will I wear today? jeans and my white halter top, I told myself. But it wasn't there.

"Janice!" I hollered. "You got my halter top?"

Sure enough, she strutted in wearin' it bold.

Why you got my shirt on?" I snapped.

"I thought you gave it to me."

"No, I didn't. Now take it off."

Aggravation from the night before clung to me like leches.

We walked to school in a slow line. I pushed ahead, not wantin' to deal with nobody. Fernando trailed behind, chunkin' rocks at my back.

"Boy, you better quit!" I yelled.

"Aww, girl, you know I'm just playin'," he laughed.

"I don't wanna play," I yelled, my body still burdened from last night's terror.

By the time we reached the schoolyard, whispers had already spread. Kids stood in groups eyes wide, staring as we walked by.

"What y'all lookin' at?" I snapped.

Tanya, my best friend, rushed to me, breathless. "Girl, you know this town. Everybody heard what happened to the pastor last night. Now they all scared of y'all."

I frowned, tired, and confused. "Scared of me? I don't even live there."

The rest of the school day went by quickly. All day Thursday and Friday, I had folks in my face at school asking questions, staring at me. I was starting to feel like some kinda celebrity.

Truth be told, I thought about changing my mind 'bout going back to Auntie Ophelia and Uncle Raymond's house as I stared out the classroom window, whispering to myself, "But I do wanna play with the new baby and besides, I might have more cool ghost stories to tell.

The school bell rang. I grabbed my backpack and headed out the door. The sun beamed down on my forehead. I looked up, smiling at the clouds, feeling like I was protected. I'm gon' be okay, I thought.

When I got to Auntie Ophelia's, she was sitting on the front porch, still rubbing her leg, eyes glossy like she might cry.

"You okay, Auntie Ophelia?" I asked.

"No, baby... my leg hurt so bad, I don't know what to do."

"I'll go get an ice pack out the house. I'll be right back."

I ran inside, but hesitated at the door. I made the sign of the cross before stepping into the kitchen, then opened the refrigerator and grabbed the ice pack. Back outside, I knelt down beside Auntie Ophelia.

Her pale legs showed blue veins through her skin. It was hot, she had on her blue shorts that were cut off right above the knee, and a light-blue shirt with several shades and shapes of blue. I sat next to her and gently pulled her leg forward, watching her face for any sign I was hurting her.

When I pressed the ice pack on, she winced a little.

"So... what time Terrcita and them comin'?" I asked.

"They should be here any moment. Sandy's asleep right now. You can play with her after she wake up," Auntie said.

Just then, I heard laughter. Terricita, Bode, and Betty came walking up the road, backpacks slung on their shoulders. Terricita and Betty both wore two pigtails that day, their dresses dropping just below the knee. Betty's was white; Terricita's was gold with blue lace trim. Bode always wore the same thing: blue jeans and a plaid shirt.

"Hey, Cynthia," Terricita called out. "How you get here so fast?"

"I don't know," I shrugged.

"Momma, you, okay?" Betty asked, glancing at Auntie Ophelia.

"No, sha... my leg hurt," Auntie sighed.

"You need me to grab you a beer, Momma?" Bode asked.

"Yes, please, son," she answered.

I leaned closer to Auntie. "You know, Auntie Ophelia, my momma does know a healer that could help you. I know you don't believe in no voodoo stuff, but from what I heard, this man works miracles. He says special prayers over folks, rubs all kinds of herbs on 'em and they get better."

"I know your momma told me about that, Circa," Auntie said softly. "I'm just scared. With everything goin' on in this house, I don't want God to punish me for not waiting on him to heal me."

"Auntie," I said, lowering my voice, "you ever thought that maybe God gave man special gifts? It's in the Bible."

She looked down, rubbing her leg. "I guess you right. Well... go call your momma Velma, tell her to get in touch with that man."

Hold this, Terrcita." I passed her the ice pack and went inside to call.

The rotary phone clicked with each number I dialed. It rang and rang before Momma answered.

"Hi, Momma," I said. "Can you call that healer man for Auntie Ophelia? Her leg still hurt."

"I told her ass I would," Momma slurred. "Me and Therese been sayin' we'd take her. She hard-headed."

I sat quiet, the phone in my hand holding up to my ear. Her speech was slurred I could tell she been drinkin' again. I took a deep breath. "Okay, Momma. I'll let her know."

I walked back outside and stood on the porch. That's when I seen Nini and some other kids from Philip Street. They stopped right in front of the house.

"We came to see the haunted house," Nini said, her arms crossed, leg cocked out, smirkin' while the others laughed.

We just stared at them. Bode cracked a crooked smile, then chuckled. "Go 'head."

They dropped their arms, strutted up the short walkway, climbed the steps, and pushed inside. The screen door slammed hard behind 'em.

Then loud screams and panic could be heard. They tugged at the screen door, kicking and crying. It was stuck, locked tight. Bode burst out laughing. Terricita and Betty sat with little evil grins on their faces.

Sandy's cry echoed from inside, woken up by the racket Nini and her friends made.

"Open up that screen door and let them fools out my house!" Auntie Ophelia shouted.

"But Momma, they wanted to go in there," Terricita said.

"Let 'em out," Auntie repeated, her voice sharp.

Terricita stood and opened the screen door. Those kids tore out faster than I ever seen in my life.

"What'd you see? What happened?" I yelled, but they didn't turn around. They just kept runnin'.

"I'll go get Sandy," Betty said, heading inside.

Auntie Ophelia sat back, sipping her beer, shaking her head. Soon enough, it was time to get dinner done, and we all went inside.

Auntie Ophelia started supper, stirring a pot of okra gumbo. The smell floated thick through the air ,savory, rich, with that little bite of spice that made your nose twitch. My stomach rumbled soon as I walked through the kitchen.

I slipped off into the other room to look at the piano, folks had been talkin' about it, Darcie Greene, and Lolita,a both swore it played by itself sometimes. I stood there staring, my hand hovering over the keys, ready to press one down, when Auntie's voice cut sharply through the air.

"Uh-uh! Don't you touch that piano, you hear?"

I jerked my hand back quickly. "Yes, ma'am."

"Raymond doesn't like nobody playin' on that piano. Auntie Le-Verta's daughter came here once and tapped on it, and he fussed all day about it. I don't wanna hear his mouth tonight. Now come on supper's ready."

We all sat down at the long table, steam rising off the gumbo bowls. The first spoonful warmed me all the way through.

"This food is so good, Auntie Ophelia. Thank you," I said, licking my lips.

Just then the front door swung open. Uncle Raymond's voice boomed.

"Fefe Goodwill! It smells good in here."

"I got your plate fixed. Come and eat," Auntie called back.

He stepped into the kitchen, grinning wide, rubbing his hands together.

"Now you know you need to go wash your hands, Raymond," Auntie fussed.

Uncle Raymond leaned over and kissed her cheek. "Better yet, I'll go shower and come back."

By the time he sat down, we kids were done eating. It was just the two of them at the table, talking low and laughing over their plates, while little Sandy crawled all over the floor. I could hardly keep up with her.

"Circa, you like watchin' Gunsmoke on Friday nights? "Betty asked.

"Oh yeah," I answered.

"Good," she grinned. "'Cause I promise you my daddy's gonna pull out some oatmeal cookies and vanilla ice cream when it comes on. Just watch."

After supper, Betty and I took to the floor, playing jacks. Sandy balanced on my hip most the time, her chubby hands reaching for the shiny little star shaped metal pieces we tossed. We played and laughed for nearly two hours.

Just like Betty said, Uncle Raymond's voice came booming from the kitchen:

"I got ice cream and cookies! Let's watch Gunsmoke, kids!"

We hollered and ran to the living room. Uncle Raymond adjusted the antenna, giving the TV a good smack on the side before turning the dial. That old set was big, heavy as a dresser, sitting sturdy on the wood floor.

We curled up with our bowls of oatmeal cookies crumbled into vanilla ice cream while the black-and-white screen flickered to life. The main character on Gun Smoke, Marshal Dillon strode across the dusty street, and we laughed when Uncle Raymond tried to mimic his walk.

The night stretched easy and slow, the house smelled of Okra gumbo and cookies. Eventually the screen went gray and fuzzy with white beads dancing across it. That was our signal time to head on to bed.

That night I fell asleep in Terricita and Betty Ann's room. I climbed up to the foot of Betty Ann's bed and dozed off quickly.

Soon, I was dreaming. I sat at the piano, fingers gliding across the keys, the music sounding so sweet it filled the room. Folks started gathering around, smiling, snapping pictures. I was grinning too, proud of the song flowing out of me until suddenly one wrong key kept ringing out.

Dong... dong... dong...

In the dream I heard Uncle Raymond's voice loud and clear.

"That's the A-O and C-2 keys. Why you playin' scary music?"

People became frightened, then scattered. The crowd ran from me; their faces twisted in fear.

I jerked awake, eyes wide in the dark. The room was quite I could hear the crickets outside. Terricita and Betty Ann lay snoring in their beds, knocked out cold.

Lord, please, I whispered to myself, don't let me see nothin' tonight.

Then, I heard it. The piano was playing.

Soft at first, then clearer, harder, and louder. Notes floating down the hallway like somebody was really sitting there playin'.

My throat felt like a frog in it. I swallowed my spit hard, heart pounding in my chest. Still, I slipped out from under the blanket, moving slowly as I crept toward the door.

The hallway was dark as midnight. I tiptoed, holding tight to the wall. A cool breeze slipped under my nightgown, brushing my legs, making me shiver. My eyes stayed wide open, too scared to blink, but too stubborn to stop. I had to see if it was true. Did that piano really play by itself at night?

At the living room entrance, I peeked around the corner.

There it was playing.

The piano keys pressing down on their own, music rolling out like invisible hands playing across the board. The bench sat empty, but the sound was alive, steady, haunting but pleasant, I wasn't scared.

I turned away slowly, praying whatever it was didn't notice me standing there. Each step back was careful, but the wood floor creaked beneath my feet. I froze when it did. Breath, I said to myself, afraid it might hear. Then, when the silence returned, I tiptoed faster. I dove back into bed, pulling the covers up tight around me. Whatever it was... it didn't care that I was there.

Twenty-Seven

The Healer of Opelousas

Velma Guillory Morris

*H*ello? *Hi, this Velma. Theresa and I on our way to bring Ophelia.*"

"I'm comin', hold on!" I hollered, wiping my apron with one hand as I hurried to the door. I swung it open and frowned. "Theresa, why you bangin' so hard on my front door? You know my husband sleepin'. You should've come 'round the back you know I stay in the kitchen."

She waved her hand. "Sha, you knew I was comin'. You should be ready. We can't be late we gotta pick up Ophelia and get her to that healer. You know how many people be lined up waitin' on him."

"Lord, let me wrap my hair real quick," I said, reaching for a scarf.

Theresa shook her head. "My God, Velma will your hair grow any longer? It done passed your butt and black as midnight. Mine long, but not nearly like yours. Funny how Ophelia's ain't near as long as ours."

"That's probably stress from that man," I muttered.

"Don't talk about our brother-in-law, Velma," Theresa snapped. "That man works seven days a week providin' for his family."

"Mm-hmm. Let me finish my beer."

"Beer?" Theresa near shouted. "It's too early to be drinkin', Velma."

"I need a drink to deal with all this ghost mess Ophelia got stirrin' up. Damn near gave me a heart attack the other night. Did you see what I saw, Theresa or you still in denial, gal?"

Her face softened. "I seen it, Velma. I wonder how the pastor doin'."

"Last I heard, he doin' well," I said.

"Oh, good," Theresa sighed in relief. Then her eyes swept my walls. "Now when you gon' change this yellow-gold wallpaper in here? Same old color forever. Same brown flower couch and everything."

"Theresa, mind your damn business and let's go."

We stepped outside and climbed in the car. As we rolled down the street, trees hung heavy over the road like they was blessin' the day. I leaned back and smiled. "It's such a beautiful day."

"Theresa, look out!" I screamed.

"For what?" she hollered.

"All them chickens in the street!"

"Aw, hell!" The tires screeched as she swerved, but we felt a bump then another.

Theresa's eyes went wide. "Lord have mercy, I think I ran 'em over."

"Well, hold up then lemme grab a few." I reached for the door handle.

"You ain't puttin' no dead chickens in my car. Duke gon' kill me."

"Dear sister, I ain't scared of your husband. Just like I ain't scared of Raymond. These chickens fresh and good."

I hopped out, scooped up a couple, and by the time Theresa popped the trunk, I had 'em tucked inside. We slid back in, both breathin' heavily.

I dug through my purse, pulled out my fifth of whiskey, and tipped it back.

"Velma, what the hell you doin'?" Theresa yelled.

"Taking a drink what it looks like?"

"I told you no drinking!"

"Correction," I smirked, "you said no beer."

Theresa's face scrunched up like a knot, her lips tight as she drove. I laughed. "Theresa, I don't know why you act like your shit don't stink."

"I don't think that!" she snapped.

I leaned back, watching her. My sister Theresa was beautiful, looked just like our mama, Pearl light complexion, long nose, wide chin, hair that waved down her back. As for Me? I favored our grandmother, Amelia LeBlanc-Guidry. Two Creole sisters, side by side, ridin' out to fetch the third.

My house was on Mouton Street, just a few minutes from Freeman. Theresa pulled up in front and gave the horn a gentle tap.

"You not getting out, Theresa? Gonna knock on the door? Or you scared you might run into your brother-in-law Raymond?" I asked, my voice dripping with sarcasm.

"Oh hush, Velma," Theresa shot back.

I leaned over and pressed my palm flat against the horn. HOOONK!

"Velma! Stop!" Theresa hollered.

"You can't tell me what to do," I fired back, leaning hard on the horn again.

She tried pushing my hand away, but she wasn't strong enough.

"Don't do that," she fussed. "You know Raymond gon' be pissed off."

"I don't care," I said, sitting back in the seat. "Can't stand his black ass anyway."

"Oh, Lord..." Theresa groaned, hopping out the car. She hurried up the walk toward the porch, then turned back and waved, laughing.

Ophelia opened the door.

"Tell Celeste to come with us!" I hollered out the window.

"We takin' her to the healer," Theresa explained.

"Yeah, that way I ain't gotta drive back over here," I added.

My poor sister Ophelia came limping out, holding her side. I could see plain as day she was hurting. Theresa tucked up under her arm, while Celesta slipped around the other side to help steady her.

"Let me get the back door," Theresa said, pulling it open.

Ophelia eased herself inside, slow as could be. Celeste bent down, lifting her legs gently so she could settle in. Theresa's car was something to see a 1960 Chevrolet Impala, light blue with gold trim. The seats were wide and smooth, perfect for a ride down a country road.

Celeste slid in beside Ophelia. Then Theresa climbed back in, cranked the engine, and reached across the dash to turn on the radio. The soft crackle gave way to music.

"Let's listen to some James Brown," she said, twisting the knob.

I turned back to Ophelia. "How you feelin', sha baby?"

"Hurtin', Velma," she whispered.

I reached over the seat, grinning. "I got a little whiskey in my purse if you want a sip."

Theresa rolled her eyes at me.

"What, Theresa?" I said, catching her look.

"No thank you, Velma. Maybe after we are done," Ophelia murmured. "Thank y'all for pickin' me up. I just hope this works."

"It will," Theresa said quickly. "You gon' feel better instantly."

Ophelia leaned forward. "What should I expect when I get there?"

I gave her a sideways glance. "Well, sha, don't be scared. This man ain't no ordinary Negro. He is black, black, skin black, eyes black, lips black. Short fella, maybe five feet tall. He wears chicken feet and things round his neck. But don't be scared. Folks fear him, but he is a good person. His heart is gold."

Ophelia settled back, her curls bouncing against her shoulders. She looked sharp in her white shorts and green tank top. She always loved her shorts.

"With everything goin' on at 1010 Freeman Street," she said softly, "I fear nothin' but God."

We all laughed, turned the music up, and rolled on down that country road.

"What we gone do about our brothers, y'all?" Ophelia asked, her voice trembling.

"I don't know," Theresa sighed. "They are sending Arthur to Angola prison. Cliff ain't been the same since he came back from the Navy. Walter, Bobby, and all of them moving to Texas."

Theresa shook her head.

I leaned forward. "Have y'all met Bobby's wife yet?"

"I've met her a few times. She seems nice," Ophelia answered.

"Velma, what did you decide 'bout your situation with the kids?" Ophelia asked.

"Oh, I took care of that a long time ago," I replied. "Herman stayin' with Ma'Mu and Potoon. Been there a while now. He gets to hang out and play with our little brother David. Loves it over there."

I leaned in, grinning. "He told me he sits right on the cabinet next to Ma'Mu while she's cookin', just watchin' her. And get this, y'all, Herman said, 'She don't even curse!'"

We all hollered laughing.

"You know, Potoon, Herman, and David stop by our house every Sunday after church," I said. "Soon as Daddy Potoon jumps out the car, first thing out his mouth is, 'Beer, quick!' in that thick French accent. True Creole folks. Lord knows I don't even understand how we kept up with our parents' half the time."

Ophelia smirked. "Well, has he learned any of Potoon's recipes?"

"Oh yes," I said. "Especially that herb tonic he makes for the men. Herman said Potoon adds sheri wine, eggs, and some other secret ingredients."

Theresa rolled her eyes, laughing. "All I hear 'round this town is, 'August and Pearl got the good stuff!'"

We cracked up again.

"Well, I'm glad Herman's happy and enjoyin' himself," Ophelia said.

"Oh yeah, sha bébé," I replied. "He and David go off in them woods, campin' like little men. And Potoon he gets up every mornin' to drive them to J.S. Clark School."

I laughed, remembering. "Herman said, 'Momma, I get so embarrassed. Me and David gotta duck down in the seat 'cause Potoon drives right up to the front in that old 1949 Dodge. Everybody lookin' at us.'"

We laughed till tears rolled out our eyes, voices loud as ever as we rolled on down the road.

Theresa squinted at the long dirt road ahead. "Velma, we goin' the right way? We been drivin' forty minutes already." The sun was beating down hard into her eyes.

"Yes," I said, pointing ahead. "Just five more minutes. Once we pass that strange statue he got by the road, we'll know we there."

"I thought you been here before," I teased.

"I have," Theresa muttered. "I just don't remember it bein' this far. These rocks tearin' up my car."

"Yeah, look at the dust behind us," I said. "Here it is turn left, right there."

Theresa gripped the large steering wheel, turned, and pulled the car into gear with the handle on the side. The old engine groaned as we rolled up the drive.

"Damn... his house is black too?" Ophelia whispered.

"Be quiet, girl. He might hear you," I hissed.

All four of us climbed out slow, staring at that dark house. Nobody said a word.

"You ready, Ophelia?" I asked.

"I guess so." She took a deep breath. I held her arm steady.

"Celesta, get her other arm," I said. I swear, that little buzz I had drained right out of me. My nerves were raw. We walked side by side onto the porch. The smell of sage and sweet incense floated thick in the air. Theresa knocked.

The door opened, and a woman stood before us skin the color of polished brown sugar, flawless, glowing. Her teeth shone white when she smiled. She wore white headwrap and a gown sprinkled with golden stars.

"Welcome," she said warmly. "Come on in. He been waitin' on y'all. I'm Shelia Mae. You must be Ophelia let me help you."

She led us down a long, dark hallway until we reached the back. The room we stepped into was bright white, almost blinding.

A man sat at the table dressed all in white. His skin was black as coal, his presence heavy.

Shelia Mae pulled a chair out for Ophelia. "Sit here. We may need the rest of y'all close."

We eased Ophelia down. The man's lips twitched as he began to speak in a low, strange tongue. We couldn't understand a word.

We sat hunched, hands pressed between our knees, the incense wrapping around us, calming our nerves even as fear crept in.

Then suddenly, his voice shifted into words we knew.

"Ophelia... you been struggling with this for some time. This thing in your leg ain't no disease. It ain't no injury. It is a dark spirit tryin' to invade your soul. The only reason the devil ain't claimed you yet is because you pray... because you believe. But I must remove it. There will be times your faith grows weak, and if you let it... it will take over."

He looked around at us. "Bow your heads. I'm gon' pray."

He lit a thick stick of sage, sprinkled holy water, and walked around swinging the smoke over us. Then he anointed Ophelia's forehead with oil, chanting louder and louder.

The light flickered. A rumble of thunder shook the walls, though the sun had been shining all day.

He knelt before Ophelia. "If it's alright, I need to place your legs on this stool. Don't think I'm bein' disrespectful. I need to touch 'em.

Ophelia hesitated, then nodded. "The pain's mostly back here," she whispered, pointing to the back of her leg. "Shhh," he hushed, pressing a finger to his lips. "I know."

He glanced at me. "Velma, get your daughter out."

I looked at Celesta. Her eyes were wide with fear, but she rose and slipped outside the door.

The healer's hands worked up and down Ophelia's leg. Her skin began to ripple like waves under the surface. His chants grew stronger, faster.

Ophelia screamed. Her body jerked.

"Hold her leg!" he commanded.

Theresa ran and pinned it down.

I rocked back and forth, whispering prayers, tears streaming.

"Oh God! It hurts! What's in there?" Ophelia cried, thrashing.

Her skin tightened, split open black liquid oozing out.

"I got it!" the healer shouted. He pulled, grunting.

"Get it out! Get it out!" Ophelia wailed.

Then with one final pull, he yanked a long, skinny black snake from her leg.

We screamed. Celesta burst back into the room, eyes wild.

The snake writhed in his hands.

"Quick,start the fire!" he yelled.

Shelia Mae grabbed matches and lit a hidden furnace in the wall. Flames roared. He threw the snake inside and slammed the iron door shut.

He rushed back. "Ophelia, are you alright?"

Her head wobbled weakly. "Water," he said.

Shelia Mae handed Celesta a cup drawn from the well. She held it to her mama's lips.

The healer placed herbs on the wound, praying over her. Before our eyes, the skin began to close, sealing smoothly.

Ophelia stirred, blinking. Then she smiled faintly. "I feel... so much better."

Relief washed over us all, we laughed, cried, even giggled at the same time.

The healer helped her to her feet. "How's it feels?"

"Like brand new. Like nothin' was ever there."

"Good. Take these with you," he said, handing her a sack filled with herbs and charms. "Place 'em in your windows, your doors. Keep prayin'."

We stepped back outside the sun had returned, shining bright as ever.

"Thank you, thank you," we said over and over.

He refused money, only nodding.

We climbed back in the car, still trembling, still amazed. We had seen the devil pulled straight out of flesh... and burned alive.

This chapter is dedicated to my Auntie Velma, my mama's oldest sister. Born February 3rd, 1930. Died May 25th, 1985, of cirrhosis of the liver.

Twenty-Eight

THE RIVER WILL FLOW

Raymond Jr. aka Bode

Stillness

Changes

New paths

"Ouch! What in the world did I just sit on?"

I lifted my leg and looked down. Sure enough, I'd sat right on
a pincher bug, and it pinched the back of my thigh something

awful. I rubbed at the sting and shifted in my chair on the front porch, eyes drifting up to the sky. The clouds were rolling in fast and heavy, like a fight at a funeral.

I thought about climbing the big oak tree out front, but today my spirit just felt too heavy. I missed my daddy. There was a time when it was me and him, side by side hunting, fishing, and stopping by Dairy Queen every Friday night for a cone. Those were the days. But now? Now all he did was work.

Daddy worked at Dimmick's Supply six days a week, breaking his back for forty-eight cents an hour. On Sundays, he drove the sweet potato truck down to Houston. The folks at that place never would give him a raise, no matter how hard he worked. Ever since we bought this house and especially after that Friday night, October 18, 1963, when Sandy was born, things had changed.

Sometimes I felt like I was the man of the house now. Tot-Tee had started stealing clothes, and Mama had her hands full with the working cleaning, caring for us and everyone else's children.

The phone rang from inside, breaking my thoughts.

Ring, ring.

I stood, brushed the dirt from my legs, and hurried inside.

"Hello?" I said, pressing the receiver to my ear.

Nothing but static at first.

"Hello? I can't hear you."

The line crackled, then a voice came clear.

"Hey, Bo-Scott. It's Uncle Rat."

"Uncle Rat! Well, hey there. What's going on?"

"I wanna come over and look at their walls," he said. His voice was low, serious. "I got a feeling the spirits in that house don't want y'all finding the money they hid before they died."

"Huh?" My eyes widened. "You think there's money in the walls?"

"Sure do. I'm fixin' to come rip down the one by the fireplace. That's where it's gotta be."

I hesitated. "Well... I guess so, Uncle Rat. But you know you're gonna have to be careful. Daddy just sealed that fireplace up. We found a hole or maybe it was a well, I don't even know but Sandy almost fell in. The smell coming outta there was something foul. Daddy sealed the whole thing and even put new doors on the bathrooms"

"He won't care once I get that money out," Uncle Rat said matter of fact.

"Alright... well, call first and let us know when you're comin'."

I hung up the phone slowly, a puzzled look spreading across my face. Did I just make the right decision? There's a reason folks call Uncle Jules "Uncle Rat." Always sniffing around, digging in holes, looking for something.

Daddy had done everything he could to protect us from this house, sealing fireplaces, building walls, throwing out old artifacts.

As I walked back toward the porch door, I thought about how everybody in our family went by nicknames. Half the time I didn't even know their real names.

Just as that thought crossed my mind, a pot flew out of the kitchen cabinet and clattered against the floor.

I froze, my heart pounding. But I turned away calmly and kept walking back outside.

We were getting used to this house, with all its evil and all its pure spirits still roaming inside.

Just last night, while I was sleeping, I felt a spirit or a ghost walking past my bed. I could hear it, plain as day, and feel the presence brush against me. At first, I thought it was Tot-Tee or Betty Ann, so I sat up to ask what they wanted. But there was nobody there. Only the sound of footsteps moving back and forth across the room.

It had gotten so common, I hardly paid any attention to it. I just pulled the covers over my head and went back to sleep.

I stepped back out onto the porch. That was always the one place I could think of clearly. My eyes drifted to the big oak tree.

"Maybe I'll climb it anyhow," I muttered to myself.

I headed toward the tree, but just as I reached for a low branch, a horn blasted.

Honk! Honk!

It was Uncle Rat, pulling up fast in his old car.

"Hey, Bo-Scott!" he hollered, climbing out.

"Uncle Rat? How did you get here so quickly? I didn't think you were comin' today. Ain't you supposed to be in the military fightin' wars?" I asked.

"Nope," he said, grinning. "I got out. Got me a job with PG&E. I'm movin' to California. Gonna take Nat with me and come back for the rest of the kids later. Now, come on help me get these tools out the car."

"Sure," I said, though something in my gut twisted uneasy.

We walked to the car. Uncle Rat popped open the trunk, and it was crammed full of tools. Looked to me like he'd been planning this for a while no way he packed all that in one morning.

I grabbed a chisel in one hand and a saw in the other. Uncle Rat slung a big brown sack of tools over his shoulder and marched inside like he owned the place.

When he sat down beside the fireplace, a chill shot clean through my arms. I rubbed at them, uneasy. The air trembled. The spirits weren't happy. I could feel it.

Uncle Rat glanced back over his shoulder, eyes wide, then locked his gaze on me.

"Don't be scared, boy, you hear?" he said.

I nodded, but my insides knotted tighter.

He started tearing at the wallpaper, paint, wood flying in many directions. Before long, there was a hole big enough to stick his head in. He leaned close, peered inside, then shoved his hand in, feeling around.

"Not one red cent," he spat. "Ain't nothin' here. I'll just move over to the fireplace."

My stomach dropped.

"No, Uncle Rat! Daddy sealed that off to protect us. "Don't do that," I begged.

"Boy, hush when grown folks talkin'," he snapped. "Show some respect."

With that, he took his chisel and went to the fireplace wall. The plaster was hard and sweat poured down his face. His forehead bunched in folds; his shirt soaked through. He kept hittin' crack, crack, crack until finally, with one hard swing, the wall gave way. A small hole split open.

The house jolted. We both fell back.

Just then, Mama stormed in.

"Rat! What the hell are you doin'?" she screamed.

"Lookin' for money," he shot back.

"There ain't no goddamn money in there!" she hollered, tossing her purse on the couch. Her eyes were wide, near wild, as she stepped closer to the fireplace. She froze, staring at the black crack in the wall.

Her voice dropped low, a whisper. "I'll be damned, Rat. You shoulda' never opened that fireplace up. Get the hell outta my house!"

Uncle Rat stood, wiping his forehead. "Ophelia, I..."

"Get. Out!" Mama cut him off, pointing to the door.

I could see she was both furious and scared.

Tot-Tee and Betty Ann had slipped in by then, standing behind me with eyes as big as a bullfrog in a hurricane. They just rolled their eyes and shuffled off when Mama snapped her head at them. Little Sandy, now just four years old, peeked in. She looked at the fireplace and giggled like it was a game before following our sisters.

Mama towered over Uncle Rat as he packed up his tools. She pulled a cigarette from her pocket, lit it with shaking hands, then crossed her arms.

"I'm callin' your wife. She gon' know what you done," she said, smoke curling from her lips.

Uncle Rat didn't answer. He just slung his bag over his shoulder and hurried out, his boot catching the seashell by the door.

My heart sank.

The foul odor seeped out again, thick and choking. Mama muttered, "Raymond's gon' be furious when he gets home."

Of course she was right.

By eight o'clock that night, thunder shook the sky and lightning split it wide open. Rain hammered the roof. I heard Daddy at the door, rattling it open, boots stomping heavy.

"What the hell happened to this wall?" he yelled. "Who opened this fuckin' fireplace?"

Mama was in the kitchen, making his plate. Her hands shook. Daddy's voice boomed louder and louder, shaking the walls worse than the storm outside. The dinner plate crashed, glass broke.

We lay in bed, listening, breath caught in our throats. I had never heard Daddy so mad.

The bedroom door burst open. Mama stood there, tears pouring down her face.

"Quick, grab your jackets!" she cried.

"What happened, Mama?" Tot-Tee hollered.

"Don't ask questions! Just do as I say!"

We scrambled, snatched up Sandy, and ran for the door. Daddy was still shouting behind us. We piled into the car, hearts pounding.

She placed the key in the ignition and turned it, praying it would roar to life. "Rrr-rrr-rrr." The engine made an odd noise then fell silent. Momma's heart sank. She gripped the wheel tighter, lowered her head, and drew in a long, shaky breath.

Lightning lit up the sky as rain beat hard against the windshield. Mama struck a match, lit another cigarette, and turned to us.

"Get out," she said.

We froze, confused.

"Out! Now! Hold hands, every one of you."

We stepped into the storm, rain drenching us. Mama's cigarette glowed red in the dark, the only light leading us forward.

"Where we goin', Mama?" Betty asked, her small voice trembling.

"To Ma'mu's house," Mama said. Her tone was steady, but her eyes gave her away. She was scared too.

We walked through the rain, hand in hand, following the glow of Mama's cigarette.

I swear, that was the night the spirits in the house woke up. Evil was lost, angry and hungry. Daddy's voice that night wasn't even his voice anymore. Something else had been released when that fireplace cracked open.

We came back the next day. The smell was still there.

Mama cleared the floor, sweeping debris into piles. For a while, things seemed quiet, if that's what one would call it, the spirits still roamed the house as usual.

But on 1010 Freeman Street, the quiet never lasted long and from that day on everything went downhill.

The gates to hell were open!

Twenty-Nine

CALL OF WARNINGS

Louis Chatman Sr. aka Papa

It was a little late, but I was gonna call old Remin anyway. It was the only time I could catch him. My son's real name was Raymond, but I liked calling him Remin. I picked up the phone and dialed one number at a time, then sat in my recliner and held the receiver to my ear.

"Hey, Remin, what you doin', boy?" I asked.

"Oh, I ain't doin' much, Dad. Just got off work," Raymond replied.

"Well, listen here," I said, leaning back in my chair, "I was thinkin' the Dodgers game comes on soon, and you and Ophelia got the best TV. We oughta all get together. That Jackie Robinson, he's a bad man! We got an African American in the major leagues now that's somethin' to celebrate."

"I know, Dad, trust me. I done already requested the day off," Raymond said.

"You got any whiskey over there, Dad?" he asked.

"Well, you know I got some," I said. "I put a little in my coffee every mornin'. Why, you want me to bring some?"

"Oh, yeah, Daddy! We gotta have some good whiskey for the game," he said.

I chuckled. "You know those girls told on me. Told your momma, Octavia, everything."

I could hear Raymond already finding it funny. "Who told what, Daddy?"

"Terricita, Ann, and Brenda," I said, laughing. "I usually hide my whiskey in the garden behind the cornfield. When your momma wasn't lookin', I'd ask one of 'em to grab it for me. Well, the other day, I reckon they got lazy. They didn't wanna go get it, it was hot outside, too many bugs, and I think they even seen a snake. So, your momma came askin' what was goin' on, and they told it all."

Raymond was laughin' on the other end of the line. "So, where you keep it now, Daddy?" he asked.

"I keep it under the house. Your momma ain't goin' under there," I said, laughin'.

"Well, invite everyone. All Ophelia's folks too. Invite everybody except for them damn ghost y'all got in that house."

"Don't worry, Dad," Raymond said. "Fefe Goodwill took care of all that. We don't have no more ghosts."

"Sounds perfect, Daddy. I'll have Fefe Good will cook up some good food." he said, sounding excited.

"And I'll bring the family stories," I said. "Lord knows I got plenty of 'em to tell about you.

We hung up laughin', knowin' the next week we would enjoy some family time, baseball, and a little mischief just the way it oughta be in Louisiana.

Saturday morning rolled around. I sat up on the side of my bed. Octavia was already up, kneeling next to her bed, praying. Judging by the look at the bottom of her feet, I didn't think she had washed them last night something she made everyone in the house do before bed: wash away the sins of the day.

"Hey, woman," I said, smiling, "looks like you forgot to wash your feet last night."

I waited for her to turn around and say something smart, but she just ignored me. I grabbed my prayer beads off the wall and knelt down to say my rosary. The floor was cold, made of solid wood. Making the sign of the cross, I began with the Apostles' Creed.

Hail Mary, full of grace, the Lord is with thee...

The rosary is a long prayer and always goes longer than Octavia's.

I stood up and walked to the kitchen.

"Here's your coffee," she said.

"Thanks, baby. So, are you going to get ready soon? Remember, we're all going to Raymond's house today for the game."

She placed her hand on her hip and sighed.

"Louis, you know I don't like going over there. Raymond and Ophelia got demons floatin' around there like wisps in the sky. You see what happened to the pastor? He ain't been the same since."

"Octavia, that was over a year ago. Raymond said there are no ghosts or demons. Come on, baby, everyone'll be there, and I gotta have my number one with me. "Besides your best friend will be there Amelia Le Blanc", She smiled at me and gave me a kiss.

"Let me get dressed," she said, smiling. Then she called out, "Ann and Brenda, y'all get up and get dressed!" "Okay, Maw'ma!" they yelled back.

We jumped in the car. I kept it clean, like always. We drove from Bellevue Street to Freeman Street, all sharp. Octavia had her little sailor hat on, looking beautiful in her dark blue top, skirt, and black Mary Jane shoes. I had on my yellow button-down shirt and black tie with black Dickie pants.

When we pulled up in front of the house, the front window was open, and laughter spilled out into the street. I turned off the engine. Brenda and Ann jumped out and ran toward the house. I walked around to Octavia's side to open her door.

She put one leg out, looked up at me, and took a deep breath.

"Come on, woman, get out the car! We're protected and covered by God's grace ,now let's go."

She stood up and closed the car door behind her. She started walking toward the house, I then quickly went to the trunk.

"Louis, what you getting out the trunk?" Octavia asked.

I pulled the trunk slightly down, eyebrows raised, the sunshine catching my face. "I'm grabbing some treats." I lifted the whiskey and cigars.

"Louis! Why you got that?" she asked, firmly.

"This ain't for me it's for Raymond," I replied.

"And the cigars?"

"Well, those are for me, baby. Now come on, let's go."

I held the whiskey and cigars in one hand, wrapped my arm around her waist, and we walked inside the house together.

"Hey!" everyone shouted.

It was good to see everyone again. The party had already started. Ophelia's dad, Potoon whose real name was August Guillory had brought over his homemade moonshine, and folks were already sipping on homemade beer.

Octavia and I made our way to the kitchen, where all the women were busy with a cook-off a competition to see who could make the best Creole dish.

"Hey, ladies!" I called.

The kitchen was alive with laughter, beer, and fun activity: Pearl, Ophelia's mom; her mother, Amelia; Velma and Theresa, Ophelia's sisters; and my two sisters, Dorthy known as Old Sally and Hazel, known as Sibby. They had everything on the stove: gumbo, fish, covillion, shrimp étouffée, turkey necks, chicken dumplings, greens, and hot water cornbread. The house smelled heavenly.

I went and sat down with the fellas in the other room.

"Turn the TV on," I said.

"The game hasn't started yet, Dad," my son LJ replied.

"It doesn't matter. Turn it on anyway. I want to see what it looks like," I said. "Raymond, they got that fancy one."

Perry walked over and turned the knob.

"Which channel, Dad?"

"The Atena ain't working," he said.

"Well, turn on the radio," I told my son Sam, we also call him Dott. "You're standing right next to it."

He turned the radio on, and we sat and listened for a moment to find out when the Dodgers would be playing. Raymond, ear close to the radio, chimed in, "It starts in two hours. We got time to fix this Atena right before the game."

The boys liked to hang out with us and enjoyed hearing the old stories. Bode, Fernando, Herman, Darcie, Karl, and Ophelia's little brother David sat around, eagered to learn from the older folks. It's important to teach these boys how to be a man, I thought to myself

I met Ophelia's brother Walter for the first time. He had two little boys with him and a daughter. Clifton also had a little girl with him.

My daughter Sally and her husband, Herbrard, had too many damn kids to count and I couldn't keep up with them all. Anyway, we sat down and began telling stories.

I turned to Herman, Velma's boy.

"What you want to be when you grow up?" I asked.

"I wanna work at Daily Motors like my grandpa Potoon," Herman said. "Not like my grandma. She worked for Miss Daisy White, cleanin' houses, only makin' two dollars a week."

"What experience you got?" I asked him.

"Well, whenever Auntie Ophelia and Auntie Theresa and my mama Velma come to Ma'mu and Patoon's house for Sunday dinner, I go outside and clean Auntie Theresa's '56 Oldsmobile, Auntie Ophelia's '56 Ford, and Mama's Buick. I shine 'em up really good," Herman said proudly.

I laughed. "Well, good job, young man."

Herman looked back at me. "What do you do for a living, sir?"

"Well, I work at the railroad now, but it didn't start off as easy as your grandpa Potoon's job," I said.

"Yeah, Dad. Trust me, I remember it well," Raymond chimed in.

We all started laughing.

LJ said, "Oh Lord, here we go. Tell us what happened, Raymond."

"Nah," Raymond said, "I'm gonna let Daddy tell the story the way he wanna tell it."

We all sat on the edge of our seats, going back and forth about who was gonna tell it the right way.

Perry jumped in. "Wait, wait! Don't forget the part when Old Ma told y'all to bring that pee with you.

We all hollered, the laughter rolling through the room. The sun poured in through the open window, and a cool breeze swept in. We were laughing and carrying on so hard I forgot the house was supposed to be haunted.

"Well, after the game, I'm gon' beat y'all at a game of dominoes," Rock said, stepping in late, wearing a brim hat dressed in a three-piece suit.

Now, Rock was just one of Octavia's many brothers, and Lord knows I couldn't stand his ass. But for today, we managed to get along. Truth be told, I believed her brothers were into some illegal mess. Her sisters weren't much better, except Lorena, my sister-in-law twice over, since she married my brother and I married her sister. The only one I ever liked. Her sister Nanny Shine, oh boy, she thought she was something special, thought she was better than everybody else. She was the only one with no kids, and she wore that like a crown. I quickly snapped out of my thoughts.

"Anyway, Raymond, I'll let you tell the story about my previous job," I said.

"Well, thanks, Dad. After all, I'm the one traumatized," Raymond said.

"Oh man, get outta here," Rock cut in.

I shot him that crazy Chatman stare.

Raymond leaned forward. "So first of all, before Dad became permanent at the railroad, he had to bid on a position. But we had to travel out of town to Ambeville, Louisiana, the coldest place in the whole state of Louisiana. Sugarcane grew tall as barns out there. When Dad got the call that his bid was accepted, he'd wake me and Perry up, tell us, 'Pack up, let's go.'

"Now Old Ma" y'all know who Old Ma is, right? Mary Fontent, Daddy's grandma."

"Oh yeah," Arthur replied.

"Well," Raymond went on, "she would make this concoction for us before we left, just in case we caught that goopy stuff in our eyes from the cold. She made us all stand around and pee in a bowl. Then she prayed over it, threw some herbs in, canned it up, and told us to take it with us.

"This is what makes the story even more crazy," Raymond said.

"Back in those days, colored folks had it worse than we do now. We couldn't sleep in hotels, and the job site didn't have a place for us to lay our heads. So, Perry and I had to pack our tents and a wash basin so we could bathe once we reached Daddy's job site. To make matters worse, we had to walk through the white folks' side of town just to get to our destination. We were scared. Daddy had us leave at night so no one would see three Black Negroes walking…"

He shook his head slowly. "Man, some nights it was so cold, Perry and I had to turn our sweatshirts inside out just to keep warm. We pulled 'em up clear to our necks, I swear we invented the turtleneck shirts."

We all chuckled, but Raymond's face grew serious again.

"So, one night, we were walkin', trying to stay warm, our bags and basins on our backs. Up ahead we noticed a group of white boys hangin' around, and we had no business being on that side of town. Daddy whispered,

'Let's cut through this corn maze and sugarcane field. We don't want no trouble.'

"So, we got to walking. The cane was tall, the stalks sharp as knives. The moon barely lit our path. That's when it happened."

Raymond's voice dropped low.

All of a sudden, this… thing stepped out in front of us. It had no face. No eyes, no mouth, just a hollow shape like the night itself had pulled together and decided to walk. The air turned cold, colder than it already was. We froze. Daddy threw his arm out to stop us and y'all know how long Daddy's arms are," he said, grinning, though his eyes still looked haunted.

We laughed, but it was a nervous laugh.

"Then it slipped behind us," Raymond went on. "We didn't hear no footsteps, no rustlin' of cane, just a heavy silence that pressed on our backs. Daddy didn't wait. He took off runnin', and we were right behind him. Man, our feet kicked up dirt, sugarcane was snappin' and fallin' every which way. It felt like somethin' was chasin' us, breathin' down our necks, though when I dared to glance back, all I saw was shadows twistin' in the cane." Raymond shook his head, half laughing, half shivering at the memory. "When we finally made it to the end, we bent over gaspin' for breath. All Daddy could say was, 'Good job, boys.' We laughed so hard, though truth be told, none of us ever forgot that thing."

He rubbed his arm as if he could still feel that night. "By the time we reached camp, we pulled out our basins, towels, and soap, got some water from the nearby river, and washed up. After the assignment was over, we'd repeat the same routine walking back at night, in the cold, cuttin' through the sugarcane. And every time, by the time we got home, our eyes were sealed shut. That's when we had to open that jar of pee and wipe our eyes with it. But you know what? It worked."

Louis Junior LJ spoke up. "Daddy, let me ask you somethin'. Why'd you even take them with you? I never understood that." "Why didn't you take me."?

I leaned forward. "Well, one you were the oldest. I needed you here to look after your momma and your sister. Raymond,now don't get mad when I say this but out of all you boys, he was and still is the strongest and the most courageous. I knew he'd fight if it came down to it."

Raymond smiled, proud.

LJ nodded. "Well then, why Perry?"

"Because he was the smallest and the scariest ," I said plain. "And if somethin' happened, I knew he could sneak back into town and let y'all know what went down without anybody seeing him."

"Daddy, that's messed up," Perry said, shaking his head.

"Well, at least I'm telling the truth," I answered. "That's why I named him Raymond after my Uncle. I told y'all this story before, didn't I?"

I looked at Bo-Scott, and he looked back at me.

"You are Raymond Junior, son. That's a heavy name. It carries responsibility."

See, my Uncle Raymond my daddy's brother was known as one of the toughest, bravest men in Louisiana. And his sister, my auntie, could cook better than anyone you ever met. Folks said her hands were blessed and she had them cooking arms.

One night, the family had gathered at their place. It was just country folks laughing, eating, and carrying on something like what we're doing now. When the evening settled down, some went home, but a few stayed the night. By three in the morning, Uncle Raymond was cleaning up, and we kids were drifting off to sleep.

That's when the nightmare happened.

Bang, Bang, Bang. A loud pounding shook the door, like thunder. I shot up out of bed, heart palpating in my neck. Out the window I saw flames torches swaying in the night, shadows moving behind them.

Uncle Raymond's face went hard. He grabbed me and my brother Charles the one with twelve fingers and shoved us toward the closet.

"Hide," he whispered. "Don't come out, no matter what you hear."

But I couldn't stay put. I cracked the door and peeked out, my skinny body trembling.

The front door exploded off its hinges. Wood broke and flew everywhere... White men ran into the house, faces twisted with hate, torches blazing.

Then my Uncle Raymond roared loud like a beast. He fought like a man born for war. He swung his fists, knocking men flat. Bodies slammed against walls, hitting the ground with hideous thuds. You could hear the bones breaking, smell sweat and blood fumigating the house, He wasn't afraid, not one bit. He was fighting for his sister's life.

But more men came. They pushed through the smoke and fire, and they got to my auntie. She screamed, a loud, piercing cry that still rings in my ears. They lifted her off the ground, her legs kicking wildly, hopeless as she begged for help.

"Raymond!" she screamed.

He turned toward her, but a blow caught him across the skull. I saw him stumble, then fall. My brave uncle, the strongest man I knew, lay unconscious on the floor.

And just like that, she was gone. They carried her out into the night.

Later, folks said they stole her so she could cook for one of their mothers. But that didn't matter to Uncle Raymond. The next day, he went searching. He knocked on doors, crossed the tracks, went straight into the south side looking for her.

We never saw Uncle Raymond or my auntie again. Some say he got arrested while others say he was found hanging in the tress, they had lynched him.

But that night, I saw what courage really looked like.

I always swore I'd name a son after him Raymond Chatman. So, when my last boy was born, I remembered my promise. That's why your brother carries the name Raymond. To honor my uncle for his strength and courage carrying his legacy.

I turned to Bo-Scott. My voice dropped low. "Now you are Raymond Junior. Don't disappoint us."

"Yes, sir," he said, his voice steady but his eyes brighten.

Everyone sat back in their chairs looking tense, don't be so tense fellows, we got threw it I said, now let's get this dominoes game going before the Dodgers come on and leave that radio playing,

Hey Fernado, yes sir grab that ash tray in the kitchen so we can light up some cigars and tell Ma'mu or Maw'ma to bring us some beers, yes sir Fernado responded.

I sat back in that gold-colored chair Raymond and Ophelia kept in their home. The light green walls looked soft in as the sun beamed on them, flowered curtains swayin' with the breeze from the open window. The supper smells good lingering in the air, Oxtails, rice, cornbread, Jambalaya, greens, potato salad and whatever else they cooked.

I passed the box of King Edward cigars to LG, and he slid it down the line until every man had one in hand.

"Now, only take one cigar," I said, laughin'. "Don't be tryin' to stick one in your pocket for later."

The men chuckled, and we all bit the tips clean off. Rock, though, had his pocketknife out, fiddlin' with it like he was fixin' to carve a roast.

"What the hell you doin' to that cigar, boy?" I spoke. "Just bite the tip off ain't no need tryin' to be all sophisticated and shit."

That set everybody off, laughter rollin' through the room like wave.

Fernando came back in, carryin' ashtrays. "Here, Papa, you can have the big one," he said, handin' me a heavy piece of glass.

"Thanks, my man. This the thickest, steadiest glass ashtray I ever laid eyes on. Where you get it?" I asked.

"Found it in the back closet," he said.

"Well, set it right here and pull up a chair. Time for you to learn somethin' about these cigars," I told him. Fernando, Herman, Bode, and David sat forward, eyes wide, smilin' like they'd been let in on some grown folk secret. They watched close as I bit the tip off my cigar, struck a match, and drew that first deep pull. Smoke curled slowly toward the ceiling, hangin' heavy over us like the ghosts themselves.

We leaned back, talkin' and laughin', throwin' bets down on the ball game. My ash grew long, too long, and I tapped it into that big sturdy ashtray.

Then oh sweet Mary mother of God.

At first, I thought my eyes were playin' tricks on me. A hairline crack slid across the glass, thin as a spiderweb. But the longer I stared, the more it spread, faster and faster, like lightning crawlin' across the sky.

Then came the sound, oh lawd, it was a sound I'll never forget. A sharp pop that turned into a deep groan, then a crack so loud it shook my chair. That ashtray split clean in half, one jagged piece flyin' across the room and slammin' against the wall so hard it made the picture frames rattle.

The room went dead quiet.

Raymond, Potoon, and I turned to each other with the same look in our eyes half fear, half knowin'. The other fellows didn't waste no time, they put their cigars out quick, like maybe that smoke had summoned somethin'. But me... I remembered what my mama, Mary Fontenot, always told me: God sends warnings. Sometimes gentle, sometimes brutal.

But this one? This one I was gon' listen to.

I stood up, lookin' at the fellows, my face turnin' serious. My heart was poundin', my palms sweaty. I scanned the room, then said low but firm,

"Somebody's gon' die."

Potoon stared back at me, worry spread across his face. "What you say?" he asked.

"Someone's gon' die," I repeated, louder this time. "Get me outta here now."

Raymond, Cliff, Lj, and Perry just sat there, starin', not sayin' a word.

"Octavia!" I hollered. "Let's go."

She came runnin' from the other room to meet me. "Why we leavin'?" she asked, breathless.

"It ain't safe here," I told her, shakin' my head. "Somebody in this house gon' die soon."

And sure, enough, one week later.

Thirty

Heaven calls one week later

Ophelia & Raymond Sr.

Now who in the world callin' at three o'clock in the mornin'?

I sat up, rubbed my face, and shuffled slowly to the phone. "Hello?"

"Hey, Daddy..."

"Who is it?" Raymond mumbled from the bed.

I covered the receiver with my hand. "It's Potoon."

"What he wants this time of night?" Raymond asked.

I just shrugged, put the phone back to my ear. "Daddy... is everything okay?"

"What? What? Oh, oh my God... oh Lord..."

The words ripped through me like a blade. My knees gave out, and I hit the floor, cryin' so hard I could hardly breathe. My heart shattered into a million pieces within minutes.

The kids came running to the doorway, eyes full of fear. Raymond jumped up, grabbing me by the shoulders, trying to lift me.

"What's wrong? What's wrong?" he kept asking, panic in his voice.

"It's... it's Ma'Mu," I spoked out, the words barely making it past my lips. "She's gone. My mama is dead."

"Pearl?" Raymond yelled in disbelief. "No-no, Lord-no!"

"Yes... yes," I sobbed, clutchin' the phone to my chest.

I collapsed against him, and Raymond held me tight. We hugged each other on that cold floor and cried together.

Thirty-One

Nobody Heard Me

Sandy

S andy, what are you doing?" Momma yelled.

"I'm washing my hands in the sink," I said. I had pulled the chair up to the face bowl, leaning against it. My hands were getting clean, but at the same time, my nightgown was getting soaked.

I looked down at the mess I had made, my mouth wide open in shock. I couldn't believe I had gotten this much water on me. The faucet continued to run, water hitting the sides of the sink and splashing outward.

Suddenly, I jumped back, pulling my hands away. "Aaaah! What was that?" I screamed.

The water was red running over my hands. "Is this blood?" I whispered.

The light flickered. I looked up just as the chair slipped from under me. I fell forward, hitting my chin on the edge of the sink.

I burst into tears.

Momma rushed into the bathroom. My chin was bleeding.

"Sandy! What happened?" she yelled, her voice full of worry.

"I, I don't know! There was blood in the sink! The light came on... this monster was in here, Momma!"

"It's okay, come on," she said firmly. "Momma gonna beat the monster's ass. Let me see your chin."

She bent down and looked at me closely. "Not so bad," she said, cleaning the cut and placing a Band-Aid over it.

"Okay, go to bed," she told me.

"I'm scared, Momma," I whispered.

"Go to sleep with one of your sisters," she replied.

So, I went and crawled into bed with Betty. She was snoring so hard she didn't even notice when I climbed in beside her. Then a loud noise filled the room, followed by a foul smell.

Betty started laughing.

"I guess she wasn't asleep after all," I thought.

"That's not funny!" I yelled; "you stink, I'm telling daddy on you".

I pulled the covers up around me and rolled onto my left side, holding one arm out of the bed like I did every night. I would sleep with my hand over my head, my fingers touching my eyelid, rubbing my nose every morning as if it were filled with ants.

I started to drift off. The room began to change. Not again, I thought. I know everybody's used to ghosts now, but I ain't they bother me too much. I'm gonna ignore it, I told myself.

My eyes were closed when I felt the heat of somebody breathing in my face. The smell was horrible. I lay there, too scared to open my eyes; my hands trembled, and chills ran clean through me.

"What do you want?" I whispered, my voice shaking.

"Your soul, Sandy. Your heart, lungs, and guts," a deep, frightening voice answered.

I shot my eyes open. They were stretched with terror. I couldn't speak. Its face was long, dark, and ashy. It had a doctor's headlight strapped to its forehead. Its teeth were yellow, broken, brittle and rotten, saliva drooling from the corners of its mouth. My arm was grabbed tight, held fast, and there was a nurse beside him I couldn't see her face, but I could clearly see her white hat and white dress. I could feel her hand on my arm, but I couldn't see it.

The monster the devil or some kind of doctor began carving something into my arm. I still couldn't yell; the pain was excruciating. It burned and burned until finally I screamed so loud I woke the whole house.

"Moma! Daddy!" I cried out. Terricita and Bode came running in. Betty sat up on the corner of the bed, too scared to come near. I tried to reach my hand out to her for help, but she was frozen.

Daddy grabbed me out of the bed and dropped to his knees beside me. "What? Why are you screaming?" he yelled.

"My arm, my arm, Daddy. He did something to my arm."

Dad looked at my arm and held it in his hand. He was angry and scared and felt helpless. My arm had brown, raised lumps all over it; it looked like ground beef scattered along my skin.

He looked up at Momma. "We gotta get the priest again," he said, getting up angry and walking into the other room.

"Let's pray," Momma said. We got in a circle and prayed. That night we all slept in the same bed, all of us together.

Morning came quickly, and I slept well. I sat up, stretched my arms with a big yawn, almost forgetting about the brown marks on my arm. They didn't hurt anymore, but it looked like they might be spreading. I pulled my sleeve down so I wouldn't have to look at them.

It was Saturday. Daddy had gone to work at Dimmicks Supply and Mama had gone to work at Ms. Cowhun's place. I went into the kitchen. Bode and Terricita were arguing over some ice cream that our grandfather, Potton, had dropped off for Betty.

"I guess Tot-Tee took it," I said to myself.

"Well, if you're going to buy for one child, you gotta buy for all of them," Mama always said that and now I know why.

I sat at the table and poured my corn flakes into a bowl with some pet milk, trying to forget everything that had happened last night. All I could hear was dad and mom talking from the next room. I sat reading the back of the cereal box, and before long

I became drowsy, my head drifting from side to side. The room softened; voices faded. In the distance I heard someone calling my name.

I stood and walked slowly around the house, listening for who might be calling me. My body felt light; each step felt like floating. I leaned toward the fireplace and looked inside. I couldn't see as far down as I wanted. The fireplace we have is not an ordinary fireplace, it leads somewhere else.

"Hello?" I spoke.

No answer. I pulled my head back and went upstairs to the room Mama never liked us to be in. I opened the door; it squeaked.

"Hello?" I called out again.

A soft woman's voice answered, faint and close. "Sandy."

"Who are you?" I asked, walking further into the room.

Then I heard other voices, jumbled and far away I couldn't make out everything they said. A man's voice muttered, "It's the same person, she didn't die."

I walked to the small desk in the corner and brushed spiderwebs away from my face that hung from the ceiling. I saw a porcelain plate with a calendar; it was opened to my birthday Friday, October 18, 1963. I tried to focus on the tiny writing for that day. Interesting, I thought. It's written in another language.

Suddenly, a loud voice outside the doorway shouted, "Sandy! What are you doing in here?"

It was Terricita (Tot-tee).

"Get out of this room now!" she cried. The door slammed in my face and as I turned to walk out. I was locked inside.

My heart raced and I started to cry. The light from the window disappeared; the room went pitch black. Writing began to appear on the wall slowly, as if carved by a cold evil hand.

Hang her, it read. She must be destroyed.

Another line carved itself: Please don't.

I screamed. "Tot-Tee! Help!"

I could hear Tot-Tee, Betty, and Bode outside the door, trying to get in. Flies covered the window. My arm burned; I looked down. Worms were wriggling from the brown, raised bumps.

"Help me Jesus, help me," I cried, falling to my knees. "Jesus!"

The door flew open. Tot-Tee, Bode, and Betty tumbled in. Bode grabbed my arm and pulled me out.

"Why did you go in there?" Terricita yelled, grabbing the back of my shirt and dragging me downstairs.

"I'm taking you to Maw-ma's house. I'm not babysitting you all day," she snapped as we went.

Terricita walked me all the way down to Maw-Ma's house without saying a single word. I was fussing the whole time, bare feet slapping against the hot pavement, the heat burning through the soles.

"I don't have no shoes on!" I cried, stumbling to keep up. She didn't care. She just dragged me along. My clothes weren't even on the right way. I barely had time to throw on a white crop top and my pink-and-white plaid shorts before she yanked me out the door.

When we got to Maw-Ma's, Terricita knocked like nothing was wrong. As soon as Maw-Ma opened the door, she changed her tune, all sweet as pie.

"Can you watch her? She's scared of the house," she said, acting innocent.

"Of course, I baby," Maw-Ma (Octavia) replied.

"That's not true!" I blurted out. "I ain't scared, she's lying, Maw-Ma!"

But Terricita just thanked her politely, threw me a hard look over her shoulder, and walked away.

I plopped down on the porch steps on Bellevue Street, arms crossed, face twisted up. I was mad.

Papa came to the door, shaking his head with a grin. "Girl, you sho' is skinny," he said, laughing loud enough for the neighbors to hear.

I glanced down at my legs, pale and bare, and felt his eyes measured me with concern.

"I ain't never seen a child look like you before," he went on. "Skin pale and white with a nappy head. You thirsty?" He hollered back inside. "Octavia, get this gurl somethin' to drink!"

When Maw-Ma swung the screen door open, the house smell slipped out with her.

Maw-Ma held a glass of milk in her hand, her apron tied neat around her waist. She bent down and passed it to me. "Here, baby, drink this."

I sipped once and nearly spit it right back out. "Ugh! What is this, Ma-Maw?"

"It's powdered milk. It's good," she said.

I shook my head, pushing the glass back toward her. "No, ma'am. I don't want it. Thank you."

Her face changed quick. She cut her eyes at me. "Get your tail in here," she snapped.

So, I did. I sat down in Papa's chair, the smell of bug spray and Roux throughout the house., watching TV beside him until Daddy came to pick me up.

Papa's brown leather chair sat right in front of the door. I could see Daddy standing at the screen door; Papa kept the door open but the screen was locked.

"Daddy!" I screamed, jumping off the arm of Papa's big chair.

"Hey, Old Sandy," he said.

I stood on my toes, unlocked the screen, and jumped into my daddy's arms. "Hey, Dad."

My father nodded toward his daddy. "Hey, Remin. I hear you still got spirits at that house of yours," Papa said. "Dad, I don't have no spirits," Daddy replied. "We had some stuff happen last night, but I reckon those kids been gettin' into things. I'm startin' to think there ain't no ghost. I ain't personally seen one."

"Well, I'll be there tomorrow," Papa said.

"Okay, Dad. I'm gonna run to the store and grab these children a treat before I head home," Daddy said. I'm excited, my daddy, Raymond Chatman Sr., the greatest man of all time, was takin' me to get some treats. We climbed into Daddy's '56 Ford, light blue, and drove off. We got ice cream and cookies and a beer, with Salem cigarettes for Momma, and then headed home.

Everyone was happy to see Daddy. We ate and talked until it was time for bed.

At 3 a.m. we heard a voice.

"Who's there? I'll blow your head off! Who's there?" Daddy's voice rang out, angry and ready to protect his family.

I jumped up and saw Daddy walkin' through the house with his gun. His face was troubled, nostrils flared. Momma followed right behind him in her floral nightgown; her curly hair stuck to the side of her head and a single pink roller sat on top.

"Get the kids, Ophelia. Go to the front room," Daddy said.

Momma scooped us up. "What's wrong, Mama?" I asked.

"Someone sat on the bed while we were asleep," she said. Raymond and I both felt it, the bed had been indented, then raised again.

"Momma, you know that was a spirit," Betty said.

"I know it was," Momma whispered, "but your daddy just wants to make sure."

Daddy came back into the bedroom. His nose still flared, but he looked calmer. "There's no one in here. Y'all can go back to bed."

Eight am in the morning. Time for church.

I could smell breakfast cooking. It was Sunday morning, church day at Holy Ghost Catholic, but first we ate. I ran into the kitchen.

"Oh no," Momma said. "Did you wash your face and brush your teeth before coming in here?"

"No ma'am."

"Well, go do it. Tot-Tee, start fixing plates." she continued.

I hurried off, brushing my teeth quickly. As I leaned over the sink, I felt a little chill slip behind me, but I ignored it. Coming back into the kitchen, that same feeling lingered like something following.

"Daddy, you not driving the sweet potato truck today?" I asked.

"No, baby. I'm tired. I'm gon' watch the game and spend some time with all you knuckleheads."

I could tell Momma was pleased. She had cooked up a spread, grit, eggs, bacon, sausage, biscuits from scratch, orange juice, and coffee.

We held hands, blessing the food.

"Pass the biscuits," I said. I slopped mine with butter and jelly.

Bode grabbed his toast and biscuits, dunked them in his hot cocoa, and slurped it up.

"That's so gross," I said.

He grinned, waved a piece of soggy bread in my face.

"Stop, that's nasty!" I tilted my head back, squealing.

Tot-Tee and Betty broke out laughing.

"Bo-Scott, leave your sister alone," Daddy said, calling Bode by Papa's nickname for him.

"I was just tryin' to share, Daddy," Bode said.

After breakfast we got ready for church.

Everyone tied on your head coverings mama said.

"Yes ma'am," I muttered when Momma reminded me.

"Do we gotta wear these all the time?" I asked.

"Yes, you do and make sure that dress is past your knee."

"Yes ma'am."

We piled up in the car and headed to church. Papa was there, and Potoon too. Grandma Pearl Ma'Mu had passed, so no more seeing her sitting in the pews.

As we settled in, I noticed a woman across the aisle with something brown and furry wrapped around her neck. "Look at her," I whispered, pointing. "Why she got a dog 'round her neck?"

"That's not a dog," Betty said.

"Yes, it is, it's doggie-dog!" I burst out laughing.

"Stop pointing at people," Momma hissed.

Tot-Tee and Bode slipped to the back with some cousins cutting church mass.

I turned my head and froze. At the back doors of the church stood a dark figure. Its long finger stretched out, calling me toward it. My stomach flipped. I turned quickly, made the sign of the cross, and slid my white veil lower over my eyes. Momma just looked at me, curious.

We went straight home after Mass. Teresita, Bode, and Betty never went to the graveyard anymore not after seeing their graves dug up, names carved right into the headstones.

Back at the house, Daddy was in front of the TV, hollerin' at the game.

"Go on and get out your good clothes," Momma said.

We changed out quick, it was hot inside, the sun blazing bright.

Before long, Potoon pulled up like always, bringing bubble gum for me, cookies and cakes for everybody else. He always gave me gum thick, hard Bozak gum.

"Beer quick," Potoon said. Momma grabbed him one.

I wished I could speak Creole French like my grandfather. Momma spoke some; she understood everything her daddy said.

Then Papa came over.

"Hey, Papa," Momma said warmly. She loved him nearly as much as she loved her own daddy.

"Raymond, your dad's here," she called.

Daddy stood, met Papa in the living room.

"Hey, Dad."

"Hey, Remin. Listen I got these palm leaves. Had 'em blessed. I'm gon' hang one above each door in this house. Go fetch the ladder."

Bode dragged it in from the yard, heavy, so Daddy helped.

I never understood why Papa needed a ladder, he was tall, arms long as his legs.

He prayed first, then set the ladder under the doorway.

"Hand me the palm leaf's, Raymond, the nails and the hammer."

I stood close, watching Papa as Daddy steadied the ladder. Papa nailed a palm leaf over every door.

"You call another priest over, Raymond?"

"Yes, Dad, I did."

"Good." Papa nodded.

"Well, I'm going to go now," Papa said.

Daddy walked him to the door.

"Bye!" Ophelia Papa yelled. "Love you!"

Wait! my momma walked out, wiping her hands on a towel. "You leaving? Well, give me a hug."

"I think I'm going to go as well," Potton said. "Love you guys."

"Love you too, Daddy," momma answered.

Everyone walked out the door, the entire family.

Not me. I stayed in the doorway. No one could see what I could see.

The demonic doctor and nurse stood right between everyone.

My legs began to shake. I was terrified. How could they be there standing among us and no one else notice? Their eyes locked on me, calling me out.

They couldn't come inside because of the palm leaves and seashell at the front door. Those sacred things kept spirits trapped and barred from crossing the threshold. Still, they crept closer.

Tears blurred my eyes. I covered my mouth to keep from screaming. Step by step, I backed away, keeping my gaze fixed on them as they drifted through the family crowd, invisible to everyone else. Evil laughter echoed around me. I covered my ears the sound was scary and causing pain in my head.

They stopped at the door, staring.

My foot hit the table. I stumbled, crashed to the floor but I never looked away. Scrambling up, I inched backward, my shoulders pressing toward the odd fireplace.

Then it came. A childlike voice, high, calling my name like a song, *Saaandy...Saaandy.* It sounded twisted and wicked.

I spun around scanning the room when suddenly a force slammed into me. Shoving me hard into the fireplace.

I fell in spinning falling deeper until I couldn't see anything. The dark swallowed me whole.

The stench of death filled my nose the smell of rot, burned skin and old flesh. Faces of the dead flickered across the walls of the pit. Screams of those murdered here clawed at my ears. Every evil deed, every hidden horror, was etched into the stones of this house, buried in the very depth of the fireplace.

I screamed until my throat tore.

"Help! Help!"

But no one heard me.

Thirty-Two

Overcome Fear with Faith

Ophelia aka Fefe

"I wish they could've stayed longer," I said as we stood and watched Potoon and Papa drive away.

Raymond shaded his eyes and squinted up at the sky. "Guess it's for the best. Look at them clouds old Fefe Goodwill, they're rollin' in fast."

"My goodness," I murmured, looking up with him. "They look like they're racin' across the sky, just ready to pour buckets and flood the street."

I'd already changed out of my church clothes into something comfortable a yellow and white striped shirt and white pants. Terricita, Bode, and Betty were running 'round the yard playing ball.

"You havin' fun?" I see. "Come on inside. It's 'bout to rain."

"Okay, Mom!" Bode shouted. He grabbed the ball and flung it; it hit Terricita right in the face. They tumbled and started fighting ' like cats and dogs.

"Stop that fightin' before y'all get yourselves punished for the rest of the day!" Raymond yelled out from the porch.

Betty just laughed. Blood was tricklin' from Bode's nose. "Go get me a towel for your brother's nose, Betty," I said.

"Yes, ma'am," she replied, and darted toward the front door. Her jet-black hair stuck up in two pigtails, she always put water and oil through it to make candy-cane swirls, though it still stood straight on top her head.

"What's your sister doin' inside the house, Betty?" I asked when Sandy didn't come back right away.

"Huh?" she paused on the porch. "Your sister Sandy, what is she doin'?"

"Momma, Sandy ain't in the house," Betty said, then handed me the towel. "Here you go, Mom."

I knelt on one knee and pressed the towel to Bode's nose until the bleeding slowed. Raymond sat beside Terricita on the porch, words of discipline turned to silence. Raymond and I looked at each other concerned that the familiar smell of Louisiana wet hot dust lingered in the air.

"Hold this to your brother's nose," I told Betty. She nodded and I ran inside. Raymond followed, his feet hammering up the wooden porch, loud and hurried.

I ran to Sandy's room and pushed the door open. "Saaandy! Saaandy!" I called. The light slanting through the window seemed to thin and go gray, like someone was slowly covering the sun.

A faint, distant cry came from the closet. My heartbeat fast. I walked slowly, the floorboards whispering under my feet.

"Sandy?" I whispered, feeling a strange mix of fear and relief.

I eased the closet door open and shoved the clothes aside. On the top shelf sat Betty's Pinocchio bank. It startled me for a second, I took a deep breath, it's just a ordinary bank Ophelia, I thought to myself, then it turned quickly. Its head swung, its glassy black eyes staring right at me and in that moment it seemed alive.

I screamed, slammed the closet door, and ran. Raymond must've heard me; he collided with me as I burst out of the room. He held me in his arms, are you okay he asked? I just started crying. Suddenly the sound of thunder the first hard drops of rain began to slap the roof, and the sky opened like a portal.

"Quick ,get the children to the back room. I'll call the priest... and one of those psychic people," Raymond said, his voice stronger and heroic.

Okay." I replied, my voice quivering. I wiped my tears and hurried down the hall.

"Come," I told the children, "Into the back room. It's safest here. Stay close and pray."

"Okay, Mama," Bode said, with eyes full of panic. "Let's go, y'all." He guided his sisters inside like little ducks.

I made the sign of the cross and shut the door behind them. My mind raced. Lord, don't let Sandy slip away. She had a wild streak,barefoot wanderer, slipping down the street when no one was looking. Dear God, not tonight please not in this storm.

The house's energy felt heavy, thick with silence except for the rain against the windows and Raymond's voice carrying low from the phone. My hands trembled as I set the kettle on the stove and reached for cups.

That's when I saw it, high on the top shelf, damn Pinocchio bank. I knew no one had put it there. A cold chill ran down my spine.

I stared at it, and my voice came out hard, pissed off. "I will find my daughter. You tell whoever took her, I'm coming for they ass ya hear."

I grabbed the cups and slammed the cabinet door.

The kettle screamed, wheeeeeeeeee! loud and sudden, "Oh, Lawd, I'ma be goddamn!" I almost shit my pants. I took a deep breath and got myself together, poured the coffee into the thick orange mugs, and carried them into the front room.

"Here," I said, setting one before Raymond. "Coffee."

We sat together on the orange leather couch. The piano brewed in the corner, and the green walls inched closer with every breath.

"The priest will be here soon," Raymond murmured. "And the psychic woman, too". "The rest of the family are out looking for her". Let's just wait here.

"That's good," I said, though my chest fluttered with every word.

Raymond looked weary, older than I'd ever seen him. "He wanted to come before," he said of the priest, "but every time he tried, he got sick. I think... The evil here kept him away." He rubbed his face and shook his head. "Fefe Goodwill, I don't know what's happening. It's hard for me to believe in ghosts... in spirits. Maybe she just wandered off. Did she have friends? Anyone she might've gone to?"

"She had an invisible friend," I said as my voice trembled low and soft. "She'd sit for hours, talking to her." The memory popped up like flash in a Polaroid camera. "One day, I watched from the doorway. She was playing with her doll; her leg twisted back in a way I had never seen a child's leg. She lifted her eyes toward the wall and said, 'Why are your eyes so red? Why are your clothes so raggedy?'"

I stepped into the room. "Sandy, who are you talking to?" I asked.

She turned to me, her face as calm as day and spoke. 'The little girl that fell in the fireplace after the doctor killed her.'

The basket of laundry slipped from my arms, clothes spilling across the floor. I'm sure she could tell in my voice I was scared, I told her, "Get up. Go outside and play."

"I took another sip of coffee, keeping my head down. Raymond looked at me. "So, when were you planning to tell me this, Fefe?" he asked.

"I was," I said, "but I didn't want you to think I was crazy."

Raymond leaned forward. "So, is there anything else you want to tell me?"

"Yes," I whispered. "There was a night that you were working late. I'd tucked the kids in, went and sat down to watch TV, had a few beers, and started to fall asleep. Then I heard a noise; it startled me, so I got up and walked into the bedroom to see if the kids were still awake. I walked in and Sandy's body was lifting off the bed like she was floating, and she fell back onto the mattress before I could even realize what was happening. It happened so quickly, Raymond. I started crying again. I didn't want to tell you; you always say everybody's crazy and that we drink too much."

Raymond put his coffee down and hugged me. Suddenly there was a knock at the door.

"Stay here, I'll get it," Raymond said."

"Hello, Ms. Aladyse. Come on in." She stepped over the threshold and paused, nose twitching like she'd caught a scent no one else could. She looked straight at Raymond. "My God... this place smells like death. How long have you been here?"

"Been here a few years now," Raymond said. "And you've been able to tolerate it?"

She walked slowly through the entry, eyes taking everything in.

"Tolerate? Raymond replied.

Child, this used to be an old hospital. The doctors and nurses here were evil, wicked. They killed more babies, more women, and men than they saved. Hell, I reckon somebody ran a brothel here, too." Her voice dropped. "Did someone run a brothel here as well?"

I stood up and answered before Raymond could. He was frozen in thought, mouth open, like he was listening to a story that he didn't want to be true. "We did some research," I said. "It was a hospital once. The people hung at the courthouse they weren't dead. They experimented on Black folks. But the cruelty didn't stop at color folks. I responded.

Ms.Aladyse kept walking around the rooms, fingertips brushing the wallpaper as if reading a sacred message, smiling at the same time. The lights began to twitch.

"The ghosts are gettin' irritated," she said. "Oh, you don't scare me." Don't you recognize me? She looked up at the stairs.

"I don't let anybody in that room."I responded.

"What room?" she asked.

"The room where they did the autopsies. The room where they did the rituals."

She paused, with an odd grin, oh I can hear it now, "On October eighteenth way back in the early eighteen-hundreds they tried to conjure a soul. A young Black girl. They thought she could tell the future. When she could not, they killed her. Do you have a child born on that date?"

Raymond's face went white. "Yes, Ms. Aladyse we do." His voice cracked.

Tears pulled at me, and I couldn't hold them back. "Where is she?". she said aggressively.

"I don't know," I replied, hunching my shoulders.

"Does this have anything to do with the head in the canal that I saw when I was thirteen years old?" Raymond asked.

"Partially," she answered. "Did someone in your family, an uncle or auntie, get taken? Was there a grandmother or an auntie stolen?"

"Yes," Raymond said. He sank into a chair. "The spirits are angry. They stole her not just to make her cook, but because she could see the future. They thought she could make them millions. They beat her, tried to break her to steal her gift. On October eighteenth, her body gave out, and they tried to conjure her back.

Because your daughter is the first in your bloodline born on that day, they think they can use her."

"An evil soul doesn't know it's dead."

I remembered the story of the canal. everyone knew about it "That head in the canal did your parents ever tell you the real reason you had to stay away?" she asked.

"That head," she said slowly, "was the result of your uncle's work. He couldn't save his sister that night, so he went into town looking for the men. He came to this house, he decapitated a few of them and threw their heads in the canal. Those men hunted him down and hung him in the trees above the canal.

" I thought to myself. She almost seemed angry about Raymonds Uncle taking revenge.

"You're named after him, aren't you?" Ms. Aladyse asked.

"Yes," Raymond answered.

She stood up so fast the chair scraped the floor. "Well, I guess we gotta find your daughter. They're going to kill her." Her fingers wiggled as she tapped the banister.

There was a knock at the door. We all jumped. Raymond straightened his back and stood up tall. "It has to be the priest," he said. "I'll get it."

He opened the door. Father Lucien stood on the porch, stopped, and made the sign of the cross.

"Raymond," he said, sharp as a blade, "get that," He spat the words,"that psychic woman outta my parish and out of your house. She's a deceiver. The devil himself."

"How do you know she's here, Father?" Raymond demanded.

"God gives some folks spiritual gifts," Father Lucien replied. "But the devil can see, too. He can mimic 'em."

"She told me things no one else knows," Raymond said.

"The devil can see all as well," Father Lucien insisted. "Did she tell you Sandy is in the fireplace and fell into a hole where trapped souls are?"

"No, she hasn't." Raymond replied.

"Of course not." Father Lucien eyes were flat, fixed, and sharp. "In the next few minutes, she'll ask you to light the fireplace."

Raymond stared in shock pure terror ran through him, then bolted back into the other room with the priest running behind him. They arrived just in time to see Ophelia strike a match and bend towards the fireplace, the flame catching and swallowing the wick. Silence pressed down thick and quick like the house itself had taken control.

Thirty-Three

Run

Ophelia

I tried several times to light the match, but it kept going out.

"Here, let me help you, Ms.," Aladyse said, putting her hand around the flame to keep it lit.

Suddenly, I heard Raymond and the pastor running into the room.

"What are you doing?" Raymond asked.

"Lighting the fireplace," Ms. Aladyse said. "It will help shed light on what's going on in this house and help us find Sandy." I replied.

I shook my head. Not understanding what Raymond was asking.

"Father Lucien" then quickly jumped the conversation and said, "She's lying, Ophelia. Don't listen to her. Put the matches away! Sandy is in the fireplace! That fireplace was used to cremate the bodies of the living and the dead, both good and evil."

"What?" I replied, looking at Ms. Aladyse. "You're going to listen to him over me, Ophelia?"

"I've been in this family for years," she said.

Father Lucien lifted his cross. "I rebuke you, Satan, in the name of Jesus! You have no power or dominion over this family."

He walked closer to Ms. Aladyse. She started backing up slowly, toward the door and down the hall. We followed her out.

The lights flickered. The walls shook; dust and debris fell from the ceiling. Father Lucien continued praying, and I prayed along with him. Raymond kept ducking at every piece of sheetrock falling from above.

Suddenly, the chandelier crashed to the floor. Raymond acted quickly, he grabbed Father Lucien, pushing him to the side, then reached for me. We both fell to the floor.

As we sat there, white dust coated our hair and clothes. Father Lucien lay against the wall, his black attire streaked with blood from his nose. Raymond pulled his arms from around me and crawled over to him.

"Father! Wake up!" Raymond shouted, shaking him.

Father Lucien opened his eyes, letting out a loud groan.

Ms. Aladyse, standing at the front door, began turning to dust. A loud growl echoed through the house.

"It's the seashell," I whispered. We sat, watching as her soul was sucked into it. It was as if an invisible vacuum had trapped the evil inside.

The house shook once more, as if we were experiencing an earthquake but we don't have earthquakes in Louisiana.

Then, silence.

"Raymond and I helped Father Lucien to his feet". He looked around, dazed for a moment, made the sign of the cross, and said, "Let's get back to the fireplace."

He led the way, praying, and we followed.

We stood in front of the fireplace. Raymond held his chin in one hand, his other arm resting across his chest. Worry and hopelessness plastered both of our faces.

"So... how are we going to get her out of there?" I asked.

"I'm going to climb down and get her while you two stay and pray," Father Lucien said.

"Where are the other children?" he asked.

"No, Father! I can't let you do that. I'll go get her," Raymond replied.

"I feel horrible. I should have boarded the entrance back up," he added.

"You had it boarded at one time?" Father asked.

"Yes, but my brother came here when I was gone and opened it back up, saying the spirits of the dead had hidden money in the fireplace and all kinds of "he hesitated, "bullshit. I didn't have time to put it back."

"It's okay, son," Father replied gently. "We'll talk about that another day."

"Now, Raymond… I can't let you go down there. It must be me."

"I've heard you say countless times that you don't believe in ghosts and spirits. How can you fight something you don't believe in?" Father Lucien asked.

"It's like accomplishing a goal for yourself. If you don't believe you can accomplish it, then it won't happen. In this case, life and death is in the power of the tongue. "Father Lucien said firmly.

"Get me a rope the ones you use for hunting and tie it around me. Bring it out the front door and tie it around that tree," he instructed.

"Ophelia, go get your other children, and you guys start praying," Father said.

"Will do, Father," I replied.

"Also, call every family member and have them start praying as well," he added.

"Yes, sir," I said, running to the back room where Terricita, Bode, and Betty were.

"Come out, guys. I need you to pray in front of the fireplace with your father and me."

"I'm not doing anything until I get my sixty dollars back!" Bode yelled. "Tot-tee stole my sixty dollars, and I've been saving it for months!"

"I found it!" Terricita shouted.

"We don't have time for this," I said. "You guys can divide the money later."

"But it's my money, Momma!" Bode cried out.

"Can we please go and pray so we can find your sister?" I asked firmly.

One by one, they walked out and sat in front of the fireplace.

Raymond ran outside to grab the rope. I looked out the window as the thunderstorm began to pound harder against the house. He struggled to drag it out of the shed, rain soaking him through and plastering his shirt to his chest.

By the time he came back in, his clothes were dripping wet. He tied the rope firmly around Father Lucien waist.

"Bode, help your daddy get that rope outside and tie it to the tree," I said.

"Yes, ma'am," Bode answered, standing quickly to his feet.

The priest gripped the rope with both hands while Bode and Raymond stepped carefully through the debris scattered across the floor. They pushed open the front door and carried the rope outside.

I stood in the doorway, watching as the rain pelted down on them. The sky cracked open with lightning, and for a moment their faces flashed white in the storm. Water dripped from their eyelashes, running down their cheeks like tears.

"You got it, Bo-Scott?" Raymond shouted over the thunder.

"Yes, Dad, It's tight on my side!" Bode called back, yanking the rope around the tree trunk and giving it a firm tug.

"Good. Let's get back inside," Raymond said.

Before leaving, he gave the rope one last pull to make sure it was secure. Then the two of them ran back up the slick wooden steps, their boots slapping against the porch, and hurried back into the house, shaking off the storm.

We hurried to the back of the room. Father Lucien stood by the fireplace as the children sat cross-legged on the floor, what we always called "Indian style."

"Are you ready, Father?" I asked.

"Yes, I am," he replied. "Keep the faith and pray as I go down."

With that, Father stepped inside the fireplace. A cold breeze rushed out as he disappeared. A dull light flickered, and faint voices whispered from somewhere deep within.

I turned to Raymond. "Do you hear that?" I asked.

"No, I don't hear anything," he replied.

I smacked my lips, frustrated. "You don't hear all the different voices?"

"No, Fefe," Raymond said softly. "What are they saying?"

"I can't make it out. I don't know…" My voice trembled.

We could no longer see Father Lucien.

"I can't see him anymore," I whispered.

"Aren't you supposed to be praying?" Raymond reminded me.

"Yes… you're right," I said.

All I could see were the gray stones lining the fireplace. Inside, a thick black fog twisted and curled. The smell of fire and burning flesh floated in the air, but there was no fire. It was quiet as a mouse.

Then the room began to shake again. The lights flickered. My mother's picture crashed to the floor.

In the far corner, a tall black shadow appeared. It darted behind me.

I jumped to my feet, eyes wide, palms and underarms slick with sweat. The room spun around me. I couldn't keep up with the shadow.

"Sit down, Fefe," Raymond said firmly.

"I'm scared!" I cried.

I glanced at the children. Their eyes were squeezed shut, lips moving silently in prayer.

I sat back down and joined them, whispering my own trembling words. For a moment, I opened my eyes and there it was. The old Pinocchio bank sat on the mantelpiece, staring back at me.

I squeezed my eyes shut tightly. This can't be happening, I thought.

The house began to shake again. The ceiling cracked and started to fall.

"Quick, get up!" Raymond shouted.

He grabbed the children as we ran for the door. The walls caved in around us, like evil itself was trying to trap us inside.

I stumbled and fell, my knee splitting open. Blood pooled beneath me.

"Fefe!" Raymond shouted.

"Keep going!" I cried. "Get the kids out of here!"

"Tot-Tee, grab your brother and sister and keep runnin', you hear?"

"Yes, Daddy," she cried.

"Daddy, should I grab the seashell?" Betty asked through tears.

"No. It's gotta stay here. Now run!" Raymond barked.

The children tore toward the door as Raymond knelt beside me. He yanked a wooden plank off my leg, ripped his shirt, and tied it tight around the wound.

"Stand up, Fefe," he said firmly. "Good Lord willin', you gotta stand." he said.

"It hurts too bad, Raymond," I cried, bent over, limping, trying to make it through the debris. "I'll just stay here with Sandy's soul and Father Lucien."

"Stop that bullshit!" Raymond roared. He scooped me up, threw me over his shoulder, and hauled me out the house. I must've gotten heavy, 'cause he dropped me on the ground like a piece of deer meat once we were outside.

I looked up my sisters, brother, and their children were all outside, along with Raymond's folks. Word had gotten out the house was caving in, and they came to help. We sat there, breathless, watching as the old house crumbled into itself.

I dropped to my knees, screaming, sure I'd never see Sandy again. Raymond tried to hold me up, but my heart shattered clean through. Everyone was crying.

Then suddenly, Bode shouted, "Look! Look!" He was jumping up and down, hollerin' so loud the air shook. We all turned and there she was. Sandy.

She stood in the middle of the smoke, thin and dirty, her face streaked with ashes, blood dripping from her nose. Smoke curled from her coarse hair. She walked toward us with her head hung low.

"Sandy!" We cried, all of us running to her. We wrapped her in our arms. She was so little, so frail, yet calm as a lamb.

Raymond's eyes lifted, scanning the ruins for Father Lucien. But something deep in me already knew wasn't comin' back.

The Morning After

The very next day, we packed our things, what little was left, and made the decision to move to California. A brand-new start.

We walked through the rubble, searching for anything we could carry. The sun was shining bright, almost mocking what we'd been through.

I prayed all night for Father's soul.

"I found Mama's picture!" I hollered, holding it high. It was untouched, like heaven had spared it just for me. "I found Pinocchio!" Betty cried. My heart sank I didn't want that cursed thing following us to California.

"Terricita, you find anything?" I asked.

"Yes," she said, "but I can't find my white sneakers. They are old, but I like 'em."

"Bode, what about you?"

"I'm tryin' to catch Gray Boie," he grumbled, chasing after the cat. "But he keeps runnin' from me."

"We may have to leave him here," Raymond said.

"Momma, I don't see the seashell," Betty whispered with concern.

I looked up, praying that Father Lucien soul hadn't been trapped inside the shell.

"If you see it, don't mess with it," Raymond said firmly. "It must stay here. On this lot. You hear me?"

"Yes, Daddy," Betty nodded.

"Hey, Maw'Ma!" I waved across the land. Raymond's mama had come to say goodbye.

"Well, y'all ready to go?" Raymond asked.

"Yes," we answered together.

We stepped off the land and walked toward Maw'Ma waiting in the street.

"There are my tennis shoes!" Terricita squealed with excitement. Her sneakers sat in the middle of the road, bright white, clean as new, one pointed one way, the other the opposite.

Her face lit up, and she dashed toward them.

"No!" Maw'Ma's voice tore through the air jagged and fierce. "Leave those tennis shoes there. Whatever you do, don't come back to this land."

We froze at the fear in her voice.

"Yes, Ma'am," I said.

We climbed into the car. Terricita kept her eyes on those shoes until the street bent, and they vanished from sight.

Fifty-Eight years later.

Ding-dong. Ding-dong.

"Oh Lord, who bangin' on my door this time of mornin'?" I muttered, pulling on my robe. I was bone-tired from stayin' up all night with Momma. Alzheimer's disease had robbed her of everything her voice, her peace, joy, and dignity.

I tightened my belt and shuffled to the door.

"Who is it?" I called.

UPS, ma'am. Got a package for Betty Chatman."

The screen door stuck. I yanked it open, embarrassed at my breath from the long night. "Yes, I'll sign," I mumbled.

The man tipped his cap. "Thank you, ma'am."

I shut the door quickly. "Look, Momma," I said, carrying the box inside. "Somebody sent us somethin'."

She didn't answer, just stared into the distance like always.

I tore into the brown paper, pulled away the bubble wrap, and froze.

"Oh my God..."

It was our seashell.

Inside was a note:

I took this from the house on Freeman Street the night it rained and crumbled. Since then, our lives have been pure hell. I realize now it was a mistake. I'm returning it to you.

My hands shook. I looked at Momma. Though she couldn't speak, the fear in her eyes said it all.

Thirty-Four

TERRICITA CHATMAN

Reminiscence

What shaped me into the amazing, family-oriented woman I am today is the fact that I had hardworking, loving parents and I was blessed with the most wonderful childhood because of my grandparents. Their parents raised them to be who they were, and through them I always felt loved and safe, especially with Dad's parents.

As a kid, I had a lot of responsibilities. But when I was with my grandparents (Dad's parents), I finally got to just be a kid. It was the most wonderful feeling, and I loved every single minute. I never wanted to go home. I can honestly tell you I believe in ghosts. There's a difference between ghosts and spirits. No matter what others may think or believe, there are such things as hauntings and the paranormal.

Forget GHOSTS. I lived it. And that experience will stay with me until the day I die.

It taught me to pray harder especially after seeing the three open graves with our names on them.

I deeply miss the house as odd as it may sound.

I don't regret my childhood. It taught me responsibility and how to take care of "you little brats."

Thirty-Five

RAYMOND CHATMAN JR.

Reminiscence

Even though the house was haunted and sometimes I feared it, there were still times I enjoyed it. I had two friends, a dog and a cat. The spirits walked by the bed so much that I wasn't even scared. The only time I felt fear was when Daddy sent me to feed the dogs at night, and he showed up with a white sheet over his head and body, running toward me.

One Christmas, Santa brought gifts for the girls but nothing for me. Tears rolled down my face, damn, Santa had put my gift in the trunk of the car instead of under the tree. Just one of the many memories I have growing up in the haunted house.

When we moved to California, I grew homesick.

I do think that somehow, all of the ghosts and all that followed were warning me ahead of time and pulling me through tough things and hard times. The good ones still guide and protect me today, sixty years later.

Thirty–Six

Betty Chatman

Reminiscene

Spirits have been around me all my life; for me, they're just a normal part of everyday experience. They come in different forms once a dragonfly hovered over me while I did my homework, and at times hundreds of dragonflies would gather and frighten me. My brother Bode (known in the book as Bo-Scott or Raymond Jr.) would sit next to me so I wouldn't be scared. He called them "big green things." Although the ghosts were present, we still enjoyed life.

I would save pennies and dimes just to buy my mom, Ophelia, a birthday presents always Double mint gum and fingernail polish. I was so excited to give it to her. The only thing that truly scared me was seeing the shadow of a man's face on the wall. I would grab my rosary beads, place them around my neck, and say the rosary; he would vanish after that. To this day I continue to see visions, but I'm never afraid.

A seashell that once lived in the house was surprisingly shipped to me sixty years later. We had intentionally left it at the house, but a family member went back and removed it. I also have the Pinocchio bank. Both items are stored in a collectible box, and my little sisters are too scared to touch them.

Thirty-Seven

Mona Rae Chatman

Remininscene

I would like to start by thanking my sister, Dona Chatman, for authoring this book; I am extremely proud of her. 1010 Freeman St. has taught me that there is another world out there where we know little about both good and evil. I believe in my dreams, and I'm able to interpret them and help others understand what their dreams mean. I have an entire book written about my dreams as well as my family's.

To my late husband Donn Desboine Jr. may your soul rest in heaven until we meet again, May 22,1964 -August 2, 2020

Thirty-Eight

RAYMOND CHATMAN SR.

Relections of Opelousas and 1010 Freeman st.

My sisters, brothers, and I were raised in the Catholic Church and were members of Holy Ghost Church in Opelousas, Louisiana. However, we also attended Little Zion Baptist Church. We learned a lot from being brought up between two different religions.

My parents spoke three different languages one of them French. We couldn't speak it, but we could usually understand what they said.

Somehow my parents knew when it was going to rain, when company was coming or when someone was going to die. They would notice changes in the moon and its color as well as the color of the leaves and when they fell. I can't say I believe in ghosts, I have never seen any myself. However, there are things I know to be true. Things I can't explain. Once I saw the head of a man in the canal on Grolee Street. Twenty years later I saw that same man near the railroad tracks. I was on the opposite side of the tracks when, somehow, the train hit him, and he was decapitated; I saw his head roll on the ground. I will never forget that day.

The only other experience I had that was supernatural involved the separation of a thick glass ash tray. My father and his ability to acknowledge spiritual warnings, knew when someone was going to die. As you read in the story my mother-in-law Pearl Guillory died the following week after my father announced the warning to the family.

My children are now in their late sixties and early seventies; they swear to this day that the house I moved onto the lot at 1010 Freeman Street was haunted.

Today I'm eighty-nine years old. I've always been active, spending most of my years working long hours and in my spare time hunting, fishing, playing badminton and playing dominos. I enjoy my whiskey just like my dad did when he was alive. My favorite Crown royal.

My thoughts to the next generations always be able to stand on your own two feet; never have to depend on nobody. At the end of the day, you're all you got.

I dedicate this to my parents, Louis Chatman Sr. and Octavia White Chatman; my grandparents, Temple Mae Glaze and Martin White; and my grandmother Mary Fontenot and Jules Chatman.

Thirty-Nine

Ophelia Guillory Chatman

Relections of my life

Hello, I'm Ophelia Mae Guillory, and yes, I believe in ghosts and spirits. As of today, I'm 86 years old. The house on Freeman Street left mc with many memories. However, the more fearful I became, the more I prayed. My faith in God has carried me through some tough times.

I grew up Catholic and attended Holy Ghost Catholic Church in Opelousas, Louisiana. All my children were Christian and went to catechism. Although I was a Christian, I believed in using salt to get rid of people and have them never return to my home. I used palm leaves too, hanging them over the doorway to protect my house.

One of my spiritual gifts was dreams. God spoke to me in my sleep, and I always knew when something bad was going to happen.

I enjoyed my beer, dancing, and playing with my grandkids until one day, in my mid-sixties, Alzheimer's robbed me. If I could tell you one thing my grandkids would say about me, it would be this: I always yelled from the back room to tell them to turn the TV down to volume seven.

My favorite sayings were: "What da shit!" "I be damn!" "Oh no shaaamee, naw... oh no sha', be'be'..." and let's not forget that long "Uhhhhhhhh."

I played Yahtzee with them and would take my false teeth out to scare them. Truth be told, I enjoyed my grandchildren even more than my own children. One morning I'll be gone, and I want them to remember me for the good times, not the woman lying in the bed in her final years.

I want to say to my daughter, Dona Chatman, the author: thank you, and I'm proud of the woman you have become. To all my children: thank you for loving me. May God bless you and keep praying

Forty

AUTHOR THOUGHTS

Impressions

I grew up hearing the ghost stories of 1010 Freeman Street. I can recall being scared to go to bed as I sat around listening to those shared stories. However, I believe every one of them. I have seen two spirits in my lifetime: a woman lying on my couch, and my grandfather standing in my doorway. I have spiritual gifts much like my grandfather, Louis Chatman. God sends me warnings when something is going to happen. I will have a dream or a physical experience, such as hearing a voice or seeing an object move with force.

I've always believed in God, but I don't confine God's word to the sixty-six books of the Bible (seventy-three in the Catholic canon). God is much bigger than we as humans give him credit for. Our beliefs and abilities have too often been contained and controlled by religion.

I'm a believer in Christ, but I can't deny the spiritual gifts I possess. I am clairvoyant, clairaudient, and claircognizant. I thank God for the gifts with which I have been blessed; because of them I have been successful in writing Soulful Echoes and this book, 1010 Freeman Street.

Forty-One

ACKNOWLEDMENTS

First and foremost, I thank God. He is the author of my life and every gift that comes with it is because of his words, I know all things are possible.

To my twin sister, Mona Chatman, this book is here because of you. Writing our family ghost story was never in my plan, but it was in yours, and your determination pushed me to begin. Once I started, it felt as if our ancestors took the lead, especially our grandmother, Pearl Guillory(Ma'mu), guiding me through every page. Along this journey, unexpected connections reminded me I was on the right path. Latecia Ricard a cousin I had never met introduced herself, only for me to realize I was writing about her grandfather a man I had never even heard of until a family friend mentioned his name. That led me to Patrick Siverand, who reached out and said, "I remember that house can I share my experience?"

His words reminded me, this story belonging to all of us who carried the memory of Freeman Street.

To my siblings Terricita Chatman, Raymond Chatman Jr., Betty Chatman, and Sandra Chatman thank you for sharing your memories and experiences of the house. Marco Sam Chatman you weren't even thought of until years later but as my half-brother, I acknowledge you and we love you.

To my cousins Lolita, Herman, and Daniel I am grateful for your time, knowledge, and stories, which added richness and truth to this book. To my cousin Akeem Guillory thank you for the research you have done on our family.

Ms. Mary Nash thank you for your shared ghost stories, Most importantly thank you for being part of our family and sharing love with my father in his later days.

Finally, to my parents: my father, Raymond Chatman Sr., for his wisdom and childhood memories, and my mother, Ophelia Mae Guillory Chatman, whose love, and presence remain at the heart of everything I do. Thank you for reading!

Forty-Two

FOLLOWING

Thank you for reading